THE GIRL WHO LOVED UNICORNS

Arthur Butt

ALL RIGHTS RESERVED

Publisher's Note:

This is a work of fiction. All names, characters, places, and events are the work of the author's imagination.

Any resemblance to real persons, places, or events is coincidental.

Solstice Publishing - www.solsticepublishing.com

The Girl Who Loved Unicorns

By

Arthur Butt

To Amelia, wherever you may find her

Chapter One

Sweat trickled between Amelia's shoulder blades, making her itch uncontrollably, and staining her kimono dark. She kept her head bowed and trudged on, clutching the two copper coins on a string tightly in her fist.

This is all which matters. Enough money to buy rice for another day.

Her brown toes made little puffs in the dirt as she plodded up the road, covering her feet in dust. She had determined not to wear sandals more than necessary. When hers wore out, where would she get more?

If only father was still alive.

Amelia's back and shoulder muscles ached. Her long black hair hung in greasy strings. She touched the coins one more time to guarantee she hadn't lost them. *Glad Tonacho-san found work for me today cleaning out his barn. Wonder if I can find a job tomorrow. Maybe Sachi-san?*

On her right, she passed the Katsumato home and veered far left of the road. She felt no fear, but...since the new warlord rose to power and her father committed seppuku, the Katsumato family was elevated, hers was disgraced. The two families did not speak to each other anymore. She cast another glance at the house and wondered what Kenchi was doing.

Amelia rounded a curve and her home rose into view. She surveyed the structure critically, noting with a practiced eye weeds and bushes grew above the windows. *Must cut those down. We need a clear view of who approaches.*

At the side of the house stood a water barrel. Amelia stopped and debated if she should strip and wash her whole body and kimono. The odor of old sweat and animal dung surrounded her like a putrid cloud. She fingered the cloth of her kimono. Once brightly colored, now time and too many washings faded the garment to different shades of grey. Even her beautiful sash was gone, replaced by an old hemp rope. She sighed. *Why bother, I'll only become filthy again tomorrow, so will my clothes. Hands and face are enough.* She plunged her arms into the tepid water up to her elbows, scrubbing her fingers and palms vigorously together, removing as much of the ingrained dirt from skin and under her nails as possible. Next, she dunked her head in, allowing her hair to fan out on the surface before rising quickly, blowing liquid from her mouth, and twisting the long strains as if wringing out a mop.

To be free, unrestrained, a drop of happiness is all I ask for.

She wished she could run away, anywhere. This small province of Japan once was named the land of the *kirin*—the unicorn. Amelia visualized herself on the back of one, her cares, worries, and hard work finished.

"Mother, I'm home," Amelia yelled, entering the front room of her home.

"Back here, Amelia," her mother called from the kitchen.

Mochitoyo-san sat at the table. Amelia hurried to her, withdrawing the string and laying the copper coins before her. "Look what I earned today," she beamed.

Her mother touched the string, her eyes clouding over. "My daughter, you do not have to...."

"I know, Mother," Amelia said, rising on her toes and still smiling, "but the extra money buys us things we otherwise wouldn't have, right?" In a quieter voice, she added, "And with most of the land confiscated there isn't much to do anyway, is there?"

Mochitoyo-san pushed the coins back. "You should save these for the teacher in the village so you can continue your studies."

Amelia laughed. "What good is it for a peasant girl to know how to read, write, and compute? I'd rather have food in my belly. Besides, I already know how. More scrolls and books can wait. Eating comes first."

The woman sighed and nodded, but did not reply.

Amelia stretched her sore arms and suppressed a yawn with the palm of her hand. "I'm going to bed," she announced. "I must get up early tomorrow. Sachi-san said he might have work for me tomorrow morning if I arrive before the sun does." She swung around toward her bedroom.

"Wait." Her mother gestured toward the oven. "You have not eaten your supper yet. You must be hungry after all the hard work you did today."

Amelia stepped over to the oven and picked up the covered bowl warming on top and peeked inside—boiled rice cut with barley, a few vegetables mixed in from the garden.

Pottage. Amelia mentally subtracted how much rice and barley was in the cupboard when she left the house this morning to work. *She hasn't eaten today.*

"Oh, no, Mother, I'm not hungry," Amelia said quickly, closing the lid on the bowl. "Tonacho-san fed me. This was part of the payment." She made a big production of rubbing her stomach and smacking her lips. "I had rice, vegetables, and even some salmon he caught in the river yesterday. We ate a feast." Amelia carried the bowl to her mother and laid the dish next to the coins. "You eat this. Like you always say, 'Dumplings beat flowers'."

The woman scanned her daughter's face dubiously, but picked up her chopsticks. "You are right. It is not good to let food go to waste. Certainly not in these times."

Amelia yawned again, twisting her back and shoulders, attempting to ease the ache. She bent over, kissed her mother the cheek. "I'm going to bed," she said with finality.

Her mother began eating. Amelia watched for a moment and then entered her room, dropping on her pallet of straw. Her stomach growled. The two half-ripe peaches snatched off their tree this morning a sweet memory. She rolled on her side and snuggled deep into the bed.

Hope I find work tomorrow. No more rice, wheat flour almost gone, too. If only Father pledged allegiance to the new daimyo....If only our land wasn't taken away....If only....

When the soldiers came to their home, her mother and father told her to hide in her bedroom. She hadn't. Instead, she'd run to the window and peeked out. She saw her father drop to his knees and draw his long knife. Then...then....

She ran to her room, threw herself on the bed, and cried until she fell asleep. When she awoke the next morning, her father was gone. He mother acted as if nothing happened, but was very quiet afterwards. For the first time Amelia noticed her mother had grey streaks in her hair.

This was once the province of the unicorn. I wish I rode one. I'd fly away, never return. We would jump over valleys, leap over mountains, travel to the farthest corners of the world. If only....

***

The vegetables in Sarchi-san's garden weren't ready to pick yet, but he found a small amount of work for Amelia to do shoveling out his chicken coop. Amelia labored, grim determination etched on her face, until the sun rose high in the sky and she was finished. When she asked, Sarchi-san knew of no one else needing helpers for the day, and with a sinking heart she left. For the morning, she received a lone copper coin and walked home, wondering if any of the other farmers in the neighborhood needed assistance so she could work until sunset and earn another copper.

On the off chance someone might want her services, she gazed down the road toward the town. Sometimes farmer's wagons broke on their way to market, and they sought people to help carry the produce to the vegetable stands, or lend a hand in fixing their carts.

On the outskirts of the village, a lone figure stood along the roadside.

Chikako.

They were friends, or rather once were friends. Her father owned a shop selling cotton, linen, and silk cloth to the people and Chikako helped in the back, sorting old cotton fabric imported from China. The girl was a year older than she, a head taller, but Chikako felt like the sister Amelia always wanted. When Amelia and her mother use to go into town, while her mother browsed among the silk and linen materials, Chikako and Amelia would talk. Occasionally, Chikako would give her cast-offs rags, so Amelia could make dresses for her porcelain dolls. When she and Kenchi walked into town together, Chikako would run out of the shop and greet both, hanging onto the boy's every word, laughing when Amelia laughed, or when Kenchi made some funny remark or joke.

All this stopped when Amelia's family fell into disfavor, their land confiscated by the new warlord, their wealth and workers taken. Her mother could only afford the cheapest cotton or hemp fabrics now to make new clothes and not much else. Chikako never talked to Amelia anymore, would walk straight into her when they met on the street if Amelia didn't jump out of the way.

Amelia sighed and continued to trudge up the road. Losing the friendship of Chikako was almost as bad as losing the companionship of Kenchi.

Three young men strolled down the hill toward Amelia, heading for the village, laughing and talking in loud voices. They spotted Amelia, halted, and pointed.

Oh, no. Kenchi and his friends. I hope they don't stop and speak to me. Amelia moved to the opposite side of the road, kept her head bowed, and continued to walk.

"Look who it is, the pig girl," one of the young men shouted. He stepped in front of Amelia, blocking her path. She looked up from their feet to the sneering faces and moved to one side, attempting to step around.

"She smells like a pig, too," another of the boys exclaimed. He blocked her from walking past while bending close and pretending to sniff. He held his nose. "Phew, what an odor."

Kenchi's lips split in a wide grin, his white teeth showing. One hand dipped into his pouch as if protecting his money, the other clamped over his face. "You're right. See the forehead and snout? She's the mother of pig girls." He took a step closer to Amelia, peeking at her between his fingers.

"Don't get too close," warned one of the boys. "Her stench will rub off on you." The two young men sauntered away, still laughing. "C'mon, Kenchi, let's go before the markets are sold out."

"You are right. Wait up." Kenchi's face grew sober and he murmured, "Sorry, Amelia." He withdrew his hand from his pouch, turned his back to her. A long string of coins dropped into the dust as he hurried after his friends.

Amelia stood frozen, watching the three recede down the hill, then stooped and picked up the string, more money than she'd seen since her father's death.

Why did he do that??

She looked up from the coins. A fourth joined the three young men—Chikako hanging onto the arm of Kenchi as they entered the town. Amelia bit her lower lip, shook her head, and then broke out into a grin when the boy pushed off Chikako and tousle her hair instead, as if he petted a puppy.

Still smiling, Amelia spun on her toes and ran home to her mother, bursting through the door shouting, "Mother, look—we're rich."

Mochitoyo-san stared back at her daughter, wide-eyed, from her seat at the kitchen table, glancing first at Amelia, and then at the string of coins, as the girl dropped the coppers on the table in front of her. A worried look of concern passed over Mochitoyo-san's features. "Where did you get this? You have not been to the town, have you?" She kept her gaze fixed on Amelia, studying her face, expecting an answer.

Amelia's mouth opened in confusion. *Why would she think I received these coins in town?* Realization struck and she closed her lips into a bitter line. *She believes I've been selling my body to the soldiers in the village as some of the other girls do when they want money.*

"It's not what you think, Mother," Amelia hurried to explain quietly. "Kenchi gave me these when no one was watching. I met him and his friends along the road into town."

"Kenchi? Kenchi Katsumoto?" The concern did not leave the woman's voice. If anything, the worry grew. "You must not speak with the Katsumotos. I told you, your father told you. Conversation is dangerous for him and his family. Associating is dangerous for us." She wagged a finger in Amelia's face. "You know better. I have told you not to talk to those people."

The elation Amelia felt melted away. Her heart sank, replaced by anger. "I know, but I don't understand why. We use to be such…."

Amelia's mother motioned her to sit. "Your father was a great samurai warrior of the old warlord's," she explained, her eyes going to her husband's sword and bow hanging on the wall. "They fought many battles together."

Amelia knew this. She'd heard the tales countless times. She nodded, wondering where her mother was going with the story.

"Your father commanded men. Once a foreigner from the far west told him about his wife, a beautiful woman named Amelia. He loved the name so much he named you after her."

"I know Mother, but I still don't see what this has to do—"

"Hush." The woman put a forefinger to her lips. "The warlord rewarded your father with all the land and peasants around here," she swung her hand in a wide circle, "and presented me as a gift to him." She smiled, remembering. "I was a cook in the warlord's kitchen. Your father and I talked previously, and he vowed he would have me as his wife." Amelia's mother smiled. "Maybe he liked my cooking. This is why he asked for me, but," she shivered, "when I saw him in his armor he appeared so big and fierce. I was afraid of him at first, until I grew to know and love him."

Amelia was becoming impatient. *I wish she'd hurry.* Amelia plastered a look of interest on her face and tried to pay attention.

"Your father was a good man, honorable and loyal. He was also a dreamer. The warlord wished to give him an administrative post, but your father begged for land. He always desired to be a farmer. He also had a vision of a unified Japan, free of war. He trained you as a samurai warrior, and because he wanted to bond his holdings and the people of this town, he trained Kenchi alongside you, although he was from another clan. He hoped by doing so he could demonstrate to all people it was not impossible for us to get along." She gave a small laugh. "He tried to train me as well, but I admit I was never very good." She added seriously, "The duty of samurai women is to protect the home while the men are away."

Amelia nodded, remembered her father telling the same thing during his instructions.

"And then the old warlord was deposed." Amelia's mother sighed. Her lips bent sadly. "Your father was also very stubborn. He refused to swear allegiance to the new warlord and instead committed *seppuku*. Except for the small parcel we have now, the new daimyo confiscated most of our land. The Katsumotos had family allegiances to the new warlord, and so rose in status and power, while we fell. "

Amelia could contain herself no longer. She blurted out, "I know *Mother,* but what does any of this have to do Kenchi giving me money?"

Mochitoyo-san leveled a sharp look at her daughter for interrupting. "The new warlord is still insecure in his power. He fights a war in the north, and many of the old warlord's men took to the forest and mountains. Your father might have gone too, if not for us. The Katsumotos have clan loyalties to the new warlord, yes, but they are not strong ones, and rumor says Kenchi has joined his army as the daimyo's newest samurai. This will make his parents proud and elevate the father still higher in the esteem of the warlord. Nevertheless, if he suspects Kenchi and his family are close to us he may believe we conspire against him, in which case, we will all be destroyed."

"Oh." Amelia never thought of clan, or the interlacing loyalties and obligations binding people together, just as she never thought what the Buddhist monks said in their temples. Her small world suddenly grew larger. "Should I give the money back?"

Her mother shook her head. "No. What has happened is done. Speak to no one about this."

Amelia breathed a sigh of relief. They would keep the money. "Tomorrow, no work for me," she announced, her face lighting up. "In the morning, I go fishing in the river to see if the salmon still run. In the afternoon, I think

I'll berry pick in the field across the road." She smacked her lips. "Pie for desert."

"I bought rice this morning at the market," her mother replied eagerly, "using the money you gave me yesterday. Tomorrow I will buy more and wheat flour to make the dough for the pie."

Amelia rose and hugged her mother. "This will be a holiday. No work and plenty of food for a change."

Her mother laughed and wrinkled her nose. "Go outside and wash, you dirty girl. You smell like a barnyard." As an afterthought she added, "Wash your kimono, too. If tomorrow is to be a festival day, you must wear clean clothing." She murmured to herself, "Maybe I should burn a stick of incense at the Shinto temple for good luck while I am in the village. Prayer cannot hurt."

Amelia knew less about the old gods than she did about Buddha, but as she ran out the door to the rain barrel she called over her shoulder, "You're right. We can use all the luck we can gather."

Amelia stripped quickly, washing her body and clothes. *Waste of money buying incense, but I guess Mother is right. I wonder if the old gods do exist or bring luck.* Living at the Shinto temple was an old woman, a *miko,* who claimed to talk to the gods. Amelia thought the woman was crazy, but then she fell into a trance, and people believed what she said and acted accordingly. *Foolishness. Old farmers believing an old woman. As crazy as believing unicorns still roam the forests and mountains.* Amelia wrung out her kimono and hung the garment on a bush to dry, shivering as a cool breeze sent goosebumps up her naked back. *Maybe at one time the creatures roamed this province, but no more. Their peace and goodwill evaporated a long time ago, as did the happiness of the land and the people.* Amelia padded inside on bare feet to find a blanket to wrap around her too thin body until her kimono was dry. *Life would be nice if the unicorns returned though, at least for a short time.*

Chapter Two

The splashing of the water echoed off the spruce and pine trees around Amelia like firecrackers exploding in the air as she lounged on the riverbank, three fat salmon full of roe flopping beside her. Wane sunlight filtered through the branches above her head, casting shadows on the earth and making the water sparkle like diamonds. She'd slept well past dawn, luxuriating in the fact she had no work for the whole day, other than the usual chores around the house before leaving to fish.

Her mother already disappeared to the market and shopping, Amelia set about cleaning the house, weeding the small garden, and feeding the chickens. Her tasks finished, she hurried to the river to see what she could catch for supper.

The salmon are still running. She caught the gleam of a red flash as one fish leaped, traveling upstream to spawn. Amelia tied the hem of her kimono tightly around hips, waded into the river up to her knees and bent over, dangling her arms into the water, waiting for supper to swim by.

When a salmon swam between her legs, using a quick flick of hands, she tossed the fish well up onto the bank and bent back over, hoping for one more of its finny kin to glide her way so she could snare another.

An hour later, she ended fishing for the morning, relaxing beneath the shade of a small maple, which spread its limb above her like a parasol. Amelia glanced up and down the path along the bank. No one else was in sight. *Might as well get a good washing in. This is a holiday and I haven't gone swimming in ages.* She stripped and stopped to examine herself.

I'll never be mistaken for a rich man's daughter. I'm brown as a nut. Skinny and small, also, and I think my nose is too large. Leaves out being a yujo, *who would want me as a play woman? I wouldn't do something so embarrassing anyway. Lousy at singing and dancing. Guess I'll be a farmer the rest of my life. What does Mother always say? 'A frog in a well does not know the great sea?' I don't even know the well.*

With a groan of resignation, Amelia plunged into the icy cold river water, grabbing handfuls of white sand from the bottom and scrubbing her whole body raw, even her hair, until every trace of in-ground dirt vanished from her body.

Clean. I can't even smell myself. How long has it been since I've been clean?

Amelia strolled from the river, wringing water from her hair and stretched out in a patch of light, letting the warm sun's rays dry her body. It felt so good to be lazy, like a smug kitten having a full belly, with no reason to rise. Amelia closed her eyes and wiggled in delight.

"Well, look what we have here." Chikako sauntered along the path next to the river. The girl stopped, hands on hips and smirked at Amelia, lying nude in the sun. "You would think a peasant girl would have better things to do than run naked through the woods like some harlot of the countryside."

"Huh?" Amelia sat up, startled, grabbed her kimono, and hastily slipped the garment over her body. "I didn't see you on the trail, Chikako. I thought I was alone." She shot the girl an embarrassed smile. "I was fishing and swimming," she said in way of explanation. "How have you been?"

"Very well, thank you." The girl gave Amelia a lewd look. "Bet you were hoping Kenchi would stroll by while you were here, weren't you? All naked and eager, anxious for him to appear."

"*What?*" Amelia's mouth dropped open. She tried to speak, but nothing came out, and finally stammered, "How...how could you...why did you think such a thing?" Her face burnt hot.

Chikako advanced a few steps, head pushed forward, brows knitting. "Don't play dumb. I see the way you hang all over him when you two stroll into town. You think I don't know what you are up too?" the girl sneered. "Well, for your information Kenchi is mine and we are getting married. So keep your dirty little fingers off him, you hear me?"

Amelia stared at Chikako without comprehension. She finally blurted out, "But...when did this happen?"

Chikako thrust her hand out, finger shaking in Amelia's face. "Oh, our wedding hasn't happened yet. Kenchi knows what is occurring, but we have not made an official announcement. However, my father is in negotiations with his parents so the time will not be long before we tell everyone." Chikako nodded to herself in anticipation. "This will be a good alliance. He is a samurai, his parents high in the warlord's favor. My father is a respected businessman in town."

The warm breeze around Amelia suddenly blew chilled and a curtain of cold mist descended over her mind. She whispered, "I wish you two the best of happiness." Pain laced her chest. Her heart sank. *Kenchi.*

Chikako continued as if she hadn't heard Amelia. "So you can stop running naked through the woods like a courtesan hoping he'll see you. Maybe if your father wasn't a fool and killed himself, you would have stood a chance, but now?" The girl smirked and shrugged, surveying Amelia as if finding a dead boar rotting in the forest. "Look at you. A skinny small half-starved rodent. Who would want something like you? Not even a cat I bet." Chikako nodded derisively at the salmon lying on the bank. "Did they die from your odor when you swam in the river and polluted the water?"

At the mention of her father, Amelia's eyes narrowed. She shouted back, "My father died by honor as a samurai should who lives by the code of horse and bow, *Bushido,* the way of the warrior. He was never a fool. He was brave and strong." Amelia breathed deeply, remembering her father's lectures he'd hammered into her about courage, honor and character.

"Oh, please," Chikako scoffed, "who listens to that rubbish? Certainly not my father or me, and if you believe in your father's nonsense you deserve exactly what you've received." Chikako swung about and walked down the path, calling over her shoulder, "Remember what I said. Kenchi is mine. Sneak around sniffing after him and you will have me to deal with."

For a long time Amelia stood still and stared along the path, seeing and hearing nothing. Conflicting emotions raced through her chest, and she shook like a leaf in the breeze, hugging herself trying to still the rage and hurt. She bit her lip, exhaled deeply, and returned to the fish still flopping feebly on the bank. Her shoulders slumped in defeat, and her strength ripped away by Chikako's words.

Chikako is wrong. My father was a good man. He lived and died by the code. I may not be as beautiful as she is, or as wealthy, but I know mercy and politeness. I know it's not right to go around insulting people for things they have no control over, or to talk badly about their dead parents. My father was a fool? Chikako is the one who is a fool, and one does not listen to the prattling of foolish people.

Shoving the aggravation aside, Amelia squatted, scaled the fish, cut a hooked branch from a tree, and strung the three for carrying. Vaguely she wondered why the monks said eating meat was wrong, but fish and fowl were fine. What was the difference? Besides, no one would pass up fresh meat if they could catch a deer or a boar. Amelia knew many people who professed not to eat red meat, but raised pigs and chickens for food. She sternly kept her mind away from Kenchi, or the conversation with Chikako. Whatever happened between the two was no business of hers. Anyway, mother forbade speaking to Kenchi, so whatever happened was not her problem. Chikako was never a friend, using their companionship to advance her father's reputation in the village by association, and get close to Kenchi to win his love. Amelia wondered if Kenchi used her too, staying friendly even if she was a miserable rodent as Chikako said, so her father would keep training him as a samurai.

Users, both of them. I should have realized, known better. Kenchi, I thought we were friends. Why did you give me money? Feeling guilty about manipulating my family and me all these years?

Faintly in the distance, the bugle of a hunting horn clamored through the trees: the soldiers of the warlord chasing an animal for sport. Amelia snorted in disgust. The high and mighty rulers of the land didn't worry about what the monks preached. They demanded and took the fattest animals from the herds and plumpest fowl from the flocks of the farmers. The choicest vegetables and fruit were confiscated and brought to the castle. The soldiers hunted at will and dined well in their lord's hall on boar and deer.

Amelia grunted and pushed herself upright. *Better hurry home and finish cleaning these fish so we can have our own feast tonight. Still have to pick berries for my pie, too. I hope Mother remembered to buy wheat flour.* Amelia knotted the cord tight around her kimono, scooped up the stick with the salmon hanging from the end, and rushed up the slippery bank to the path.

Mochitoyo-san was home and busy in the kitchen as Amelia sauntered through the door. "Plenty of rice,"

Amelia's mother announced, "and I bought wheat flour, too." She eyed the fish Amelia carried. "Sushi?"

"Full of roe," Amelia replied, holding up her catch and beaming.

Mother and daughter grinned at each other.

"Berry picking now," Amelia said, snatching a wooden bowl from the cupboard and laying the salmon on a cutting board. "I'll be back."

"I will cut up the fish and start on the dough," her mother agreed. The woman glanced outside. "Do not be too late. The sun is setting and the sky is growing dark. You know how I worry about you at night when you go out. So many bandits roam the land now. The province is not safe for a man at night, let alone a woman."

"Won't be late, and don't worry. If I see strangers I'll run the other way," Amelia replied, hurrying outside. "Besides, I'll be across the road in the field in sight of the house. I'll be fine."

Sharp thorns stuck to Amelia's clothing as she wandered her way into the field, ignoring the pricks the bushes left on bare legs and feet. She kept walking, head lowered, searching for a spot loaded with ripe, wild raspberries, and squatted. Amelia started picking, eating as many of the fruits as she tossed into the bowl, face red from the juice, while her hands and arms turned scarlet from the pinpricks and scratches of the thorns.

The hunting horn blew again, louder, issuing from the dark forest abutting the field, accompanied by the baying of dogs in hot pursuit. Amelia looked up, annoyed, scanning the trees for signs of the hunters or the hunted. *Still tracking? I wish they'd leave the silly beast alone and return to the castle. I hope they don't ride this way, either. I'd better hurry up. The last thing I need is for soldiers to find me here while I'm alone. Mother is right and the warlord's men are as bad as the thieves are, maybe worse. It's growing dark and I have enough berries for two pies.*

At least the soldiers will scare any outlaws away. Amelia glanced at her bowl overflowing with raspberries, and then checked the time. The sun already gone from the sky. *Didn't realize how late I've stayed out. Almost dark. Enough.*

Amelia stood, groaning, arched her back, and picked up the bowl. She took one last glance at the field, scanning the grass and the dark forest beyond for bandits or soldiers.

In the gathering dusk, a pinpoint of white light appeared emerging from the woods. The glimmering halted, swung back and forth like someone signaling with a lantern, and then stopped and fixed in Amelia's direction.

The radiance grew larger, took form, the waning glitter of sunlight shining off a unicorn's horn.

Is it true? Oh, Lord Buddha, it is. A unicorn—how beautiful!

Displaying unerring accuracy, the unicorn continued to bear down on Amelia's position. The girl fell to her knees, arms outstretched, holding her breath in awe, hoping for the animal to edge nearer.

The unicorn stopped ten paces away, studying Amelia, showing intense curiosity and doubt, sniffing the breeze to catch her odor.

Amelia reached out her hands and wiggled fingers. "Come here, baby. I won't hurt you."

Taking mincing steps, the unicorn approached, nuzzling Amelia under an arm and knelt, placing her head in Amelia's lap with a contented sigh.

A surge of joy and happiness shot through Amelia. All the wonderful things of life coursed through her body in rapture, combining into a glowing spark of love in her heart and mind for the animal. Still gazing into the unicorn's brown eyes, she stroked the alabaster hide, caressing the animal with small scratches behind the ears, and cooing in a low drone.

Amelia stood and so did the unicorn. She walked around the animal, examining the beautiful coat from all sides. An arrow protruded from the left flank, drops of red staining the white hide in a thin line down the leg.

"Oh, gosh, someone's shot an arrow into you. You poor baby." *The warlord's soldiers, they were stalking unicorns. Of all the miserable...!*

As if to confirm her thoughts, the hunting horn blew again accompanied by the braying of the hounds. "We have to get you out of here—quick," Amelia exclaimed, already fretting what to do about the animal, "but I must take the arrow out first." She patted the unicorn's head. The animal gazed back with trusting eyes and a soft nicker. "This won't hurt a bit," Amelia said, repeating a phrase her father use to say when Amelia found a splinter in her hand or foot. She examined the wound carefully.

The barb had not penetrated far into the skin. Deep enough to stick into the hide and make a messy wound, but not enough for a debilitating injury. Amelia gripped the shaft below the head between thumb and forefinger and slowly worked the bolt out, attempting to be as careful as possible. She felt the unicorn's flanks shiver, but the animal did not struggle or attempt to leap out of her grasp. After a moment, she'd withdrawn the arrow and dropped the barb into the stickers with distaste.

"There, all better. Mama fixed," Amelia exclaimed. The baying of the hounds stopped abruptly and changed into a confused whining. "The dogs have lost your trail," Amelia commented, listening, "but the warriors may still be tracking you." She scratched the unicorn on top of the head. "We must hide you now. If the hunters still follow your trail they will arrive any moment." Amelia scooped up the bowl of berries, tucked it under one arm, the other hand grasped the unicorn's mane and tugged. "Come with me." She started walking briskly toward her home, shooting quick glances over her shoulder for the hunters or their dogs. The unicorn ambled at her side, a slight limp in her stride, but no other sign of distress. They crossed the road, and in the gathering twilight, Amelia paused, thinking. *Where can I hide you the hunters won't search?* There was little choice. The land was flat, only her home and the old barn breaking the landscape. *Can't take you inside. To the barn.*

Amelia yanked on the unicorn's mane again. "C'mon. Let's make you disappear." She led the animal to the barn and swung the door open wide. The inside was dark and smelled faintly of cow dung and musty hay, except for a few farming implements, old baskets and hemp sacks, vacant. The oxen they once owned to plow the fields died of old age, and the family never had enough money to replace the beast. The stall sat empty. His absence had not distressed Amelia. Her family did not possess enough land now to need the ox. What small amount they worked, Amelia dug up using pitchfork and shovel. Amelia lent the extra work scant thought, but was glad they hadn't discarded the hay, leading the unicorn to the pen and commanding, "Lay down."

The filly's head bobbed in agreement, as if she understood, and approached the stall. The animal sniffed the hay curiously, released a sneeze, and cast a dubious glance at Amelia, before stepping cautiously inside, turning around, and folding her legs beneath her.

"Good girl," Amelia cooed, piling hay on top of the animal until the creature hid from view. "Now you lay quiet here and don't make a sound, or move a muscle," she cautioned. "I'll be back."

Amelia snatch up the bowl of berries and hurried to the house, out of breath.

"Stop right there, girl." Three warriors approached on horseback, pulling up between Amelia and her front door. "Who are you?" the rider in the middle demanded

brusquely, glaring at her from his mount as if she were an insect he meant to step upon.

Frightened, Amelia looked into the men's faces and quickly lowered her gaze to her feet, bowing her head in a position of servitude.

The warlord's soldiers. High-ranking samurai by the dress of the men, too. I'm in trouble now. I wonder what they want of me?

"I'm—I'm Amelia, noble sir," she stammered in a low voice. She flicked her head in the direction of her home, still not looking up. "I live here, sir."

The door of the house flew open and Amelia's mother peered out. "Amelia? Daughter?" The woman took a timid step, gazing into the growing twilight and surveying Amelia and the riders, terror mirrored in her stance. The old woman quickly dropped her head also.

One of the riders, a captain by his dress and manner, leaped off his horse and swaggered over to Amelia with contempt. "We hunt a beast from the forest and field beyond here. Our dogs lost the scent at the river, and the spore went away at the road." He stared at Amelia, taking in the red stains on kimono and hands. "Have you seen the animal?"

They are the hunters I heard in the woods. The blood. The unicorn's blood covers me.

Terror knotted in Amelia's belly, racing upward along her spine to lodge in her neck. "N-No, noble sir," she stammered out. "I was alone in the field berry picking. I heard noise, horns blowing and dogs barking. I grew frightened, and left. I saw naught of any beast." Amelia held out the bowl of berries as proof of her story, and laid the container on the ground before the soldier for his inspection if he willed.

"My daughter and I were making a pie to celebrate our good fortune of having such a wonderful lord as we have now," Amelia's mother put in quickly, glancing up, wearing a sickly grin and dropping her head again. "We are poor peasants and know nothing of hunting beasts. We listen to the priests and do as they command and do not eat red meat."

"Hmmm…" The captain reached out and grabbed Amelia's wrists in his hands, yanking them up in front of his nose, and peering at her palms. His gaze swept over her filthy kimono with a grimace. "Your arms and clothes are stained red, girl. No doubt from the blood of the beast we seek. You are lying to me. Now tell the truth or you forfeit your life and your mother's. Where is the beast?" He released Amelia's hands and rested his fingers on the hilt of his sword.

Amelia's mother gasped. Amelia's body shook. Tears crept into the corners of her eyes. "Oh, no, sir. I do not lie." She thought quickly. "The stain is juice from the berries and the blood pricks from the thorns. I fear I ate as many as I picked, and was quite scratched on my hands, arms, and legs, also." She looked up so the soldier could see her face and held out her hands and arms, and then quickly lifted the hem of her kimono to reveal dirty scratched ankles and feet. Amelia dropped her head again. "See, my face is all red too." She waited breathlessly; sending a prayer to Buddha and the older gods of Japan, the samurai would believe and not question her further.

"Hmmm…"

"Daiki," one of the riders shouted, obviously impatient at his companion's failure to receive an answer, "it is dark and we cannot track your beast anyhow. The peasant girl knows nothing. Can't you see she is terrified? If the wench knew anything, we would have heard the story by now. Let us ride to the castle. The hound master has already returned to the fortress."

Daiki's lips bent in coiled defeat. He studied the earth, shoulders sagged in resignation as the hopes of a kill vanished. "Perhaps you are right," the soldier sighed at last.

"The beast has eluded me again, but I will have its horn if the search takes me the rest of my life. You may place a wager on my words." He glared at Amelia and her mother. "If you see this beast, a filly unicorn, report the fact to the castle. Understand me? Tell the guards at the gate Captain Daiki ordered you. They will inform me."

Amelia bobbed her head up and down until she felt dizzy while staring at her feet. "Oh, yes, noble Sir Captain Daiki. I'll remember and report anything I see at once. Of course, sir, as you command."

As Daiki remounted his horse he shouted to Amelia's mother, *"You too old woman. I'll be back."* After those parting words, the three wheeled their mounts and rode off into the gathering darkness of the forest toward the warlord's castle.

Amelia stood trembling, head lowered, until the drumming of the horse's hooves ceased, willing her heart to slow its pounding and breath to return to normal.

Her mother ran out into the yard and grabbed her arm. "My daughter, into the house. They are gone. Quickly before they reappear and ask more questions." The woman jerked her forward toward the doorway.

Still afraid to glance around, Amelia reached down and snatched the berries, scrambling up the stairs into the house behind her mother. "You saw nothing of the unicorn the samurai hunted?" her mother asked, still visibly shaken by the encounter with the warlord's soldiers. She hurried to the window and peered out, searching the yard and the field beyond for signs of the warriors.

"No Mother," Amelia denied. "As I said, I picked berries and saw nothing. When I heard the bugle of the hunters I fled here at once."

Don't quiz me anymore, please. If I tell you the truth, you'll be terrified and make me give the unicorn up. Those soldiers will kill the poor animal for her horn.

Amelia still held the bowl. She dropped the container on the table next to a bowl of dough, changing the subject. "Let's hurry and make our pie. I'm hungry."

Mochitoyao-san released a sigh of frustration and swung away from the window. "I am too old for this," she muttered. "I wish your father was still alive." Taking slow steps, the old woman walked to the bowl, rolling the dough out and fitting the crust into a pan. "Go light the stove," she ordered Amelia.

While they waited for the pie to bake and cool, Amelia and her mother rapidly ate: a thick porridge of rice, vegetables, and pieces of the salmon Amelia caught. Amelia fretted, hardly tasting the food, wishing the pie cooked so her mother would go to bed. The time was late when they finally finished their desert and sat back, groaning contented sighs.

Amelia scraped the last smears of berry juice from her plate with her hand and sucked her fingers, pretending to stretch and yawn. "I am stuffed. I'm going to bed, Mother. I'll see you in the morning."

Mochitoyo-san suppressed a sigh of satisfaction also. "I go to sleep, too, daughter. We have had a busy day and ate well."

Amelia wandered off to her room, and listened tensely for her mother falling asleep. When the gently snoring of the woman issued from the bedchamber, Amelia stood, slipped quietly through the kitchen and tiptoed to the back door of the house. Silently she swung it open, and ran through the dark to the barn, guided only by the illumination of the moon, which was full and bright. She needed no light to see the way, but the shadows cast by the brilliance seemed to hold unspoken dangers, as if a soldier lurked in each one. Amelia hurried to the stall out of breath where the unicorn hid. Brushing the hay aside, first, a shiny horn appeared, and then the unicorn popped her head up shaking hay from her mane.

"You are safe now. The soldiers have gone away."

The unicorn gazed back at Amelia with adoring brown eyes. *"I love you."*

Chapter Three

The thought rung loud and clear like a bell in Amelia's mind. She gasped. "You speak?"

"Of course. I am a unicorn. A girl unicorn. Only girls can speak. We are very smart." The animal peered at Amelia curiously. *"My name is Lan Ying. What is yours?"*

"Uh…?" Amelia was so startled, for a moment she forgot what her own name was. She finally blurted out, "Amelia," feeling foolish. Lan Ying cocked her head to one side, expecting Amelia to add something. *What does she want me to say?*

The answer finally dawned on Amelia. A crazy thought ran through her mind. She added, "I'm a female, too. A girl, but I don't think I'm very bright. I am fifteen years old."

Lan Ying bobbed her horn up and down as if already knowing this. *"Amelia,"* the unicorn repeated, savoring the name in her mind. *"Pretty."*

Amelia automatically replied, "Thank you. How is your wound feeling? May I see?"

Lan Ying unfolded her long legs and stood, stepping out of the stall and walking into a shaft of moonlight filtering in through a window. The unicorn swung around and presented a hindquarter to the girl for inspection.

In the dim light, Amelia barely made out where the arrow pierced the alabaster hide by a dark red blotch marring the coat. She touched the hair tentatively using one fingernail and scrapped gently. The blood was dried and flaked off, but the wound itself disappeared.

"You're healed!" Amelia exclaimed in amazement running one hand over the unicorn's flank, brushing off the dried blood while searching for the wound in vain. "How…?"

"Unicorns heal very fast," Lan Ying replied as if this were common knowledge to everyone except Amelia. Her horn swung toward the barn door. *"We can be killed, but only a virgin can capture and ride us. Those three wished to kill me for my horn. Our horns have great power and can heal, too."* She gazed at Amelia. *"This is why I ran to you. You are a virgin. I can sense the purity. You are mine and I am yours. You may ride me if you wish."*

"Me?" squeaked Amelia. "How far can we go?"

"As far and as fast as you wish," the unicorn replied. *"You need but think and I will take you there. My fillies and I often explore new places. I do not mind traveling at all."*

Visions of racing over moon lite landscapes flashed through Amelia's mind. The same dream repeated every night when falling asleep. China and India lay in her grasp, even the far off lands from where the mercenary who gave her name sailed. Amelia grinned with excitement at the thought of seeing strange, far-off places and peoples.

The moon was setting. *It's still early morning. No will be awake yet. No one to see.* "Sure, when you're feeling strong enough. I mean when your wound…."

"I will always be strong enough to carry you. You are my rider now," came the soft reply. Lan Ying shook her head of the last bits of straw and ambled to the barn door, pausing, while waiting for Amelia to catch up.

Amelia had ridden a horse before, but always holding onto a saddle horn to mount, and stirrups for her foot as a boost. As the unicorn stopped in the darkness, Amelia halted at Lan Ying's side, contemplating the best way to scramble onto the unicorn's back. She took a step to the rear and ran forward with a springing leap, attempting a sprawling landing along the unicorn's spine while grabbing onto the mane. She tried pulling herself up onto Lan Ying's shoulders, kicking her legs and grunting from exertion. Amelia made the trip halfway and slowly slipped to the ground again.

A soft chuckle echoed in her mind. *"Either I am too tall, or you are too short. I see we both have some getting used to each other. Here,"* The unicorn bent down, folding her front legs beneath her chest. *"Now try mounting me. Hold onto my neck, hop, and kick your leg up and over. If this does not work I suggest we find a ladder or rock for you to stand on."*

Amelia studied the unicorn's back, now even with the top of her head. "If you say so," she replied dubiously. "First let's try the hop." She took a fast skipping run, leaped, and grabbed Lan Ying's mane, kicking one leg across the unicorn. Amelia landed hard on her chest, started sliding to the other side, and desperately righted herself, wrapping her arms around the unicorn's neck in a tight hug, and clutching her thighs to Lan Ying's sides as hard as possible.

Amelia's heart raced. She was actually on the back of a unicorn. The sweet, spicy odor of the animal's coat flooded her nose. The warm, soft hide pressed tightly against her body.

"Well, sit up, and let go of my throat, you are choking me," Lan Ying said, miffed. *"I will not buck you off. Besides, we have not even moved yet."*

"Oh." Amelia still clutched tightly to the unicorn, arms and legs locked around Lan Ying's body in a death grip. Grinning foolishly, she released Lan Ying's neck and sat straight.

I never realized how far down the ground would look from up here.

"Where do you wish to go?" The unicorn's muscles tensed as Lan Ying pranced about in a circle, tossing her head, which made the spiral horn bob up and down, glimmering sparkles in the dim light.

"Uh..." Where did she want to go? Amelia glanced at the sky. The moon had set. False dawn brightened the sky. China and India were too far away—for now. "The village," the town the first place entering her mind. No one would be on the streets yet. If the two hurried, they could ride down the main street. Amelia's eyes narrowed and a devilish grin passed over her face. Maybe one person would be on the road, or looking out her bedroom window. Chikako. *Wouldn't it be great if the witch saw me riding a unicorn? The sight would show her and Kenchi I don't need their friendship. I don't need anyone. I have a unicorn to ride and love.*

Lan Ying set off at a fast trot, Amelia bouncing up and down on the unicorn's back. A broad smile swept over her lips and she suppressed a nervous giggle as the cool morning air rolled over her body. A giddy, tickling started in the pit of her stomach flowing up to her chest. The breeze of the unicorn's passing ruffled her long black hair into a twisting cord and Amelia had trouble keeping a straight face as they rode across the field. The two hit the main road and the unicorn broke into a gallop, flowing over the surface of the way as if they skimmed on the top of the water. Amelia felt no sensation of movement, yet houses and fields flew past, a flipbook of movement while she stood still. The small town rose rapidly into sight. They passed the Buddhist temple in the middle of the village, the large, ornate doors tightly shut against the night. No lights showed in the windows to prove the inhabitants moved about or awoke yet.

"Can we slow down?" Amelia asked, swinging her head back and forth, attempting to view every doorway and window in sight from her new angle. "I want to see the shops as we pass."

"Of course, however I do not think we should go too slowly." The unicorn's head twisted from side to side also in distress, peering down dark alleyways. *"We make*

an easy target if hunters are about. I have taken an arrow to my rear once already this week. I do not need another bolt in my tail."

And I don't want to be seen and recognized, even by Chikako or Kenchi, Amelia thought. *What would happen if some shopkeeper peered out his window, saw me riding a unicorn, and the news returned to the warlord, or Captain Daiki? What was I thinking? He would have my mother and I killed for lying.*

Amelia rode on, nerves taut to the breaking point, indecision screamed in every fiber of her body. Should she tell Lan Ying to turn around and leave? They already traveled halfway through the town. The distance was as far out as in.

The streets stayed deserted, however, and the unicorn slowed to a fast walk, trotting along the empty main thoroughfare. Amelia kept searching doorways, more concerned for people watching rather than the contents of the storefronts, but most were shuttered tight, a few lights shown from second story windows where the shopkeepers lived above their stores in the rear of the buildings; early morning risers eating a quick breakfast and preparing for the long workday ahead.

"A wagon approaches."

Amelia swung her attention from the stores to the street ahead—a farmer transporting produce from his garden to sell at one of the vegetable stands in the market. He walked next to his ox-cart, drowsing as he stumbled along. The beast ambled down the middle of the road, as sleepy as the farmer was. Neither ox nor man observed the approach of Amelia and Lan Ying.

Amelia ducked low, burying her face in the unicorn's mane. "Oh, we can't be seen. Do something."

"Me?" Lan Ying swung her head around to stare at Amelia in surprise and snorted. *"What do you expect me to do?"* The filly said as an after-thought, *"Unicorns do not*

turn invisible, you know. We are much too pretty to hide ourselves. Our glory should be seen by everyone—except hunters shooting arrows, of course."

"Great." The farmer and his cart drew nearer. Amelia hid her face deeper into the mane of the unicorn so he wouldn't recognize her and thought hard. She shouted into Lan Ying's ear, "Run fast. As fast as you can."

"That I can do."

A sudden lurch rocked Amelia, hurtling her backward on Lan Ying as the unicorn accelerated with blinding speed. She clutched onto the mane, yanking hard to pull forward again as the long hairs whipped her face, half-blinding her in the process.

"Hey, cut it out and stop tugging on my hair. You hurt."

"Sorry." Amelia released the mane and wrapped her arms around the unicorn's neck in a tense hug instead, squinting her eyes as dust and bugs flew into her face.

Out of the corner of her eye, Amelia caught a glimpse of the farmer straightening up at full attention, a startled expression crossing his features as she flashed past the wagon. The oxen kicked in fright, bolting and overturning the cart, spewing baskets of vegetables and the surprised farmer onto the road.

Then the end of the village appeared. Lan Ying slowed to a gallop and Amelia was able to sit upright again, spitting dirt and hair from her mouth, and brushing the long strands off her face. "Next time tell me when you're going to sprint," she complained, scrubbing grit from her forehead.

"But you said—"

"Yeah, I know what I said."

Dawn was breaking. The rising sun painted long orange stripes across the sky in different shades. Amelia and Lan Ying raced over the landscape. Shadows receded as the approaching morning and the green countryside revealed the far vista to their eyes. Before, two mountains rose from a pale white fog, towering over the surrounding terrain, shrouded in low clouds at the peaks.

Growing short on time, but what a beautiful view. I would love to see those mountains. "Lan Ying, how long would it take to reach the mountains so I can see everything?"

"Not long at all," the unicorn replied. *"This time no complaining how fast I run, but hang on tight, though,"* she reminded Amelia gruffly, tossing of her head, *"and not to my mane, please."*

The unicorn accelerated again, not at the torrid speed shone before, but still fast enough so they seemed to drift over the fields and leap brooks, as if the obstacles approaching were mere toys set in miniature. The mountains grew steadily closer and taller, looming giant-like in Amelia's vision. Soon the two climbed past streams, rivers and waterfalls, which danced along the slopes in sparkling ribbons of silver.

"Enough. Stop." A level area the size of a small field stretched around Amelia, a drop-off on one side displaying the landscape below. Rugged, high peaks on the other edge jutted into the sky. Lan Ying made mincing steps to the brink of the incline, sniffing the rocky ground as she walked.

Spreading out in clear view, the land stretched as far as the eye could see, altering into a haze at the horizon. In the foreground, the village and neatly separated velvet green fields surrounding the buildings appeared as if tiny scenes tossed across the countryside. "This is beautiful," Amelia, drew an intake of breath. The cool breeze blew her hair, and she pulled her kimono closer, stretching upward and shading her eyes with the right for a better view of the town and farmhouses. Interspersed among the emerald squares of pasture and crops, small blotches dotted the land, the dwellings of peasants who worked the earth for a living.

Amelia picked out the road leading from the town to her house, tracing the lane backward to find her home among the other scattered dots.

"What the…?" Where her house should be a pale grey smoke covered the area, spreading in soft swirls to conceal the small patch of their land. Amelia's eyes widened in disbelief and growing horror, realizing what this could only mean. *"Fire,"* she breathed. "Lan Ying, we must return home as soon as possible. My house is on fire and my mother is in danger."

The unicorn swung her head to stare at Amelia. *"I sense trouble in your tone. Have no fear; we shall fly like the fastest hawk."*

Lan Ying swung on her hooves and plummeted down the hill amidst a scattering of rocks and dirt, Amelia clinging onto her neck. All the while the girl breathed to herself while her heart hammered in her chest, "Let everything be alright. Please, Buddha, let my mother be okay."

They sped over the earth, across emerald fields and dirt roads. Lan Ying slid to a halt at the edge of the house. In front of Amelia the smoldering remains of her home sat, blackened beams still glowing red in the embers. The small barn a dark hulk of smoking ruins.

"Mother? *Mother—Where are you?"*

Amelia heard no reply.

"Your mother is not here. The woman is—gone."

"NO. She must be here somewhere." Amelia leaped off Lan Ying and dashed forward, coughing as a stray wisp of acid smoke blew in her face. She sprinted around to the rear of the smoldering ruins and gazed over the small patch of land they cultivated; positive she would see her mother standing in the field expecting her. A growing sense of

desolation ignited in her breast; a plaintive moan arose in her throat, a wail ripping out over the countryside.

"MOTHHHHER."

A moist nose nuzzled her in the armpit. *"She is gone. I sense it."* Lan Ying stood behind Amelia, her soft brown eyes gazing at the empty stretch of earth also.

Wetness gathered at the corners of Amelia's eyes and dripped down her cheeks, leaving faint runlets in the dust on her face. "Why didn't someone…the neighbors…..No one came to help." She fell to her knees, another high-pitched keening scream escaping her lips. Amelia stared at the unicorn, her stomach twisting into a cold knot. "Where is my mother? Do you know?"

Lan Ying lifted her head, nostrils flaring, ears cocked. *"The woman is not dead. I do not sense her in the ruins of the house or barn."* The unicorn made a slow circle, sniffing the breeze. She stopped, nose pointing across the field in the direction of the woods. *"That way."*

Amelia traced along Lan Ying's gaze. Her muzzle aimed straight through the forest to the warlord's castle. "The soldiers from last night," Amelia mumbled. "They must have returned this morning and found the blood trail leading to the barn." Horror and recognition seized her. She said, "They have taken my mother prisoner, and it's my fault."

"How can the abduction be your fault?" the reply from the unicorn reverberated in Amelia's mind. *"You have done nothing wrong. You were not here."*

"I rescued you," Amelia whispered back, placing fists to her mouth, attempting to hold back a torrid of tears. "I lied to the soldiers. They must have learned the truth."

The unicorn shook her head and snorted. *"I do not understand. Since when is saving me a bad thing?"*

Amelia bit her lower lip and balled her hands at her side, refusing to reply. She sank to the ground stricken in silence. She didn't know what to do anymore, who she was, where to turn for help. *I'm lost—Lost. Father, Mother, what do I do now? Someone, please tell me.*

Lan Ying continued, *"And I am not certain your mother is at the castle, or was taken prisoner, only she traveled in this direction."* Again, her head swung toward the forest.

The unicorn's words broke Amelia out of her misery. Her mind, paralyzed by fear, pushed back the blackness and she began to think coherently again. *Maybe Lan Ying is right. Of course, if soldiers attacked the house and set my home on fire, Mother would have run across the field and into the woods to escape. The forest is the only safe place to hide around here. All else is cleared farmland and she would have been seen by the men.* A glimmer of hope flared. *Who would know what happened this morning? Of course, old Tonacho-san. He sees and hears everything in the area.*

With renewed confidence Amelia rose. "C'mon, let's take a ride." Lan Ying knelt and Amelia leaped up and wiggled onto the unicorn's back. "Down the road and to the left."

Wisps of silver smoke curled out of the Tonacho's chimney from the cooking fire. Amelia surveyed the barnyard for signs of life and then beyond to the neatly plowed fields. A lone figure bent over, industrially hoeing away at weeds between the lines of vegetables. Amelia nudged Lan Ying forward past the building to the edge of the tilled rows and shouted, *"Tonacho-san."*

The old man painfully straightened and looked around at the sound of his name. His eyes lighted on Amelia and Lan Ying, widening in surprise and shock. He first exclaimed, "Where did you find a unicorn?" then he shook his head in dismissal. "It does not matter. Go away." He held his hoe like a spear and waved the shaft over his head. "You are in danger, and you place me in danger as well by being here."

"Huh?" Lan Ying halted. Amelia stared at the old man in surprise. "I would never…I don't understand what you're talking about."

"You saw your house?" Tonacho-san took a step forward, holding the pole across his body as if he would lunge at the first false move of Amelia or Lan Ying, and gestured angrily in the direction of the glowing remains of Amelia's home. "Your arrest has been ordered by the warlord himself, a reward offered, captured, dead or alive. The same is true for whoever is seen helping you." He shot quick glances left and right to the adjacent fields to see if anyone else watched. "Now go. You and your spirit animal leave. I do not wish to be killed or have my house burnt to the ground as yours was." He stopped suddenly and eyed her suspiciously. "For all I know you may be a demon already, killed by the daimyo's men and reborn to life to bear me to the next world." He stuck his whiskered chin out belligerently and brandished his hoe, dug his toes into the soft earth, prepared to a fight for his life. "If so, you will not find I walk willing to the grave."

"But, I have no intention of hurting you." Amelia shook her head. Tonacho-san was right, and standing here arguing did not make the situation better, but before leaving, one question remained. She asked in a soft voice, "My mother? Is she dead? A prisoner? Please tell me, I have to know if my mother still lives."

The old man paused. "A prisoner, I think, of the warlord's," he replied in a kinder voice. "When I first saw the smoke rising from you home I rush to help put the blaze out. Your mother was led away by the soldiers." His voice grew angry again. "Now go, I say, before my fate is the same as hers."

"Thank you," Amelia choked out. As the nightmare of loss continued to engulf her, Amelia murmured to Lan Ying, "Let's go back to the house. Maybe we can find something to salvage."

As the unicorn clopped up the road, Amelia kept repeating to herself, "What do I do? Where do I go? How will I survive?" until the questions took on a beat of their own, matching in some horrible way the treading of the unicorn. Her past consisted of scorched timber and cinders, the future cloudy and bleak at best. She was lost, adrift in a world suddenly cold and without hope.

The fire had burnt out; a few smoking beams among the black ash all that remained of her once beautiful home. Fallen debris covered the earth where her bedroom once stood, but Amelia managed to make her way to their small living room. *Nothing much,* she admitted to herself in disgust, digging through the cinders using a stick. Close to a wall, half buried in the dead embers, Amelia unearthed her father's *katana*—his samurai sword, inside the scabbard, somehow unharmed by the blaze. Amelia kept digging, hoping to find his bow as well, but the weapon was gone, destroyed in the fire, as was his quiver of arrows. Eagerly, Amelia grasped the scabbard and wiped the ashes off on her kimono.

She stood, transfixed, among the destruction of her home, eyes focused on the past remembering her father saying, "Samurai wives and daughters must learn the use of weapons to protect the household when the men are at war." She'd nodded silently and spent hours practicing the use of the bow and sword with Kenchi. Amelia also recalled him saying, "The duty of a samurai is to take revenge on those who attack us. For if we do not defend ourselves and those we love from evil, who will do it for us?"

"Father, I have failed you," she muttered, wetness streaking her cheeks anew. "I did not protect our home as I was told." Dark marks singed the heavy leather belt, but the rawhide remained strong and intact. In a daze, Amelia buckled the blade around her waist.

The weapon hung heavy on her hip, almost touching the ground. Amelia drew her father's sword and gazed at the shiny steel, running delicate fingers along the flat of the blade. "Created in the crucible of birth with fire, folded over again and again for strength. Beaten on the anvil of life to give the weapon meaning," she whispered as the tears flowed unchecked down her face. Amelia slipped the katana back into the sheath and straightened her shoulders. "I failed you once Father, and Mother. I shall not do so again. I hope I am as strong as you."

Amelia didn't know what would happen in the future. Every man's hand turned against her. One thought fixed clearly in her mind. *I must rescue my mother.*

An urgent whinny snapped Amelia from her trance. *"They come."*

Chapter Four

"Oh, no." Amelia stumbled out of the ash and ran to Lan Ying's side, scanning in every direction. "Who?"

"Soldiers. I can smell the odor of man sweat on their leather, the clinking of weapons against armor. We must leave before they attack us and capture you as well as your mother." The unicorn knelt. *"Mount."*

Amelia leaped, throwing one leg over the unicorn and grasping onto the mane. She searched the landscape desperately for a place to hide, her hair whipping back and forth as she hunted for a safe place out of sight. "I don't know where to go," she moaned at last. "I have no family now." A reward was out, no one would help, no relatives or clan to shelter for protection. Fear of the unknown clutched her.

"I will take you to safety," Lan Ying replied with assurance, and started trotting away from the ruins. The horned head swung to Amelia, liquid brown eyes gazing adoringly. *"You saved me. I will save you. I love you. We are together. This is the truth of our world."*

They crossed the field Amelia so recently picked berries in without a care in the world at an angle toward the dark forest. Behind, Amelia hear angry shouts, orders to halt upon pain of death, as arrows peppered the ground around the two. The unicorn sped up, streaking around trees and bushes, leaping over boulders as if they were pebbles. Amelia kept her head ducked, afraid she'd be slapped in the face by the branches from the trees they swept past, or tangled in the thorny vines the unicorn miraculously flitted through unscratched. The towering pines and maples shrank away, replaced by open ground covered by amber grass waving in the breeze. Amelia looked up. Ahead lay a wider, darker forest, somber trees like specters crouched to swallow unwary travelers. A stark peak rose in the distance capped with a tip of white snow. "Suicide Forest," she breathed. "Mount Fuji, sacred to the gods, birthplace of *Kuninotokotachi.*" She yelled at the unicorn at the top of her lungs to make herself heard over the rush of the wind, "Is that where you're taking me? *Aokigahara*—The Sea of Trees? Demons infest the place, the ghosts of the dead and malicious phantoms stalk its darkest recesses, waiting to haunt any who enter. Only the bravest venture in and even then many do not emerge to tell what horrors dwell in the shadows." A sensation of bugs crawling over her skin ran up her spine. Unimaginable terror clutched at Amelia's throat, eyes widening at the thought of the specters of the dead stalking among the dark trees, or demons lying in ambush to snatch the unwary such as she from the unicorn's back and render flesh and soul.

"You are good and your heart is pure," Lan Ying replied while galloping, the stark forest drawing closer with each muffled hoofbeat. *"You ride on a unicorn whose essence is as noble as yours is. You have nothing to fear."* She added sarcastically, *"Besides, it is still daylight. Everyone knows the spirits do not stir until night."*

Amelia wondered how untainted her soul really was, and what was to prevent the ghosts from waking early or a demon tying her up in a rocky crevice until dusk. She gulped as the forbidden forest drew nearer. *I hope I'm pure. After my thoughts today about what I'd do to the soldiers I'm not sure anymore.* Sound deadened as they entered the woods, a shroud of silence blanketing all noise. Even the chirping of birds and the scurrying of small animals was absence, as if they too shunned the malignant trees and bushes. No rustling of insect life marred the stillness. Only the rapid thumping of her heart and the beating of the pulse in her ears told Amelia she was still alive and in the real world, and not a ghost traveling in the nether regions. The atmosphere was chilled and damp, the kind of air felt in a crypt, which crept into ones body to make the bones ache. Lan Ying found a faint trail in the gloom, more of a dry streambed than path, and climbed upward over stones and protruding roots. Amelia gasped. The stinking corpse of a man leered at her from against a boulder next to the bank. Faint wisps of grey hair still clung to the decomposing putrid skull and chin. For the first time Amelia heard a noise, the low drone of flies buzzing over the body, as maggots squirmed out of sockets where the eyes should have been.

The grey kimono rotted into shreds. Moss and vines twisted around the torso, reclaiming the body as the earth waited eagerly to pull the remains back into the ground to a stony grave. Amelia squeezed her eyes shut and buried her face into the unicorn's mane, afraid to look anymore and fighting hard not to vomit at the rancid odor. *Ubasute—his people left him to die. The yurels will greet him here. His angry ghost will seek me out along with the other shades who have died in this place. Please don't haunt me. I didn't kill you. I didn't kill any of you. I am good. I am good.*

Amelia peeked left and right, refusing to keep her gaze on the rotting corpse. Out of the corner of her eye, to the left, she saw a flash of movement, a pale shifting fog gliding through the air between the tree trunks, but when she swung to stare directly, the mist disappeared. *Is my imagination playing tricks on me? I did see something, I did—I think.* A low moan floated from the right accompanied by the crash of a tree and the shriek of a woman. Amelia twisted in the direction the screech originated from but found only the dark boles of the forest. *Oni—Demons. Buddha protect me. They will eat my soul. I know they will.* Amelia squeezed her eyes shut again.

Still Lan Ying climbed, as sure as a mountain goat over the rough terrain, heading deeper into the silent forest. Amelia refused to open her eyes, sure at any moment she'd feel the grasp of boney fingers on her shoulders, or the fetid breath of a demon on her neck, as the attack she was sure would happen finally arrived. The gasping of her breath rasped too loud in her ears and drowned out any other noise. After what seemed an eternity the unicorn halted.

"We are here."

Amelia took a shuddering breath, unsure of what to expect. She lifted her head, squinted her eyes open, and peered about, positive ghosts of the dead or fanged demons encompassed her eager to dine.

They stood in a small cool glen. To one side a waterfall tumbled from the heights draining into a small pond, the tinkling of the water murmuring like silver bells. A clear stream gurgled from the pond, running downhill through moss-covered rocks and into the dark forest. On the other side of the clearing, the land dipped into a lush green meadow, the chirping of birds floating faintly in the air. From her vantage point in the glen, Amelia barely made out the faint contours of the terrain below. The air felt warmer, too, then in the forest; a soft velvet glove covered by the odor of honeysuckle and wild roses filled the breeze.

"This is beautiful," Amelia exclaimed, straightening on the unicorn as far as possible and craning her neck in all directions to have a better view of the landscape. "I never knew such a place like this existed in the world."

"The glen is sacred to the unicorn, and protected by us against all evil stalking the surrounding forest," Lan Ying replied with the faint ring of pride in her thoughts. Her horn jabbed in the direction of the pond. *"Beyond the waterfall is a hidden cavern. You will be safe inside. The cavity is the womb of the earth from which all unicorns galloped in the great stampede of antiquity."*

For the first time Amelia noticed a stony ledge around the base of the pond curving behind the water cascading from above. She slid off Lan Ying's back and took cautious steps toward the rock face, being careful not to slip on the wet stones. "No ghosts, right?" Amelia asked, only half in jest as she looked at Lan Ying. "No demons? Spirits? Remember, you promised." She peered along the ledge toward the black opening.

"Go." Amelia felt a prod on her bottom as Lan Ying nudged from behind with a sharp horn. *"Not even as much as a fearsome mouse or a snake, I promise. Unicorns never lie,"* she chided, her nostrils flaring and flicking her mane in mock anger.

"Hey, you hurt," Amelia yelped, rubbing herself and throwing a glare backward at the unicorn over her shoulder. Lan Ying stood patiently for her to hurry up. "I'm going, but you don't have to be so rough. A simple, 'Please move,' would be sufficient." Amelia strode forward along the ledge, attempting not to show the fear lucking inside.

The rush of the water splashing into the pond drown out all other noise, even the echo of Lan Ying's hoofbeats on the rock. Spray moistened Amelia's hair, damping her skin. The curtain of falling water dimmed the sunlight, making sparkling green shadows glisten off the wet stone. Amelia paused, holding out a hand and collecting spray in her palm. "This water is warm," she exclaimed, extending an arm into the liquid and allowing the flood to splash over her fingers. "Why is it warm?" A tingling started in her skin, burning, her hand turned red. Amelia snatched her arm out of the flow. *"Ouch.* This stuff hurts. Is there something mixed in? Poison? Acid?"

"Which reminds me." Lan Ying stepped forward, shoving her spiral horn into the flow. Golden motes flashed off the tip, traveling up and downward through the liquid, glistening flickers changing the color of the water to a light yellow before becoming clear again. *"There, this is better. The water will not hurt you anymore,"* the unicorn announced with a nod as she withdrew the horn. *"You humans are such frail creatures. Someone should tell your emperor to allow unicorns to rule Japan. We are much*

more durable and wise. This would be good for the kingdom and the people much happier."

Amelia disregarded Lan Ying's statement and asked, "What did you do?" She cautiously slipped her hand into the mist again, ready to jerk out fingers at the slightest discomfort. This time the water was warm and soothing. The stinging in her skin halted as if the burning never was.

"Hot water is forced up from the earth below through crevices in the rock," came the smug reply, *"and mingles in the cold rushing from the river above. The flow gushing through the cracks, however, contains great earth magic. It will not harm animals who are part of the natural world, but to humans who do not live in harmony with nature, the liquid is poisonous if drank or even touched. My horn contains healing powers granted to me by the gods. The magic took the enchantment out, making the water harmless for you or any human. This is the reason those soldiers hunted me. For the medicinal properties of my horn."*

Amelia's eyes widened. "Is there anything else dangerous I should know about? Poisonous snakes, maybe? The *mamshi*?" She scanned the water and the rocks searching for any reptiles, which might lurk in the crevices or swim in the depths of the pond.

"I told you, no snakes. The fall was the only thing unsafe. In fact, the same heat warming the water also warms the cavern, keeping the cave dry and comfortable summer and winter. The earth provides well for us here as long as we abide by its rules. Now—KEEP MARCHING. I am becoming soggy from the mist, and my mane frizzes after the hair dries." To emphasis the point, Lan Ying shook her head, spray Amelia with droplets of moisture from the nape on her neck. *"See? It is already becoming curly. I am going to look like I have a bush growing on me."*

"Hey, I'm moving." Amelia hurried on until she stood before the opening of the cavern. Taking hesitant steps, she entered, searching the floor for rocks that might trip her. The opening was narrow but broadened into a vast space having a high vaulted ceiling. Sunlight filtered from cracks in the rock, changing the darkness into gloom she could see in. "This is perfect," Amelia said as she swung in a slow circle, examining the top, sides, and floor. Her eyes came to rest on a corner. Built along one edge, someone arranged flat rocks to construct a crude stone oven. More rocks were piled strategically for shelves as high as a man could reach, on which tightly bundled packages rested. On the ground, the occupant dug out a space and encircled the hole stacking stones for a fire pit. Hey, a person lives here." Amelia stalked forward and scanned the cavern for signs of life, and then the living spot more closely. A pallet containing dried grass lay along the wall with kindling stacked for the fire. Large chunks of lava rock scattered about for sitting, even a rough wooden stool rested by the simple bed.

"A human once stayed here," Lan Ying acknowledge as she walked toward the fire pit, *"a holy man."* The filly paused; head cocked, thinking. *"He was a Buddhist monk? The unicorns deemed the man pure of heart also. He thought good thoughts, and disturbed nothing or no one. But he has departed back to his ancestors years ago, before I was born. No one has resided here since."*

Slowly, almost hesitantly, Amelia moved about the space, afraid the ghost of the monk might linger in this place and be angry if she disturbed his belongs. In one dark corner, she spied two objects making her eyes light up—a bow and quiver of arrows. Amelia threw caution aside and eagerly ran forward, grasping both, and held the two up to the light. "Using these, I can hunt," she exclaimed to Lan Ying.

"In this forest you may not hunt," the unicorn replied firmly. She shook her head. *"The killing of warm blooded animals is forbidden. This is a tradition of the unicorns and one the monk approved of."*

"But—what am I supposed to eat then?" Amelia frowned. Her stomach rumbled. At the mention of hunting, she remembered her last meal was the night before and she'd missed breakfast.

"Well, fish and fowl are allowed," the unicorn conceded glumly, *"but nothing wearing fur. We have our rules, you know. We do not want some foolish hunter to mistake us for deer. Would not do at all to have humans running about shooting arrows at unicorns, now, would it? First, it is a squirrel, then a rabbit. Next thing you know I have a bolt in my rump again."*

Amelia cocked her head to one side. "Birds and fish aren't animals?"

"Not our kind of animals, anyway. Noisy and not too bright, I would say. The unicorn snorted in revulsion. *"Why, have you ever had a bird fly overhead and...?"* A shiver ran along the unicorn's back, as if the subject was too revolting to continue talking about. Lan Ying said, *"You can eat snakes, lizards, and frogs, too. No one likes slimy, creepy creatures."*

"Yuck. Neither do I for that matter," Amelia replied, and stuck out her tongue in disgust. "At least not to eat, anyway."

Hunger still fresh in her mind, Amelia marched out of the cave carrying the bow and arrows, determined to catch a meal. She continued to walk until she arrived at the beginning of the meadow. Lan Ying trailed and stood by her side while Amelia studied the tall grass, checking for movement, and feeling the breeze in her face. "Been a long time since I fired an arrow," Amelia commented, selecting a bolt from the quiver and fitting the notch into the string. She tugged on the cord experimentally and nodded. "I haven't shot one of these since my father died. I doubt if I can hit anything at all." Amelia gazed across the field. "I wonder if there's anything to hunt."

"I know one way to learn," Lan Ying replied. *"Stay quiet and be prepared to shoot, but remember, nothing wearing fur."* With those parting words, the unicorn cantered into the meadow, kicking up dust from the tall grass as she trotted and releasing loud whinnies.

Amelia waited tensely, hardly breathing, eyes narrowing. Holding the bow in one hand, she drew the cord and arrow back with the other. A flurry of wings beat into the air and a brownish-red pheasant launched into the sky from under the unicorn's legs, streaking past Amelia's line of vision in a blur of color.

Amelia took careful aim, tracking the fowl, and released the arrow whispering a small prayer. A soft screech echoed across the meadow and the bird plummeted to earth.

"Got 'em!"

Grinning broadly, Amelia ran forward and retrieved arrow and pheasant, holding the bird up for Lan Ying to see. "Acceptable, right? No fur."

The unicorn ambled forward and sniffed at the pheasant. *"Quite alright. I would never eat the thing, but humans—well, what can you believe. I have heard you people can consume anything, the same as pigs and rats."*

Amelia shrugged and walked toward the cave. With a straight face she replied, "Well, at least I'm in good company, but what can you expect from creatures who walk on two legs? Besides, think of it this way, eating birds leaves more grass for you and the other unicorns to dine on."

Lan Ying's head reared up, her eyes widen in surprise. *"You are right. I never thought of that."*

Within the hour, Amelia gutted the bird, plucked the feathers, and had the fowl roasting in the crude oven. As the sun settled over the western mountains leaving long fingers streaking the sky, she laid back and examined her next move.

The faces of her parents floated in her mind's eye. For some reason Amelia's vision settled on her father. Until the last, he'd always figured out a way of solving problems and achieving his goals—except for the final end when he was left no choice. Amelia stared into the glowing embers in the oven. His sole flaws, his unwillingness to compromise his principles. His undying loyalty to friends and the character of a samurai warrior were his downfall. She knew he tried to cooperate with those around him, even crossing clan allegiances, by his act of training Kenchi. He thought extending a hand of friendship to the young man was sufficient to bring the waring fractions of their domain together—only closeness wasn't enough.

Kenchi. Playmate, companion—a hope of maybe more at one time? His kindness the other day still flowed in her mind, and then she remembered Chikako's words at the river and her fists balled at her side. Kenchi would marry Chikako in the future and this was the end of might-have-been. Now he was the enemy, and probably used her and her father all along to acquire the training he would never receive otherwise. His father's clan aligned with the new daimyo, sworn to him. Amelia never thought of family loyalties before. She was still a young girl and the world of political intrigue never entered her mind. Why the hate and fighting? Why the distrust of each other? Weren't they all one people giving allegiance to the emperor? He was the descendant of the sun god himself. Why didn't he make everything right, or the shogun?

Amelia clamped her eyes shut and shook her head, black hair flying back and forth like a whip, as she tried to clear her mind of useless thoughts. This was going nowhere. How would she rescue her mother from the new daimyo?

"Lan Ying, do you know of any way to enter the warlord's castle?" Amelia said. It was crazy to ask, but who knew what magic the unicorn was capable of producing when she put her mind to the task.

Lan Ying was busy nuzzling the wrapped packages on the shelves, sniffing curiously at each one before examining the next. At the call of her name, she turned her head toward the girl. *"The front gate always works for me when I want to enter a castle."*

The sides of Amelia's mouth slumped down. "No silly. I mean a way to sneak in without anyone seeing us. A secret way. A hidden passage? Uh—or, you know. A magical way, maybe? Can you walk through the walls and materialize inside? A unicorn way."

Lan Ying ambled over. *"The fortress is well guarded. The warlord has many troops patrolling all entrances. Besides, unicorns do not sneak. We are too handsome a beast to cloak ourselves and hide. Everyone must see how perfect we are so the animal kingdom can sing our praises and marvel at our beauty."*

"Then how can I release my mother from there?" Amelia replied as her face twisted in frustration. "I don't see how?"

"Knock at the front gate and ask politely?"

Amelia's voice broke as she sputtered in dismay and glared at the unicorn. "Oooh—you're no help at all."

The unicorn nuzzled her with a soft nose. *"I love you."*

In spite of her anger, Amelia found herself smiling as she gazed into the unicorn's soft brown eyes. She reached up and hugged Lan Ying around the neck. "I love you too, baby, but I can't walk up to the daimyo's castle. I would be arrested and killed." She pictured herself striding up to the gate, asking for her mother's release. Amelia cringed at the thought what would happen next as the guards seized her.

"You will not know unless you try, but if you do not wish too, then the only other choice is to vanquish the warlord in combat and take your mother back by force."

"WHAT?" Amelia stared at the unicorn in disbelief, unsure if she'd heard Lan Ying correctly. "Defeat the warlord in battle, you said? And how am I supposed to do that?"

"How should I know? I am a unicorn and as such abide in peace and harmony with all living creatures. We do not do fights. War is a human thing. Eating fresh grass is much nicer and tastes better. I would try asking politely first though. Much easier and faster."

What the unicorn said was absurd. How could a fifteen-year-old girl defeat a warlord single-handedly? Even if she could raise a following, maybe some of the old daimyo's soldiers who knew her father, if she could locate such, would be not enough. Amelia's temples pounded. Tension built in her shoulders and radiated into her neck. The day was too long, too much happened to try thinking rationally. "I gotta sleep," she muttered to Lan Ying, standing. A wave of dizziness swept over her as she staggered to the pallet of grass and threw herself down.

Mother. Father. Kenchi. What do I do?

***

Amelia glanced at the kimono drying on a rock in a thin shaft of sunlight filtering through the branches. She'd spent the morning gathering large supplies of firewood gleaned from the fallen trunks of trees on the forest floor, and laboriously hauled armfuls to the cavern. Afterwards she bathed in the pond, scrubbing herself raw with sand, and given her single worn garment the same treatment as well, while marveling how the earth magic in the water made everything so clean. Large rents marked the length of the fabric, the hem a tangled mass of strings and knots. Amelia picked up the cloth and held the kimono against the sunlight. In some places, the light shone straight through.

"Soon I'll be walking around naked," Amelia mumbled to herself, shaking her head in misery. "Then what do I do?"

Lan Ying raised her head at the sound of the girl's voice. The unicorn trotted to the pond and nuzzled Amelia inquiringly. *"Something is troubling you?"*

"Yes. See?" Amelia lifted up the gown. "Nothing but tattered rags. If I ever venture into one of the towns, the villagers would laugh me right out again. I look like a beggar—a poor one."

Lan Ying sniffed the wet garment. *"The garment smells like you. Your odor clings to the fabric."*

Amelia put the kimono to her nose and inhaled. *"Phew.* You're right." She pushed the cloth away to arm's distance. "Thanks for telling me. It's not only a rag, but I can't get the stench of my sweat out of this tattered scrap either."

"Well," the unicorn replied, reasonably, *"Your hair is quite long. Not as beautiful as my hair, but why wear clothes at all? I do not and no one laughs at me. I think you would look beautiful covered in your mane if it were longer."*

Amelia suppressed a giggle at the thought of her hair wrapping around her skinny body. "I really would be a sight then wouldn't I, naked, my hair covering my chest and hips, riding a unicorn."

Lan Ying shook her head, perplexed at Amelia's reluctance to abandon clothing. *"If you insist on covering your body in dead things, and you do not like what you wear now, put on something else. I do not see why this upsets you."*

"Like what?" Amelia snapped back. She shook the cloth at the unicorn. "This one gown is all I have. They don't grow on trees, you know."

Lan Ying swung her horn toward the mouth of the cavern. *"The monk left many bundles. Some of the packages contain clothes. I can smell the fibers of the plants. Maybe one will fit you."*

"Really?" Amelia shot a look at the waterfall and cavern mouth beyond, eyes wide. She nodded. "Thank you. I never thought to check." She rose and padded inside the cave, barefoot and naked; her kimono left on the pond bank forgotten in the rush, and strode to the shelves where the bundles lay.

"Try this one." Lan Ying's horn poked one soft package wrapped in deerskin and tied by a string. *"This bundle smells clean and fresh."*

Amelia's fingers tore at the knots and pushed back the wrappings. "Oh, my," she breathed, holding up a pure white kimono and sash for the unicorn to see. She shook the garment out to get rid of the wrinkles and draped the cloth against her body. "The gown fits," Amelia exclaimed in delight, beaming at Lan Ying, "and the material is so beautiful." Her fingers caressed the fabric and she slipped the kimono on. Without tying the sash around her waist, Amelia held her arms out and twirled in a circle. "White is lucky, too, like you are," she informed Lan Ying, smoothing the cloth with her fingers. "The color stands for purity and truth." Before the unicorn could reply, Amelia ran outside to see how the gown looked in the brighter sunshine.

Minus the sash, the garment bellowed out behind her like the wings of a white dove. Amelia spread her arms wide, giggling, and shouted, "Look at me, I'm a bird." She kept running, making circles, until she reached the meadow revealing a panoramic view of valleys and hills stretching before her.

Lan Ying galloped up. *"You run fast for a human."*

"Not really," Amelia gasped, out of breath. She pointed toward a town in one of the valleys. "Down there are people who can run much faster than I can."

The unicorn followed her hand. *"Those people? They do not move swiftly at all."*

"Where?" Amelia craned her neck, searching the landscape for the people Lan Ying referred.

"On the road. The humans are all tied together like horses by the neck and being led." The unicorn studied the chain of bodies. *"I do not see how the creatures could run at all secured like animals. In fact, I saw one stumble and fall before he was jerked back to his feet."*

Amelia spotted the road and traced the length until she made out a line of figures trudging their weary way on the path. *"Prisoners,"* Amelia spat out the word, eyes narrowing, attempting to make out individual people. "The warlord has taken more captives to work his fields and fight in the army." Her jaw muscles clenched and lips compressed into a grim line of frustration. "Oooh, I wish someone would try and stop him for once. The man is a devil—*Evil*. He has no compassion for anyone at all."

Lan Ying swung her head to Amelia. *"You are someone. Why do you not try?"*

"Me? How could I stop him? He has an army; all I have is a unicorn."

The unicorn snorted. *"And that should be enough for anyone, but you have a bow, also. You have arrows. You have a sword,* and *a unicorn to ride. This is more than most have, and most important, you want something done."*

"True, but...." Amelia stopped in mid-sentence. *What Lan Ying says is right*, she thought. *Maybe I can't raise an army of warriors and defeat the warlord, but someone must put a foot down somewhere. Why not me? I can't get my mother released, but maybe I can save those poor souls down there from the same fate as hers.*

Amelia spun around and stalked back to the cave. "C'mon, Lan Ying. We're going for a ride."

The girl entered the cavern and returned a few minutes later with sash firmly knotted around the kimono, her father's sword buckled around her waist, the quiver of arrows slung over her back, and bow clutched in hand. Possessing more strength then she knew, Amelia clambered onto the back of Lan Ying before the unicorn could kneel. She patted Lan Ying on the neck and said in a determined voice, "Okay, you. Let's see if we can strike a blow for truth and justice."

Chapter Five

The downward slope through the Sea of Trees was rocky, craggy outcropping kept protruding from the earth like bones, and the forest threw out tentacles of trees and roots as if to slow anyone from escaping its grasp. Low hanging branches and vines whipped out of nowhere, clinging to Amelia, ropes of the dead wishing to keep her bound until nightfall.

Lan Ying and Amelia zigzagged their way around ledges of boulders and the tangle of the forest, until they hit the flat leaving the trees behind and open country before the two. The unicorn increased her pace to a gallop, and the road the prisoners tread on flashed into view. Lan Ying sped along the dusty lane until the gang of captives and their guards were plainly visible in the distance. One soldier marched behind the line, a single warrior on either side covering the flanks. The commander of the procession marched in front, occasionally casting a glance to his rear, reassuring himself the column kept up and in order. Amelia tugged an arrow from the quiver and fitted the notch into the cord.

"Slow down some," Amelia shouted to the unicorn. "I want to do this quick, but not this fast. I can't shoot straight with you bouncing up and down."

Lan Ying's breakneck speed slowed to a gallop, the gait as smooth as a whisper. Amelia drew back the arrow, and taking careful aim, released the bolt at the rear guard. The moment the arrow zipped away, she snatched the sword from its scabbard.

A reverberating, "*THUD*," echoed in the air as the arrow hit home, and the rear guard released a scream of pain, collapsing to the ground. Amelia howled a savage cry of triumph, feeling the blood lust rising in her soul to avenge her father's death and the abduction of her mother. By chance or purpose Lan Ying's shoulder smacked into the flanking soldier, bowled over the guard as the filly galloped past and up the line of prisoners. The captives halted in their tracks, open-mouthed as they gaped at Amelia, who yelled like an avenging angel of death, dressed in pure white, streaking by the column, her sword raised overhead. As she drew abreast of the front edge of the captives, the commander spun around to investigate the screaming and faced Amelia in shock. Amelia bent low, and using all her strength, swung the sword in a wide bolo chop across the man's throat. With a gurgling cry he dropped.

"Okay, baby," Amelia whispered into Lan Ying's ear as the unicorn slowed to a trot, "let's go back and see if we can free those prisoners."

The unicorn turned in a wide circle and cantered back to the line of captives, who watched the two in awe. Fear etched their faces, not knowing what to expect. Three of the prisoners dropped to their knees dragging others to the dirt, heads bowed in a position of servitude and respect.

"I believe I broke the guard's shoulder when I bumped him," Lan Ying remarked. *"He is slow to rise and I feel his pain. Humans are such frail creatures, are they not? None of you would last a minute in horse tag. My fillies and I would smash you like worms. The fourth man still stands. Beware, he holds a weapon."*

"I see him," Amelia replied. She replaced the sword and notched another bolt. "Be prepared to dodge." She covered the samurai with an arrow.

The lone guard held his bow also, steel head pointed directly at Amelia's chest. Lan Ying trotted closer, the girl and soldier locking eyes, stiffening in anticipation to see who would shoot first. The tension in the back of Amelia's neck grew the nearer she approached the samurai and prisoners, but still the man made no gesture to either shoot his arrow or drop the bow in surrender.

Finally, with mincing steps Lan Ying stood next to the captives. Amelia was forced to make a decision—drop her bow to reach for her sword in order to cut the prisoners loose from the ropes binding the column together, and leave herself defenseless, or shoot and try to kill the guard before he shot back.

The man lowered his bow and Amelia saw his face for the first time.

"Kenchi."

"Amelia."

Her hand quivered and she slowly released the tension on the cord, aiming the point of the arrow toward the ground, the joy at seeing her friend quickly changing to caution mixed with anger. "We have always been honest to each other. I am going to put away my bow so I can release these men." Amelia kept her eyes steady on the young warrior, hands shaking. "Will you kill me?"

"You know I will not." Slowly Kenchi eased the draw on his bow also. His bolt aimed at his feet. Even at this distance, Amelia saw the sweat on his upper lip, the trembling in his arm. He chuckled mirthlessly, "Besides, I am outnumbered." He looked first at Amelia, and then at Lan Ying, who stood with horn lowered, snorting fiercely, and pawing the ground as if hoping for the command to charge.

Amelia released a sigh of breath she didn't realize she held and did the same, slipping the arrow back into the quiver and draping the bow over her shoulder. She slid the sword out and shouted to the prisoners for all to hear, "Hold the ropes up tight so I can cut your bonds."

As if her voice broke a spell embracing the prisoners in a trance, the bound men cheered and lifted the cords up from their necks attaching them together. Amelia rode down the line of captives, swinging her sword and slicing through the bindings. As she reached the end of the procession, a sharp thought from Lan Ying rang in her mind.

"Beware."

Amelia looked up. Kenchi had his bow drawn, arrow pointed straight at her head. He released the bolt.

Later, Amelia would say the arrow sped at her in slow motion. She could actually see the shaft twisting in the air as the missile drew nearer. Then the arrow zipped past her ear and a piercing wail arose from behind her and Lan Ying. Amelia whipped around.

The guard who Lan Ying knocked down stood five feet behind her, frozen. One hand clutched the arrow in his chest, the other a sword, lifted high over his head to strike. The soldier crumbled to his knees, dropping the weapon from limp fingers and grabbed the shaft, attempting to pull the arrow out before he fell on his face, driving the barb deeper into his chest.

"This was the first man I have ever killed. One of my own." Kenchi stood before Amelia, stony faced. His features showed no regret but a tear trickle along the side of his cheek.

"I have killed also, today. This too, was the first time I have committed such an act," Amelia admitted in sorrow, seeing her pain reflected in the face of the young warrior.

The two young people stared at each other, embarrassed by their emotions, and spoken admissions, not knowing what else to say an afraid to say anything more.

The silence was broken by one of the captives, a farmer by the look of him, who approached Amelia and Lan Ying. "Thank you, Lady." He bowed deep. "Without your help the warlord would have taken my life from me, put me into one of his mines, digging until the end of my days."

Amelia raised her voice and addressed the rest of the captives. "You are all free now. Return to your homes and farms."

A burly, middle-aged man with a harelip retorted, "We cannot return to our towns or anywhere. The daimyo will arrest us, and this time our punishment is our deaths for escaping him the first time. We are fugitives lacking food, or a place to live."

Amelia realized this was true. She'd never thought about the fate of the men once she freed the prisoners. If the captives showed their faces anywhere in the domain of the warlord he'd have each beheaded.

A tall man bearing a scar across his face laughed gruffly. "So we shall be outlaws, bandits who rob the rich and take what the wealthy carry. What of it? I was once a soldier in the old warlord's army. Fighting and killing are no great matter to me. If being a criminal mean my life or theirs, food in my belly or hunger, the choice is easy."

A few, "Ayes," of agreement echoed from the other men. Amelia said, "You were a soldier of the old warlord's? My father was too. A great captain. His name was Yuto—Yuto Mochitoyao. He fought for many years with the old warlord."

Scarface studied her closely and nodded. "I recognize you. He brought you to our camp one day. I remember him holding your hand as the men practiced archery and swordplay. Your father was my captain and I respected him dearly as did all his men. I heard he was dead, acting as an honorable samurai should, showing character and courage, committing seppuku rather than swear allegiance to the new ruler."

Amelia nodded. "Yes, what you heard is true. He refused to bow to the warlord and compelled to die. The warlord has also captured my mother and holds her in his castle as one of his new servants. I mean to force her release."

The scar-faced man turned to another with a questioning look, who nodded, then said to Amelia, "My name is Haruto." He shoved a thumb at the other man. "This is Sota. If you wish, we will fight to free your mother. Your father was a brave and good man. We both served under him and would help if we could. As samurai we understand retribution must be delivered to the new daimyo for his acts of dishonoring you." He broke out in a loud laugh. "Besides, we have nothing else to do now, no home, or captain to follow. It would be good to reap revenge on our new daimyo and show him the cost of making us desolate."

Sota rubbed his right fist into his left palm. His death-like eyes glistening with excitement. "Revenge against the warlord is fitting. He killed many of our friends. This will be his turn to see his people suffer."

"Uh, yeah, I guess so," Amelia said, taken aback by the vehemence of his tone and the hungry expression on his face. "Sure, you can help me free my mother. I'm going to need all the assistance I can get."

Haruto and the other men stripped the guards of their weapons and whatever provisions they carried. The warrior returned, swinging a sword experimentally to acquire a feel for the blade. He eyed Kenchi darkly and said to Amelia, "What should we do to this one? Kill 'em?"

"No."

The young man smiled faintly and dropped his hand on the end cap of his sword, ready to draw his weapon in defense of his life if necessary.

"Are you sure? He was one of our guards, the warlord's man," Haruto said. "You cannot let him run free. He will report back to his master what transpired here, and lead soldiers to recapture us." His tone left no doubt he wished to kill Kenchi and finish him as soon as possible. Sota started to edge around the others to stand behind the young warrior.

Both men stared at Amelia waiting for a decision. "He is my friend and he saved my life," she hurried to explain to Haruto before a fight broke out. "If he reports what we do here, then so be it, but I will not have him harmed." To Kenchi Amelia said, adding as much vehemence as she could put into words, "You are free to leave and return to your family, Chikako, and the new daimyo." A thought struck her, and Amelia drew herself high on Lan Ying's back. "If you are to inform the warlord of what I have done, tell him also this is but the first of many attacks 'till he frees my mother. Until he does I will give him no quarter or peace in this land."

Kenchi's mouth twisted into a scowl as he surveyed Amelia, Haruto, and Sota. He said in a low voice, "I am afraid I cannot inform him of anything. I have killed one of my companions. If I return and tell the warlord you released me, he will suspect I collaborate with you and wonder why I did not die alongside the rest of the men." He shrugged. "He will kill and torture me if I tell him the truth, and my family as well." Kenchi took in the measure of the former captives standing around and listening. "I am now as the people here, homeless, and seeking employment. You appear to have the beginnings of a small army. Do you need another warrior?"

"I would not trust him," Haruto scrambled to protest in a loud voice. He said to Kenchi, "How do we know you will not turn spy? This lady," he nodded to Amelia, "said you are her friend, and I believe she believes this is true, but where do your true loyalties lay?"

"When Mochitoyao-san brought Amelia to the training camp, I accompanied the party. You remember seeing Amelia. Do you recall me as well?"

Haruto rubbed his chin and squinted his eyes, studying Kenchi's face, thinking back. "Now that you mention the fact, I do recollect another child accompanying the two." He appraised Kenchi in a new light and nodded. "You've grown some, boy."

Kenchi broke into a smile, the tension in his body draining. "I guess so, but that was years ago. Mochitoyao-san taught me everything I know. He was my master. My first loyalty is to him and his family—Amelia and her mother. This is a trust I cannot sweep away and still call myself a true samurai warrior." He said to Amelia, "You believe me? I would join you in this endeavor and see your purpose through to the end, no matter what your end might be."

"Huh?" The idea never crossed Amelia's mind Kenchi might wish to fight alongside her. He was a different clan, the enemy, now taken by Chikako as a husband-to-be holding a bright future; his family was an accepted part of the new order in the domain. He humiliated her in front of his friends. "Are you sure?" Amelia said at last. "Your father, mother? What will they think? You own both honor and respect also."

Kenchi replied seriously, "My parents would rather see me alive than commit seppuku, and my father always held great admiration for your father after he started training me to be a samurai warrior. My relatives will tell everyone I am dead, and understand why I stand by you."

Amelia nodded in recognition of his words. *I suspect he fears I will shoot him in the back if he tries to leave, but I will take him at his word. Even though he used me to continue his training with my father, still, he saved my life, and I owe him this much.* "Of course you can join me if you wish. I will be glad of your strong arm at my side." Her gaze swept the rest of the men. "Anyone who desires can join me." *Oh, dear. Where am I going to put all these people?*

Of the twenty men Amelia rescued, ten decided to enlist in her cause, eleven counting Kenchi. The rest casting their lot to a bandit's life in the wild, or venturing back to their homes, hoping their clan would hide them and the warlord would not discover their whereabouts, or forget about the captives entirely during the chaos of the larger war.

The troop set off across country, Amelia leading the band in front on Lan Ying, the men trudging behind trying to keep pace with the prancing unicorn, who continually swung her head around to snort at the group in frustration for their slowness.

"These clods move like turtles," the unicorn commented in disgust to Amelia when one of the older men begged for a rest halt, *"turtles walking through mud, and they smell of man odor and red meat."* A shiver ran the length of the unicorn's coat. *"At this rate it will be two days before we return to my soft meadow, the nice sweet grass, and scented air. Humans—HUMPH."*

"Lan Ying, what a terrible thing to say," Amelia exclaimed, her lips twitching. "These men were victims of the warlord, no doubt beaten and half-starved along the way. I wonder how the prisoners can walk at all." She snickered and patted the unicorn on the neck, whispering, "They do smell, but give the captives a chance to wash in the pond. I'm sure the man stink will go away." A thought struck her. "The water will not hurt the people?"

"The magic should, polluting the water with their male stench, too. No liquid, no matter how pure will ever wash away the odor of man reek. Nevertheless, my horn has made the fall and pond safe for smelly men, also, but I could never understand why you people have not gone extinct long ago." Lan Ying shook her head in bewilderment and issued another snort. Amelia caught, *"When we walk through the trees I bet the odor will not go away, but cling to the leaves and bark of the forest for a week like donkey dung,"* before the unicorn focused her attention along the track the party trailed.

Amelia rode in silence, feeling comfort in the presence of Lan Ying and her cryptic remarks. She tried to wipe away the destruction of her home, how to survive, and concentrated on the future and rescuing her mother from the warlord. The ideas would not form. *Leave it alone. I shouldn't force the thoughts. Think of something else for a while.* She said to Lan Ying, "What did you mean by horse tag and your fillies? You have fillies?"

If a unicorn could be said to chuckle, Lan Ying did. *"Of course. My age mates. We were all born in the spring of the same year. A puny human would never stand a chance when we gather together to play."* She paused and then said, *"One day you can meet my friends and see for yourself, but I warn you, you must ride on my back if the girls become too rambunctious. I do not want you hurt."*

"Me, neither." Amelia lit up in admiration. "Must be nice having lots of fillies and other unicorns your own age to talk to."

"Of course." Lan Ying looked at Amelia soberly. *"Do you have fillies?"*

Amelia shot a fast look behind her at Kenchi. A picture of him embracing Chikako flickered across her mind's eye. "I thought I did," she replied quietly, "but I guess I was mistaken."

The unicorn tossed her head. *"I will introduce you to my fillies. My friends will like you even if you are a human. Remember, stay on my back when we play, I do not want you trampled in the stampede."*

Behind them, Haruto fell in step beside Kenchi. "You and this girl Amelia are friends? How well do you know her? The girl does not seem old enough to fight, certainly not true warriors." He took in the measurement of Kenchi. "For that matter, neither do you."

Kenchi winced at the warrior's remark, but replied, "As I said, her father was my master. Amelia and I trained together since we were children. Her parent's farm lay next to my parent's farm. Her father taught us all he knew—bow, horse, and sword. Amelia held a katana, her father's sword, before she could walk, and a *naginata* not long after. Why do you ask?"

Haruto watch the stiff back of Amelia as she rode on Lan Ying. "The girl is determined to rescue her mother. I wonder how long the determination will last. Many people start having grand schemes, but in the end, most falter. I do not want to begin a war against the new daimyo and have my fighting fall to nothing."

Kenchi released a hearty laugh. "Do not worry about Amelia's resolve. You knew her father. He trained her, not only to be the wife of a samurai, but to be a samurai in truth. When we first learned the use of the bow, she was unable to drag the string all the way back. For weeks, Amelia carried the bow, tugging on the cord, building her muscles, even sleeping with the weapon. Her fingers bled from pulling the string. Eventually she was able to draw the cord all the way to her cheek without strain." Kenchi pointed a finger at Amelia's back. "That girl will not give up. She will strive to free her mother until the woman is safe."

"Or until we are dead," mused Haruto thoughtfully.

"Of course," Kenchi agreed. "Is this not what courage is all about?"

"She is so young, though. How can a girl, not even a woman yet, have such determination. The thought seems impossible."

Kenchi reached deep into his mind and remembered an old Japanese saying Amelia's father use to say. "You knew Mochitoyao-san, fought with him. One time when he first started training me and I could not use a sword, I asked, 'How can the son of a farmer become a samurai?'"

Kenchi smiled to himself. "He replied to me, 'Sometimes a kite breeds a hawk.'" He nodded to Amelia. She rode stoically on Lan Ying, face locked in determination, staring straight ahead at the mountains in the distance. "Look at her. This time the hawk has bred an eagle."

"A fledgling eagle," Haruto corrected drily.

"Nevertheless, an eagle."

Amelia led the small column, thinking the same thoughts as Haruto. She'd taken on the responsibility for these men, accepted their need to avenge themselves against the warlord. If the prisoners died in her service, their deaths were her fault as surely as if she took a sword and slayed each one. Was she willing to carry the blame and guilt? She possessed no idea how to rescue her mother, how to provide for the people. Her best choice was to tell the captives to disband before the war started, and save themselves. She should do the same. How could anyone think to battle the ruler of their province?

"What troubles you now?" Lan Ying looked at her as the column marched along. *"The impossible odor of smelly men? I told you they were foul!"*

"No, it's not any odor." The doubt Amelia felt bubbled up inside her and poured out over the unicorn. "Just thinking. If these men help me rescue my mother and they die, the destruction will be my fault. What right do I have to ask anyone to sacrifice their lives?" Amelia's forehead wrinkled into a series of creases as she concentrated on her thoughts. "I have no plan, no knowledge of warfare, not even where our next meal is coming from. I don't even know how to start."

"You will learn as you go," Lan Ying replied with certainty. *"When you were a baby you could not walk, then you learned. Afterwards you ran. This will be the same. As for the men,"* the filly cast a baneful eye at the captives puffing along behind her and Amelia, *"the creatures will make their own choices. These males obey their free minds, and will leave as quickly if they do not agree how you act."*

"You think I'm doing the right thing, then?"

"Unicorns never lie, and I am your truest friend. I love you."

The sun settled over the western horizon, and day transformed into dusk. The small party entered the Sea of Trees, the men shooting frightened glances over their shoulders. Weird howls and moans echoed through the forest, and even Amelia felt a creeping sensation up her spine as if bugs crawled along her flesh to lodge at the nape of her neck. The sweet smell of attar from the grave wafted from the carpet of leaves and twigs littering the earth, calling the living to join the dead in decay.

"Are you sure we are safe?" Kenchi jumped as an eerie cry reverberated along the darkening slope. He twisted to confront whatever menace issued the call, and clutched the handle of his sword tight, ready to draw the weapon if attacked by an unseen demon.

"I–I hope so," Amelia stuttered. "I stayed here yesterday and last night. Nothing bothered me." He mouth hardened into a thin line. "As long as you are pure of heart and have never deceived anyone for profit or false gain you have nothing to fear." She watched his face, positive her statement would invoke a reaction of fright from the young man if he used her. When Amelia didn't see the apprehension expected mirrored in his expression, she relaxed and worried about the other men in the troop. *Maybe he is truthful. I bet Chikako lied. I wonder if Lan Ying's protection extends to the rest of the warriors.* She patted the unicorn's head. Since their discussion of the slow progress of their party, and the debate about her mission, Lan Ying strode steadily ahead, refusing to acknowledge the presence of the ex-captives.

Suddenly one of the men in the rear of the formation released a blood-curdling yell, scratching at his face as if a swarm of bees attacked him, and scurried off into the surrounding darkness, howling in pain. Another screamed, raised his hands, fingers curled into claws fighting an invisible foe, and trailed him into the night.

"Should we go after those two?" Haruto asked as he drew his sword. Sota did the same. The faint crashing of bodies and curses reverberated among the trees, casting echoes in all directions as the men stumbled through the brush and tripped over rocks in the darkness.

"They have been judged unworthy," Lan Ying's thought drifted sadly to Amelia. *"The spirits of the forest have claimed the two as their own. Their souls are not pure and are fodder for the demons. They face the judgement of the evil their minds wrought during life, and pay for the wickedness in everlasting death."*

"Oh, my. I never thought they might not be worthy!" Horror of what she'd done shot into Amelia's chest. She counted the remaining men. *Have I rescued these poor devils only to have each killed in these woods?* "How about the rest, Lan Ying? Are the others safe? If I knew I was bringing the prisoners into danger, I would never have told the captives to join me."

The unicorn's shoulders gathered in a shrug. *"We shall see. This is not your fault; rather the evil deeds wrought in the past returned in kind. If the men who follow you have performed malicious acts, they forfeited their souls to the next world as well."*

"It's no use," Amelia said to Haruto, who peered fearfully into the darkness. As an afterthought, she said to the rest, "Think pure thoughts and all the good works you have done in the past." Amelia bent low, tapped Kenchi on the shoulder, and felt for his hand. His fingers entwined hers. "I may have misjudged you, my friend," she whispered to Kenchi, "but sharing my favor can't hurt."

Those were the only loses. After another mile, as twilight blackened into true night, the party reached the waterfall and cavern without further mishap. Breathing a sigh of relief, Amelia dismounted by the pond and beckoned the men to the ledge. "Walk behind me. We'll be safe here." She crossed her fingers, praying Lan Ying was not mistaken about the potency of her horn as the water sprayed on the men in a mist.

The band entered unharmed. Amelia groped her way to the fire pit and started a small blaze. When the fire crackled, throwing weaving phantoms on the ceiling, she waved in a circle around the cave. "Well, this is the place. Make yourself at home."

The men wandered about, exploring the recesses of the cavern in the dim light. Kenchi asked, "Food?"

Amelia put her hand to her mouth. "Oh, dear. I never thought of food. I have nothing."

Haruto, who'd walked directly to the shelves and examined the vessels and neat bundles stacked upon each other with interest, strode over carrying a big clay jar. "We will not starve," he exclaimed, holding up his prize and shaking the vessel vigorously, producing a loud rustle. "Rice, and plenty of it. I found two more containers also. We have the provisions from the guards, too. Tomorrow we shall stalk the countryside and hunt game. I am sure in these woods we can kill deer, boar, and hare. Easy pickings I'd say, and good eating for hungry men."

Amelia looked around the cavern in distress, afraid Lan Ying might have heard him. "Oh, no! You mustn't." Her gaze traveled to Haruto and Sota, shifted to Kenchi seeking support. "The spirits of the trees have forbidden the killing of anything wearing fur. Only fish and fowl may be hunted and eaten in this place." The men gathered around closely to listen. "I do not know what would happen if we killed animal in the forest," Amelia explained carefully. She watched the faces of each person. "And I would not care to find out. I have no desire to end up as the two who the demons took and ate this night." She gazed meaningfully at the men to let her words sink in and impress each of the force of her edict. "Many fish live in the pond; more swim up the river from the ocean. The meadow holds birds. I killed a pheasant there yesterday. No doubt quail, duck, and geese are present also. I haven't investigated the rest of the land, but I'm sure we can gather fruits and vegetables, too. Maybe rice growing wild in the field. We must explore the area tomorrow and see what we can learn if we are to stay here for any length of time and survive."

Amelia waited for a reaction. Kenchi nodded in understanding and strolled over to the pit, tossing more wood into the flames until the fire burnt bright. "If those are the rules of the forest, we must abide by what the spirits require. As you said, I do not wish to become a plaything for a demon who desires to feast on my soul." The rest muttered in agreement in low voices, shooting frightened looks toward the entrance to the cave as if evil ghosts lurked at the opening, listening to the conversation.

Kenchi waved Amelia over to the fire and sat cross-legged. "I think we'd better discuss how to rescue your mother before retiring for the night." He patted the space next to him. "Do you have a plan? I confess I know of no way to accomplish such a deed."

Amelia took a seat next to him. The men noticed the two preparing to talk, hurried over, squatted, and formed a circle around the fire pit. "No," she admitted after all assembled. "I've tried to think of one, but the last two days have been so hectic. I haven't had the time to really devise a scheme for her release." She stared into the fire watching the glowing sparks rise, the flames pasting a red sheen on her face. "Rescuing my mother will be impossible unless you or one of the men know a way." Amelia glanced around, hoping one of the ex-captives would throw out a suggestion or idea she hadn't thought of.

The warriors looked at each other in puzzlement. Haruto spoke up. "We could storm the castle. If we are lucky and quick enough, maybe we could enter and slip over the walls before the sentries even realized what was happening."

Low words circulated, discussing the idea. Kenchi said, "A frontal assault would never work. I have been to the warlord's fortress. Soldiers guard every entrance. More line the corridors at strategic points, and along the walls. We would not go ten feet before discovery."

"We might sneak in," suggested Sota, giving a sly nod. "Disguise ourselves, perhaps as farmers or merchants making a delivery to the castle."

"Attack like a *Shinobi*?" Kenchi replied in disgust. "Without honor? We might, but then we are no better than the warlord, and we lose all respect."

"Who cares about respect," said Sota, spitting into the fire. He wiped his mouth with the back of his hand. "The idea is to rescue the girl's mother, right?" He waved an arm in the air. "We can worry about face after the two are reunited again and we are safe from reprisal."

A chorus of "Ayes," arose from the men around the fire.

"Wouldn't work in any case," replied Haruto. "The farmers and merchants in the area are all known to the guards by person or name and carry passes. Before we walked through the main gate, the soldiers would arrest us, hold us for questioning, and kill the pack of us as spies. Besides, we need weapons to fight." His lips moved wordlessly as he counted around the circle. "A few swords and four quivers of arrows—"

"Five quivers," Amelia put in, touching the bolts and bow slung over her back.

"Five quivers of arrows," the warrior corrected with a faint smirk, "will not be enough."

Lan Ying ambled into the cavern while the men spoke. She thought to Amelia, *"If you are not going to ask politely for your mother's return, and you cannot steal her away, I hate to admit it, but you need more of these men, and will have to take your mother back by force."* The unicorn snorted and shook her mane in chagrin. *"I cannot believe I suggested more men in my cavern."*

Amelia shot a startled look at the unicorn. Would locating more warriors be possible? Yesterday the idea would have been absurd. Who would obey her? Now, she had eight, no, nine counting Kenchi, ten including herself, who were willing to die to save her mother.

"Where can we locate additional troops to help us?" Amelia asked Kenchi, "If we did recruit more, how could we arm those who we found?"

The young samurai rubbed his chin, thinking. Finally, he replied, "More fighters are no problem. All hate the warlord, although most are farmers or shopkeepers not trained in combat. A few like these," he motioned toward Sota and Haruto, "still exist, the remains of the old daimyo's army. Men would join our cause if the former warriors knew we wished to fight the warlord. Weapons are another problem, though." He paused, thinking again. "I know of a village by the coast where such would be found. I heard the samurai speak of a town in camp. The warlord is moving troops there. He has already brought in supplies of food and weapons to have provisions ready when the soldiers arrive. If we hurry, we could raid the stores before they are heavily guarded."

Amelia's eyes lit up. "How soon before the rest of the warriors reach the town? Where is this village? How far?" It was possible. Maybe, just maybe, she would raise an army of her own.

Haruto asked, "How many soldiers are there now? Do you know? Remember, there are only nine of us, three warriors, five farmers, and one girl. Not even a healthy troop of samurai."

"A day's journey from here," Kenchi replied eagerly, leaning forward and trying to answer both Amelia and Haruto at once, "and the warlord is still gathering his troops. The guards are conscripts, under the supervision of a samurai, from what I understand. The time before the troops are reinforced?" He stared at the ceiling of the cavern, his lips moving wordless as the thought. "Three – four days, maybe? I am not sure, but no time soon."

"Gives us a chance to plan," Amelia said quickly, hardly able to contain her excitement. She checked from Kenchi to the older warriors to see their reaction. Haruto and Sota bobbed their heads in agreement.

"True," mused Haruto. "Don't want to rush off like a bunch of children on an outing." He nodded to himself again and muttered, "We could pull this off. We could."

Amelia gasped, her heart beat quicker. She reached out and placed a hand on both men's shoulders. "Let us make it so."

Chapter Six

The next day was spent exploring the territory around the cavern. Parties set out searching the meadow for herbs, vegetables, and whatever fowl the archers could flush using bows. Another group began construction of fish traps, while a third wandered the forest for nut and fruit trees.

Kenchi and Amelia stayed close to the cavern, hauling in more firewood, constructing sleeping platforms for the men, and rifling through the bundles left by the old monk.

"Mostly books and scrolls," commented Kenchi as he placed another unwrapped bundle aside. "All Chinese. I wonder if this monk of yours traveled from China originally to spread their new religion, or sailed there to study the texts with other monks and journeyed back carrying new knowledge."

"I don't know," replied Amelia. She gave a curious examination to the kimono she wore, wondering if the weave would indicate the place of manufacture, but was not skilled enough to make out small differences. She did notice one thing, however. "For all the riding I did yesterday, and sweaty work today, no dirt has clung to the fabric. Look." Amelia held the hem up and shook the material in Kenchi's face while stroking the cloth in wonder. "It's still clean."

The warrior strolled around her examining the kimono himself. "You are right," he said at last, "not a stain anywhere. Hmm… I wonder." He took in the books with a sweep of his vision and back to Amelia. "In China white signifies death. If he were Chinese, I wonder why he would choose such a color, and why the fabric holds no mark."

"In Japan white is purity and truth," Amelia murmured, fingering the cloth as she rested on one of the rocks. "Is death then purity and truth? Aren't those virtues one in the same?"

"Death of the flesh is the ultimate fate and truth of all living creatures," Kenchi replied soberly, sitting opposite her. "In this respect, the completion of the flesh is pure. Nothing taints the end of one's life once the body has expired." He issued a slight chuckle. "You cannot be a little bit dead, can you?"

"I guess not," agreed Amelia. Suddenly, she could no longer keep from blurting what had been on her mind since the freeing of the captive men. "What is the real reason you decided to come here? You could have contrived some excuse for the warlord; hit yourself with a rock on the head and say the prisoners knocked you unconscious. Cut yourself using your sword and claim overwhelming numbers defeated you—something. Why really did you cast your fate with me and these men?"

"I—I see how the warlord treats the people of this domain, even his own soldiers and kin," stammered Kenchi. "I am ashamed. I have too much respect for myself to treat people as if they were vermin for extermination at the slightest whim. I even hear my parents mutter the same thing when the two think I do not listen." Kenchi found cause to study his boots, the shelves containing unopened bundles, and then his boots again, refusing to look Amelia in the face. "There were other reasons, too."

"Oh? What other reasons?" Amelia kept her head down also and said in a low voice, "and what about Chikako?"

"Huh?" Kenchi glanced up sharply in surprise. "What does she have to do with this?"

"A few days ago I met her by the river. Chikako said her father and your parents negotiated to arrange a marriage between you two." Amelia fidgeted with the kimono. "There is still time for you to return. I will not blame you."

Kenchi laughed so hard he began to choke. "Sorry," he said at last in relief, gulping air. "My father mentioned he was approached by Chikako's father. She is all right, I suppose, for a merchant's daughter, but all Chikako hears is the clink and rattle of coins, too quick to fawn on the powerful for the slightest favor. I told him the girl was not worthy to be the wife of a samurai. True, a woman must maintain the household accounts and spend wisely, but when I marry, I want a woman steeped in the tradition of bow and horse. One who is able to use a sword as well as a brush."

"Oh." A spark leaped in Amelia's chest but she kept her voice impassive. "I suppose so. Being a samurai is a heavy responsibility, and one would want a wife able to defend the home, as a proper samurai woman should. What other reason, though, could you wish to stay and help me?"

Kenchi clasped his hands together and stared Amelia in the eye. "Well, we were always—close. I cannot stand by and see you fight alone against this evil man, especially when you wish to save your mother. You do the honorable thing and I would help, if I can."

"Oh." The way he said "close" sent a tingle of excitement along Amelia's spine. She blushed and examined his boots. "This means you will help me? To tell you the truth, I doubt the rescue of my mother can be done, but—I must try."

"You will succeed," Kenchi whispered with sure knowledge. He kept his gaze steady on her. "It will take you a while, but I know you. Remember when your father taught us the use of the *naginata?*"

Amelia clapped her hands together and laughed. "Oh, I hated the weapon. For a long pole, with a blade at one end, the thing was so *heavy.* I don't know how you managed to wield the shaft with the weight on the tip, and I carried the women's smaller, lighter version, the *ko-naginata*, and it was heavy enough.

Kenchi leaped to his feet, making wild gestures in the air. "You practiced night and day, though, like this. Even slept holding the weapon if I remember. Nothing would stop you from learning how to use the *naginata* until you mastered the moves. This will be the same. Nothing will halt you until you achieve what you want."

Something akin to joy stirred inside Amelia. "Thank you. With you by my side and your belief in me, anything is possible."

Kenchi and Amelia wandered outside still reminiscing about the old days.

Haruto had brought back sturdy branches from the forest and constructed crude *bokkens,* wooden practice swords, for the men to use who were not familiar with swordplay. He and Sota swung furiously at each other, demonstrating the various chops and parries used in combat.

Kenchi and Amelia watched for a moment alongside the other men. "When was the last time you practiced dueling?" Kenchi asked.

Amelia thought back. "About two years ago. I practiced a while after my father died, but without him, or you, to train against, I gave up. Running through the moves day after day by myself grew so boring."

Kenchi flushed pink and snatched two of the bokkens from the ground and tossed one to Amelia, guilt rushing into his breast he'd not continued practicing with her, even though the fault was not his. "If you are going to fight you should practice. Hacking away from the back of your unicorn may be okay in a battle against unskilled opponents, but if you meet another samurai you will need all the skill you possess."

"You're right." Amelia hefted the bokken, getting the feel of the weapon. She slipped her sword from the scabbard and laid it reverently on the grass, replacing the blade with the bokken. Kenchi did the same. Amelia took up a position opposite the young warrior. "Let's duel."

They faced each other, bowed, and squared off. With a flick of his wrist, Kenchi drew his sword, slashing at Amelia's midsection. The girl leaped back nimbly whipping out her own sword. The two circled warily, waiting for an opening.

Kenchi leaped in using an overhand chop. Amelia countered, letting her wooden blade slide down Kenchi's and swiping at his stomach. Kenchi blocked and the two backed off again.

Remember what father taught me. Take my time, search for an opening.

Slowly, the old moves returned to Amelia as the muscles recalled the twists and turns learned from long practice. She blocked out the noise around her, the chirps of the birds, the comments of the men watching, centering her whole attention on the man before her.

For every thrust Amelia used, Kenchi knew the counter. The same master trained both. The pair practiced together for years. After ten minutes neither one was able to strike a blow against the other.

"HOLD."

Haruto stepped between Amelia and Kenchi. "You both fight well, but to improve, you must fight someone better." He clasp Kenchi on the back. "I will spar against you for a while, young pup, and see how you do."

At the name "young pup," Kenchi's ears turned pink. The other men laughed, and one made a barking noise. Kenchi grinned good-naturally and said, "Yes, Sir, I will try and learn all you teach me."

The faced each other and began trading blows. Kenchi was fast, but Haruto was as fast, his wooden sword flashing at Kenchi's head, stomach, and legs in a never-ending series of strikes. Kenchi tried a feint to the old warrior's head, meaning to change at the last minute to a cut at the belly. He found himself dodging backward just in time as Haruto's bokken zipped past his nose to within an inch. The old warrior chucked and stepped close to Kenchi, their swords locked above their heads. "Made you jump, huh, Pup?" Kenchi smiled back, and then doubled over in pain as Haruto brought his leg up and smashed the young man in the ribs with his thigh and knee. Haruto stepped back and stopped fighting, dropping his wooden sword to the ground. He felt Kenchi's side. "No ribs broken, but let that be a lesson to you. Always expect the unexpected." He took a deep breath and helped Kenchi stand upright. "You are good, and as you learn you will become better, if you are not killed beforehand."

Sota spoke up. "Lady Amelia, why don't you take Kenchi back to the cave so those ribs of his can rest?" He checked the sky gauging the time by the sun. "We are done here for the day, and there's still much to do before the sun sets."

Kenchi protested he was fine, but Amelia took his elbow. "Sota is right. We can always practice tomorrow and we haven't finished constructing all the sleeping platforms yet."

As Kenchi and Amelia walked to the cave, Kenchi kept muttering, "I should have been watching. I saw your father do the same maneuver to another warrior in a demonstration. An old trick, he told me afterwards. He said he would teach both of us one day how to do the move, but…." He glanced quickly at Amelia and fell silent.

My father possessed many things to teach us, Amelia lamented silently to herself. *I wish he'd lived long enough to show us everything he knew. Oh, Father, I miss you so.*

They entered the cavern, Amelia and Kenchi lost in their own thoughts. One of the men broke the silence, the hare lipped farmer named Yuki, rushed into the cave behind Kenchi. "*Rice*. I found rice growing wild in the meadow, and the grain ripe for picking." He beamed at Amelia and Kenchi, rocking back and forth on his feet in excitement. "Enough to feed an army, if necessary. We will never know starvation in this place. I found wild onions also."

As the day progressed, the rest of the parties drifted in carrying wild game birds and fish, excitedly talking about the bounty this paradise provided to those who looked. Pheasant cooked on a spit, along with pottage and salmon baked in the oven, made for a hearty dinner. After the company ate their fill, the men relaxed around the fire pit and planned their strategy for the attack on the supply depot.

"The village lies here," Kenchi drew a crude map in the dirt using a long stick," along the coast."

"I have been there," acknowledged Haruto, "a long time ago when I was young. Small place, a fishing village, but good seafood. Why is the warlord massing his troops there?"

Kenchi nodded. "As you said, good seafood and plenty of it, also rice. The harbor is deep and well protected against storms. The perfect place to keep his troops until he needs the men at the front. He can bring more troops in by the sea and the town sits on the border. His base of supplies will be close when he attacks his neighbors and in case of defeat he can evacuate his troops by boat, if need be."

Haruto grunted assent and studied the drawing. Amelia said, "I have never been there, but I know of only one road, along here by the shore." She took the stick from Kenchi and drew a squiggly line along the coast, from there another line inland to the Sea of Trees, and stabbed the middle. "We are here. How are we going to travel all this way without being seen, or caught once we've made our attack? The distance must be twenty *ri*. If we disguise ourselves we are sure to be stopped and questioned by one of the warlord's patrols."

Kenchi said eagerly, "I have studied maps. We go this way." He took back the stick and drew a diagonal line from the cavern to the village. "On the farmer roads and paths through the hills. The soldiers patrol, but not in numbers; too many paths and not enough men. If we leave early, we can be there by morning the next day before the sun rises. This is when the guards will be at their sleepiest and not expecting an attack." He slapped his hands together. "We attack, grab what is needed, and scat before the warlord's people know what happened."

"How will we find the supplies in the dark?" Amelia shook her head. A premonition of wrongness stuck in her mind. "I do not think this is a good plan. Not thought out enough, anyway."

Kenchi waved a hand indifferently. "The weapons and supplies are still in wagons. This is a small village. How many wagons can there be having soldiers surrounding them as guards?"

Amelia looked at the crude sketch again and then at Haruto. His face was impassive, covered in flickering red shadows from the dancing firelight.

I have to make a decision. These men give me no answers. This doesn't feel right, but Kenchi acts so sure. "Are you positive this will work? We don't know how many soldiers guard the wagons, we've never been over these roads before. What happens if we become lost, or we do run across a troop of soldiers? Maybe we should delay and scout the area first to be sure."

The men fell quiet and waited on Kenchi to reply. "We can be sure of nothing, Amelia. We do know one thing, if we do not act swiftly, more troops will arrive and then our one chance of gaining weapons will be lost. Talking if fine, and we can talk all night and into next week, scout the area until we know every path, but if we are to start this venture, we must start somewhere and not discuss the point to death."

Amelia sighed and stood. "Okay. We leave the first thing in the morning before daybreak. We'd better sleep, then. Tomorrow will be a long march."

As she lay on her pallet of grass, Amelia breathed a silent prayer: *Buddha and the ancient spirits as well, let this be the right choice. I am so afraid the battle will go wrong.*

***

The trek in the early morning hours was precarious. No road led out of the forest in the direction the company wished to journey, fallen trees blocked the way, and outcroppings of boulders forced the party to make detours. The troop forded freezing streams, but by noon, Kenchi and Haruto located a footpath angling in the same direction they traveled and the marching was easier, although the men need hike single-file in many places. Gradually the trampled earth broadened until the path turned into a well-worn wagon route. Additional small roads joined the one they trekked, some running down from the mountains, others leading to the coast. Amelia stayed in a constant state of agitation, fearing attack by patrols, apprehensive of taking the wrong branch of the lane.

"See?" Kenchi walked beside Amelia and Lan Ying, "I told you." He jabbed a finger along the trail. "Farmer's road," he said cheerfully. "If what I remember is correct from the map I saw, more will merge, all leading to the coast."

"I know. I hope this is the right one," Amelia complained. "We've already passed two roads, are you sure we are still on the right one?"

Kenchi hesitated and then said, "Of course," he replied with confidence. "I told you, I saw a map."

"I am glad he knows where we are going," Lan Ying thought to Amelia. *"I do not."*

"You don't know where we are?" Amelia said in distress. Her one belief was the unicorn always knew their location, and whatever happened would bring the party back to the cavern and safety.

"Of course I know where I am," issued the curt reply. Lan Ying stomped one hoof firmly on the dirt to emphasis the point. *"I am here."* Her head twisted and the horn pointed downhill to the right. *"The sea is this way. I can smell the salt water, but where this path leads to, I do not know, or where here is, I know not also."*

A twinge of anxiousness shot through Amelia. "You can trace your way to the cavern, though, right? We're not really lost."

"Of course I can," a reply snapped back. *"I am a unicorn, am I not? We are of the earth and can always find our way back to some place we have been. The Sea of Trees is known to all."* Lan Ying fired a glance at Kenchi, and then twisted her neck to survey the men marching behind her. *"Not like silly men who chase off into the wild not having the slightest idea of where they are."*

Amelia breathed a sigh of relief. At least if Kenchi and Haruto couldn't locate the village the party could make their way home.

More paths combined into the one the column marched and branched off. Only once did Amelia meet another traveler, an old farmer leading an ox-cart full of empty baskets that once might have held vegetables, plodding up the path toward their party. He halted in surprise when he saw Lan Ying and the rest, ready to bolt when Kenchi hailed him. "Ho, good sir. Is this the way to Komi village?" The young warrior smiled broadly, keeping his hand well away from his sword and strolled forward.

The old man eyed Kenchi suspiciously, but nodded. "Yes." He shoved a brown hand along the path from the direction he'd come from, "about three more *ri*. You'll hit another road on the right, broader than this one. Lead you straight to the village." He craned his neck, checking the men and their weapons. "You are the warlord's soldiers on patrol? I hope you catch the bandits plaguing these roads. Man can hardly take his produce to market without being attacked."

"Oh, no," Kenchi hastened to say. "We are, umm…guards for the fair young maiden." He hooked a thumb at Amelia who stared back in surprise. "This lady is to be a bride of a prince in China. A boat will meet us at the village sent by the prince himself, he is so eager to wed. Can't you tell? The girl is dressed all in white and rides a unicorn, showing her virtue and virginity to the world."

Amelia lowered her head, blushing and covering her mouth so her grin wouldn't show.

"Of course, I should have guessed." The farmer bowed low to display his respect. "May the spirits bless your union," he said to Amelia.

"Thank you," she replied, trying hard not to burst out laughing while attempting to act as she imagined a modest maiden should on the way to her wedding.

The party traveled on, located the next path as night descended in the sky. Kenchi and Haruto walked ahead, carrying pine branches dipped in pitch used as torches to light the way. A full yellow moon rose as twilight changed to evening providing more illumination.

The path took a wide bend avoiding an outcropping of stone. As the party trudged around the turn, they entered a flat clearing offering a clear view of the ocean beyond. Below, faint lights flickered like fireflies in the night.

Komi village.

Amelia studied the moon. The sphere was sinking low in the sky. Tension arched her shoulders in anticipation of the coming raid. She hunched low over Lan Ying's back. "Enough time to survey the village, locate the wagons, and prepare ourselves," she announced to the party at large. Amelia checked the men. They were as tense as she was. "Let's move out."

The troop crept down to the village. Two dogs ran out to greet the warriors, quickly silenced by arrows. Amelia winced inside when she hear the mongrel's dying yelps, but steeled herself, blocking out the cries. *This will not be the last. Please, no more tonight.* Amelia whispered to Kenchi, "Pass the word, no unnecessary killing."

His lips compressed into a bitter line, but Kenchi nodded silently and murmured into Haruto's ear, who spread the orders to the rest.

The band weaved their way along narrow mud alleys between shacks until the group halted at the main street. Amelia rode out onto the road, glancing quickly up and down the lane before retreating into the obscurity of the covering buildings. From her vantage point atop Lan Ying, she made out the low burning glimmer of a campfire at the end of the town. The shapes of tents and wagons flickered in the shadows.

"We must circle around the village. Someone is sure to see us if we walk up the street," Amelia said in a low voice. The band silently faded back to the edge of town and worked their way through fields until Amelia, Haruto, and Kenchi were satisfied they'd passed the wagons on the road. A lone guard made his sleepy way around the camp, appearing and disappearing among the carts and picketed horses. Faintly, the low drone of soft singing flowed in the air as he attempted to keep himself awake.

"I will challenge the guard to a duel," Kenchi said as he stood erect and rattled his sword in the scabbard to guarantee the blade was loose. "This is the honorable way." He made as if to step out into the street.

Haruto reached out and grabbed the young man's shoulder, jerking him roughly back under cover. He whispered loudly, "Are you mad? You will alert the whole camp with the fighting."

"But how then...?"

Haruto waved Sota forward and murmured into his ear. The man grinned, nodded eagerly and ran off. "Now we wait."

"For what?" Amelia asked, nervously watching the guard.

"You will see."

The delay was not long. The guard ambled behind a wagon. A minute passed, and then another. Sota appeared clan in the soldier's armor and waved, a bloody knife still clutched in his hand.

"I do see," Amelia said tensely with displeasure in her voice. "Let's finish quickly before more must die."

As silently as wraiths, the warriors approached the sleeping camp. Sota already hurried to a cart, rifling through the interior. He waved his hand over his head. "Get the horses. This one has weapons aplenty," he whispered eagerly in a hoarse voice. "Provisions, too."

Two of the men ran to the picket line, calming the horses and unhitching the animals at the same time. Pressure built in Amelia, her body shook. If the camp were to wake up now, it would be a disaster. "Hurry," she breathed.

After an eternity, the horses were hitched into the traces. Kenchi and Haruto sat in front, the rest of the men climbed into the rear of the wagon. The farmer, Yuki, held the straps, gently pulling the horses along, whispering encouragement in a soft voice, and stroking their heads to keep the animals calm. The band circled around the town again through the fields and up the slope, heading to the trail. The squeaking and groaning of the wagon wheels echoed unnaturally loud in the false dawn darkness. Amelia was sure any moment she'd hear the guards yelling the alarm as the camp awoke and discovered the death of the guard and the theft.

It wasn't until she reached the path and began climbing into the hills, that Amelia squeezed her eyes shut and breathed a sigh of relief as the butterflies left her stomach.

We did it. No one was hurt, and we didn't have to fight. We actually made a successful foray. The raid was so easy.

"HALT."

A soldier stood in front of Amelia and Lan Ying, blade drawn. More materialized around the clearing. "What do you have in the wagon?" the leader demanded, advancing on the party. He sheathed his sword, but the rest made no move to copy his example.

Amelia froze. An arrow zipped past her shoulder and embedded itself in the man's chest.

"RUN."

Yuki leaped to one side, drawing a long knife and rushed one of the soldiers. Haruto snapped the reins of the horses. The animals bolted and the wagon sped past Amelia up the trail in panic, while Kenchi leaped off to engage the enemy. As he raced by Amelia, he slapped Lan Ying on the rump. "Go. I will hold the soldiers as long as I can."

Amelia reached out, extending a hand. "Mount behind me. You can't stop them all." Three soldiers advanced on Kenchi waving swords and screaming.

Lan Ying reared, snorting. *"No. He may not mount me. Only a virgin may ride a unicorn."* The unicorn jumped along the path after the wagon without casting a backward glance at the troops or Kenchi.

"I can't leave Kenchi to fight alone, he'll be killed." Amelia tumbled off the unicorn, stumbled to her feet, and drew her sword. Issuing a cry of rage, she sprinted to the fighting men, blade drawn high ready to strike at the first soldier she met.

Kenchi engaged the three warriors at once. Yuki tumbled into the darkness fighting blindly, but shouts rang out as he attacked pursing soldiers who stumbled through the bush to kill him. The wagon bounced along the trail, not even the creaking wheels heard over the fighting.

"Ahhh!" A screaming fury with long black hair brushed past Kenchi and leaped at one of the warriors, hurling an overhead chop. The soldier blocked the blow and swung back at Amelia. She sprang aside as the blade swished within inches of her belly.

Kenchi shot a startled look at Amelia and attacked his two opponents with renewed vigor, but nevertheless he and Amelia retreated until they fought shoulder to shoulder, battling for their lives as a net of steel weaved around the two.

"Foolish humans. So stupid." Lan Ying contemptuously shoved Amelia and Kenchi aside, lashing her iron-hard front hooves at the soldiers. One warrior caught in the chest flew backward, arms wind milling, stunned by the power of the blow. Another shrieked in pain as the unicorn's horn speared him through his right breast, the force spinning the soldier around. He staggered off into the brush leaving a trail of blood on the leaves. Lan Ying punctuated each blow with, *"Stupid, stupid, so stupid."*

The third warrior held his ground for a moment bravely, but seeing two blades and the murderous horn aimed at him, turned and fled into the forest toward the town.

"You should learn to be more like unicorns," Lan Ying chided Amelia. *"Kind and gentle."*

Kenchi and Amelia bent over double, gasping for breath. Sweat dripped down Amelia's nose and stung her eyes as she huffed between gulping lungful's of air. "Yeah… Kind… Gentle… Like… You."

Lan Ying walked over and sniffed the soldier lying on the ground. He moaned, fumbling weakly in the dirt and attempted to sit up without success. *"This one lives."* The unicorn swung her head in Amelia's direction and nickered in confidence. *"You see? Unicorns are kind and gentle. No one died."*

Amelia ignored the filly's remark and cleaned the blade of her sword on a handful of leaves. She asked Kenchi, "Are you alright?"

"Yes." He surveyed the clearing, searching for signs of life. "Where is everyone? What happened to Yuki? The wagon?"

"Dunno." Amelia cupped her hands. "YUKI."

No answer.

Kenchi yelled out, "HARUTO?" Only echoes returned. He grasped at Amelia's kimono. "Haruto and the others have fled in the wagon. Our men must be halfway to the cave by now. We cannot wait for Yuki. The day is growing light and the rest of the guards will notice the thief and search, if the soldiers are not already doing so, or the one who fled will tell his comrades where we are. We must leave. If Yuki lives he will find his way to the cavern."

Amelia and Kenchi started walking. "Haruto and the wagon must be ahead of us." Amelia kept straining, rising on her toes to peer along the trail. "I'm surprised he hasn't sent anyone to locate us, or paused somewhere along here for us to show up."

A troubled expression passed over Kenchi's face. "Haruto may not be able to. If one squad was out, there might be more. I never thought any soldiers would patrol the back trails, but if the warlord has ordered, I fear our men were captured."

Chapter Seven

"This is my fault," Kenchi kept complaining as the three trudged along the trail. "I should have realized patrols would be stationed in the woods in case of attack." He said softly to Amelia, eyes pleading for her to understand, "I am sorry. Forgive my stupid error. I do not know how I could be so foolish. I fear my poor judgement has cost the lives of our men."

"Not your responsibility," Amelia replied stoically, staring straight ahead. Defeat lay like a blanket on her, smothering all hope. She halted and cocked her head, listening. Besides the birds twittering and the buzz of insect life, no other noise broke the silence. "The blame for this mess is mine. I had a bad premonition about the raid from the first. We moved too hastily, didn't know the true lay of the land, or the strength of the enemy, not even what patrols the warlord ordered out or when. I will not make the same mistake twice."

"There will be a next time?"

"Of course," Amelia replied. She took a deep breath, pushed the defeat behind her, and cleansed her mind of any doubt. Amelia swung on Kenchi like a tigress at bay. "This changes *nothing*. Do you understand? We learn from our mistakes, recruit new soldiers—find weapons. I have yet to rescue my mother, and I will not stop until I know she is free and safe."

They arrived at the bend in the road.

"No wagon," Amelia commented, surveying the lane in both directions.

"Too many wagon and cart tracks to be certain if one of the marks is ours," Kenchi said. He made a circle, searching the dirt and shook his head hopelessly. "We have not come across wreckage of the wagon, though, or traces of a battle. No soldiers have brought the wagon back this way containing our men or bodies. A good sign. Perhaps Haruto and Sota have escaped after all and we will meet our troop later. We can hope."

"Lan Ying, can you tell?" Amelia asked.

The unicorn shook her head. *"All wagons smell the same to me. Dead and musty. The scent of man stink hangs on the trail, but I do not know if the humans I sense are your men or not. I have not had time to familiarize myself with their individual odors yet."* Lan Ying snorted and a thought drifted to Amelia. *"Which is something I am not looking forward too."*

At nightfall, the diminished party reached the Sea of Trees, tired and half asleep, but discovered no sign of their companions along the way. In her eagerness to reach the cavern, Amelia did not hear the moans and strange noises of the forest in the dry streambed. Her mind kept wandering back to the disastrous battle and the fate of her people, her blood running cold each time she thought of their death or capture. As Amelia, Kenchi, and Lan Ying reached the cave, Amelia scanned the clearing in the dim moonlight for indications of people or the wagon.

Nothing.

"No one is here," Amelia whispered. She fought an overwhelming desire to run, screaming the names of the men through the night, somehow thinking if she yelled loud enough Haruto or Sota would materialize out of the air before her eyes, and everything would be okay once more.

"Perhaps the wagon will arrive later," Kenchi suggested kindly as he saw the anguish on Amelia's face. "Let us go inside and build a fire, cook food. I am hungry, so are you, and when the rest of the men arrive I am sure everyone will want to eat also."

Amelia nodded silently. *Buddha, let the people live. Have I murdered those men because of my own carelessness?* A swirl of guilt descend on her. *Their blood is on my hands, the blame for their deaths lays on my soul.*

Kenchi started a fire while Amelia concocted a pottage of rice, vegetables, and leftover fish from the previous day. While the two ate in silence, each lost in their own thoughts. Amelia found herself nodding, her chin bobbing up and down as she struggled to stay awake. She jerked her head up and looked over at Kenchi. He slumped, snoring soundly where he sat.

I can't fall asleep. What if the men arrive? Or, the warlord's soldiers? What if the enemy trailed us back here and attack while we sleep?

Amelia's head nodded again. A soft, wet muzzle nudged her neck and shoulder. *"Dawn has broken,"* Lan Ying's soft thought drifted to her. *"Sleep. I will stand guard. No one will pass while I watch over you."* The unicorn took up a position across the entrance to the cavern, swishing her tail, head lowered, the horn as menacing as a sword blade. The filly looked at Amelia who staggered to her sleeping pallet and collapsed into a tiny ball. *"I love you."*

The next morning Amelia woke thinking the previous day was a nightmare, until she sat up and glanced around. Kenchi stood impatiently next to Lan Ying at the cave entrance, but the rest of the cavern was vacant.

Amelia scrubbed at her eyes, stretched and yawned. "No one? Did we sleep all day and night?" she called to Kenchi anxiously.

"Yes." He scowled at Lan Ying, "No one arrived yet, and your unicorn will not allow me out of this cave to check the trail either."

"I guard the entrance as I promised," the thought drifted primly from the filly, adding a shake of her head. *"I am a unicorn. No one has passed me. Unicorns are faithful and always keep their promises."*

Amelia rose and ran to Lan Ying, laughing and hugging her around the neck. "Silly. Kenchi is like my brother. He can enter or leave anytime he pleases."

Lan Ying moved out of the way, her head held high. *"I would have let him leave, but he refused to say please. Men are so rude. Males do not know the first thing about being polite."*

"Did you ask him to say please?" Amelia's lips twisted up at the edges.

"Of course not. Why should I? I assumed he knows proper manners. He is a samurai, I heard. Besides, he is a man. I only speak to women and not many of those."

Kenchi watched this one-sided conversation in amazement. "You can speak to the beast? The unicorn understands what you say," he blurted out.

"See what I mean?" Lan Ying snorted and glared at the young warrior. With contemptuous dignity, she swung around until her rump faced Kenchi, her white tail twitching. *"Beast indeed. I knew there was a reason not to speak to him. Very rude indeed, but what can you expect from a male."*

Amelia switched her attention from Kenchi to Lan Ying and back again. "Yes, I can talk to my unicorn, and she speaks back," the girl said. "I think you insulted her. Her name is Lan Ying, not beast."

"Oh." Kenchi made a deep bow, grinning, at the unicorn's rear. "I am sorry Lan Ying. I did not know you had a name or understood what I said. I am young and foolish when it comes to unicorns. You are the first one I ever met face to, uh…umm, face. Forgive me for my ignorance. My mistake will not happen again."

"Humph."

Amelia slapped her hand over her mouth and hurried outside, snatching Kenchi's arm on the way and waving him along. When they were out of Lan Ying's sight, she whispered in his ear, *"Don't worry, it's okay. She'll get over it."*

The sun was well risen in the Eastern sky. Amelia scrambled onto a boulder, scanning in every direction as far as she could for their missing companions. Seeing nothing, she cupped her hands and screamed, *"Haruto—Yuki."*

Faint copies of the names repeated to her, swallowed by the Sea of Trees.

Amelia slid off the rock. "They....They all can't be dead, can they?" she said to Kenchi, sniffing back tears. "At least some of our people should have returned to the cave by now if any are still alive."

"Still too early," the warrior hurried to assured her. "Remember, the trail narrows and the horses will have trouble navigating the path, especially at night. I do not know about Yuki, but if I were Haruto and he still has the wagon, I would find a safe place to hide during the day, and camouflage the wagon from prying eyes. The warlord's troops are still about patrolling, and the patrols will search every road in the area."

"You think—here?" Amelia glanced quickly left and right as if expecting a troop of soldiers to appear out of the forest sprinting toward the cave and waving their swords.

Kenchi chuckled and shook his head. "No. We are too far away from where the battle was, and only fools and desperate men like you and me would voluntarily venture into the suicide forest night or day."

"Maybe I should ride back and search for Haruto and the rest," Amelia said suddenly. "Our men might be hurt, or lost. In the darkness who knows which way the horses might have ran. Maybe the wagon broke down and they have no way of repairing it. Going to the village I was lost."

"Returning to Komi village would do no good," Kenchi replied. He reclined against the boulder and spread his hands wide. "Where would you look? Not in the town, or on the road. As I said, Haruto probably hid during the day to avoid detection by the patrols, and if you rode far enough you would meet soldiers yourself. Having you captured is the last thing we want, right?"

Amelia dropped next to him, brushed her long hair out of her face and stared in despair at the white clouds barely seen through the tree branches. With a sigh, she found a piece of lava and heaved the rock into the pond. The pebble landed making a plunk, shooting ripples out into a circle. "What can we do then; nothing?"

Kenchi located a stone also and heaved the rock into the water next to hers. "Wait," was his simple reply.

"We still have pottage from last night," Amelia said dully, pushing herself erect. "We should eat before the food goes bad."

"I saw green tea in one of the bundles," Kenchi offered, standing. "I will start a fire and boil water. We might as well make ourselves comfortable. This will be a long day."

The sat in the cave and ate in silence. Amelia looked up from her bowl and asked, "What do we do if the men never return?"

Kenchi placed his bowl and chopsticks down. "As you said, we recruit more," he replied promptly. "The warlord confiscates many farmers' property to hand over to his favorites. Yours was not the only land seized and home destroyed in the *han* the warlord rules. Many landless men and women wander alone through the province, merchants and samurai too, whose clan ties are in disfavor." He rubbed the knuckles of his right hand into his left palm. "This is why so many bandits roam the province now. The robbers started as displaced warriors. We will find many who will rally to your banner if allowed the chance, never fear."

For the first time that day, Amelia smiled. "Before people run to my flag, I need one first." She put a finger to her mouth, eyes narrowing. "What should my symbol be?"

"Well, I know you need a unicorn on there somewhere," Kenchi joked, casting a furtive glance over his shoulder. "Lan Ying would never forgive you if you did not, and I would receive all the blame. I am sure."

Amelia bobbed her head in agreement. "One white unicorn." She glanced down at her kimono. "I'm dressed all in white, also, but the banner can't be *all* white. No one would see me or Lan Ying."

"White on black, then," Kenchi replied. "A silhouette of you astride a unicorn on a black background, with black outlines."

"Perfect." Amelia clapped her hands together and leaped to her feet. "Now if only I can find the materials. I wonder if there's anything I can use in those other bundles. I don't remember seeing any drawing material, but I'm sure the monk must have a writing box containing ink and brushes."

Amelia spent the balance of the morning, and well into the afternoon, rummaging through the monk's wrapped bundles, locating ink, brushes, and cloth for her flag. While not busy measuring, sketching, and cutting, she kept running outside the cave, listening and clambering up on the boulder, watching for any sight of the men returning.

Kenchi stalked the forest and meadow with bow and arrow, searching for game birds until lightning streaked across the sky, and a booming thunderstorm broke out, cold sheets of rain changing the day into night. He stomped in late in the afternoon, hair wet and shivering, but carrying a brace of quail slung over his back. "Caught these birds just before the rain started," he boasted, "and look—" from his pouch he produced six peaches, "found a tree on the way back, too. The fruit is ripe. I remember how you always use to grab a peach from the tree in your front yard when we went walking." He took a bite from one and handed another to Amelia.

"I love peaches." Amelia seized the fruit and ripped off a hunk with her small sharp teeth. "Yummy." Juice trickled down her chin. She swallowed, wiped her mouth and licked her palm, asking, "You didn't see any sign of the others, did you?" Before Kenchi could reply, Amelia shook her head, frowning, as if she said something funny. "Of course not. Those would be your first words."

Lan Ying wandered in, shaking herself vigorously and spraying drops of water all over Kenchi. The filly ambled over to Amelia and sniffed at the banner, nudging the cloth with a damp muzzle. *"Painting?"* She studied the outline of the unicorn and issued a humorous snort. *"Is that supposed to be me? You made my ears too long. It looks more like a donkey with a spear sticking out of my head."*

"Oh." Amelia held the banner up for Kenchi to see. "What do you think? Have to wait for the ink to dry before I put the flag on a pole. Hope the pigment doesn't run when the banner gets wet."

More thunder rumbled and lightning flashed, brightening up the cave from the mouth and cracks in the ceiling. Amelia jumped and released a yelp.

"Big noise," Lan Ying commented, undisturbed, as she peered at the cavern entrance. *"The gods must be fighting among each other or angry at someone."*

"I hope not us." Amelia cringed as another thunderous explosion rocked the air from outside. "Oh, my." She moved closer to Kenchi and Lan Ying as if the nearness of their bodies would protect her from harm.

Kenchi squeezed her shoulder and then squatted, plucking the quail, and skewering the birds with a green spit over the fire pit for roasting. Amelia knelt down next to him. "We should save the feathers," she said, scooping the mess into a pile. "We can use the quills for something.

Next time catch a goose. Those feathers are the best for fletching arrows if we are forced to make our own."

The warrior kept plucking, but glanced up, grinning. "I will do my best."

Lan Ying watched, bored. *"I will be back,"* the unicorn said to Amelia.

Another clap of thunder rocked the cavern. "You're going out in this? Why don't you wait, it's dangerous out there. You'll get hit by lightning and soaked with freezing rain."

"Let her go," Kenchi said after listening to Amelia speak to Lan Ying, "but keep her away from me when she returns. Your unicorn has made me wet enough already."

"I am a unicorn. Unicorns fear nothing." flicking her tail, Lan Ying strolled out of the cave and into the rain with a backward thought to Amelia. *"A bath never hurt anyone, especially a smelly man."*

Night fell by the time the two finished eating. Lan Ying wandered into the cavern, dripping water, mud up to her knees. Kenchi back hastily away from the wet unicorn. Amelia jumped up. "Oh, you poor thing. I told you not to go out. You're soaked."

"I will dry," a calm reply came back. The unicorn edged toward Kenchi and shook herself vigorously.

Kenchi dried himself with the sleeve of his kimono, and went to clean up the scraps of their dinner when shouts and curses rang faintly from outside the ledge. Amelia threw a quick look at Kenchi and dove for her sword. The next moment Haruto stumbled into the cave, dripping wet, trailed by the rest of the men, who cursed as loudly as he did at the tempest outside.

"By all the Shinto spirits who dwell in this forest, *we made the trip!*" Haruto bellowed, wringing out water and mud from his hair. "Blast this rain. I thought we would drown tonight in the storm. I swear for the last mile we did more swimming than walking."

"Haruto!" Amelia dropped her sword and flung herself on the man, disregarding the wet and dirt covering his body, and then embraced each of the other warriors in turn with the same enthusiasm. "We thought you were dead. What happened?"

Kenchi was pounding the men on their backs, laughing. "You rascals. What a sorry sight you are. Where have you been?" He grabbed Sota by the sleeve of his soggy kimono and dragged him to the fire. "Sit." He waved the men to the pit and threw on more wood. "Dry yourselves and get warm. You must be freezing. We want to hear your story."

"Almost got ourselves killed," Haruto said as he sat and made himself comfortable on a rock. The men headed to the fire, huddling around the blaze, rubbing arms and legs to return circulation to their frozen bodies, and holding their hands out near the flames. "When we took off from the battle we missed the turn-off for the main trail in the dark," the warrior said, shaking his head. The rest of the warriors chuckled in remembrance and tried talking at once, until Haruto held his hand up for silence so he could continue. "Went straight ahead into the hills and found ourselves lost. By the time we realized we were on the wrong path it was broad daylight. We were so confused as to the right direction, and afraid the captains would have patrols out searching for us, so—" he shrugged and raised his hands in the air in a sign of helplessness, "we kept going straight, trying to place as much distance between the town and us as we could. Eventually we reached a farmhouse. The farmer hid us."

"Pretty wife," Sota interjected with a grin. The rest chuckled and bobbed their heads in agreement; low murmurs and snickers passing around the fire.

"Yeah. He has been hiding her too, from the warlord's soldiers," Haruto said, taking hold of the discussion again, nodding. "Those hill people are *mad*. The farmer almost slipped a knife into my ribs before he realized we weren't the warlord's men. The warriors have been stripping the farms bare, food, males of fighting age, women to cook and service the army. Anything the warlord thinks he can use, he takes. In most cases without payment."

"I thought as much," Kenchi said. He murmured to Amelia, "This could be the beginning of our army." Her attention flashed from Haruto to Kenchi and then to the old samurai who began to speak again.

"Anyway," Haruto continued, gazing around the circle, "when the sky opened up, we figured the time was safe to start again. The farmer took us on a different road than the one we approached on, shorter from his place to here, rather than walking back to the turn-off the way we hiked the first time. He left us, but we lost the trail in a jumble of boulders. The path failed when we were almost here, and we got swung around in the dark again." He rubbed his chin. "Curious thing, while we were debating which way to go, a point of light appeared through the night. At first, we thought you searched for us with a lantern in the rain, but the light didn't approach, and when we called out we heard no answer." He scanned Kenchi's damp apparel. "You weren't out looking were you, youngster?"

Kenchi shook his head in denial. "No, neither Amelia nor I were seeking you tonight. I was out hunting earlier in the day, but ran back here when the sky started to storm."

"You'd be a fool to stay out in this weather anyway." Grunts of agreement returned from the rest of the men. Haruto raised his hands for quiet. "The light started to retreat into the dark and we figured we scared the person. Anyway, we decided whoever held the lantern must live close by and we could beg refuge for the night until the rain finished so we followed, hoping to catch up. Eventually we discovered landmarks we recognized. Don't know what happened to the light. If it wasn't you two I don't know who was out in this storm." He took a deep breath and swung his arms wide, encompassing the party, "Here we are."

Amelia breathed a sigh of relief. *They're safe. Thank Buddha. Wonder who was wandering around carrying a lantern. Wait, he said a point of light? Or, should I say, thank Lan Ying?* She shot a quick peek at the unicorn who quietly swished her tail, still damp from the downpour. Amelia decided to ask later, in private. She said to Haruto, "Did you see any signs of Yuki?"

"You mean the farmer?" Haruto glanced around as if realizing for the first time the man wasn't present. "No. We thought he was with you. Where is he? He hasn't returned either?"

"Lost in the fight. We hoped he would be back by now." Kenchi peered toward the cave entrance. "Where is the wagon? You brought the supplies, I hope, after all the trouble we went through to steal food and weapons."

"Of course," Haruto answered. "That was the whole point of the raid, wasn't it? Was a hard time bringing the animals through the forest, what with the trees and all, especially when the trail grew so muddy. Half the time the wheels stuck in the ruts and we had to push the cart out, but we brought everything here, horses and all. Enough rice to feed fifty men for a week, steel arrowheads, swords, spearheads. We can equip a small army if we can recruit enough fighters. We should raid again soon." Murmurs of agreement circulated among the warriors.

Amelia's eyes flared, the muscles in her jaws locking. *How could these men be so stupid? Doesn't Haruto realize they almost died by acting too hasty? Take our time, plan, check and double check. If the warlord and his men are afoot, this is the time we should be silent. Never again will I rush into a fight not knowing first what the enemy does, or when he does it.* "We will not raid again until we explore every trail, every footpath of the place we attack," she leaped to her feet and said fiercely. "I will not stand for another disaster as this. Understood? We may have gained supplies, but otherwise the foray was a fiasco."

The vehemence in Amelia's voice shocked the men into silence. Haruto drew back, startled, but nodded solemnly. The rest hung their heads not saying a word.

"We must have spies," Amelia continued. "People who can inform us what the soldiers are doing, where the warlord will do it, and how many warriors there are. I want to know when the patrols leave a village and return. We need to understand why the troops assault one farmer and not another, and who these people are. Every detail of the enemy's thoughts. Only then do we strike. Do I make myself clear?"

She received nods of agreement.

Amelia took in each man by eye, especially Kenchi. "This will require much planning," he said thoughtfully, "and I do not like the idea of using spies. Kanuho's are," he paused groping for a word, "without honor."

Amelia understood what he meant. A true samurai warrior always tried to prove his self-worth. Kenchi saw no dignity in hiding and sneaking. "We fight from weakness," she said at last, "and for courage, to do what is right. I will judge myself if what we do is wrong, as you will judge yourself. If in the end we can say, 'I have done right,' then the use of spies has been justified."

Sota made as if to speak, but Haruto laid two fingers on his sleeve with a slight shake of his head. Kenchi said nothing but looked pensive. Amelia felt she'd won her point and surveyed the two older warriors. Now was a good a time as any to see if the men would obey her wishes. All of the returning warriors were tired, dirty, but in good spirits. "Fine. Now before you and the men relax you have one more task."

"But we just…." Haruto began until Amelia glared at him. "What?"

"I want to unload the wagon. Our supplies shouldn't be left in the rain. The rice will grow moldy and the weapons rust. We must tend to the horses. Bring everything inside. The horses, too, and see if there is anything to feed the animals. They're the beginnings of our cavalry. Before we're done we'll need one of those also."

In response, issuing good-natured grumbling, the men filed out. Amelia watched the warriors warily, not believing Haruto and Sota obeyed her orders without more than a slight mutter. She trailed behind, determined to help and set a good example for the rest. Kenchi reached out and grabbed one arm. "You should stay here inside the cave. The night is cold and wet. Troops are for unloading wagons, not generals."

"Am I a general now?" Amelia asked in surprise.

"You acted like one. You have an army—sort of. Your people conducted a successful raid, right? No matter how disastrous the foray went, our raiders still returned safely carrying supplies." He flashed one of his grins at her. "Might as well start boiling rice. I am sure the men are hungry."

Amelia giggled. "Do generals cook dinner for their troops?"

Kenchi shrugged. "How should I know? I have only met one general—you."

Two days later Yuki appeared at the head of a caravan.

One of the men ran into the cavern where Amelia, Kenchi, and Haruto sat planning their next move. *"It's Yuki. He has returned and brought more people."*

Amelia leaped to her feet, as did Haruto and Kenchi. "Who?" began Kenchi, but the warrior darted outside again.

"Are we betrayed?" asked Haruto, placing his hand on the grip of his sword, a worried expression clouding his face. He stalked to the entrance of the cave and peered out.

"I don't think so," said Amelia hurrying to catch up, "not willingly. He fought the soldiers."

"If he was tortured he would have told the soldiers everything," Kenchi yelled to make himself hear over the splashing of the waterfall. The three hurried along the ledge. "The warlord is known for using red-hot pokers on his prisoners when he wishes answers and does not care if he wastes his victim."

Amelia heard shouts of greetings and the babble of excited voices long before Yuki rose into view, weaving through the trees calling out to the rest of the warriors. Behind him like a dark snake, was a line of carts drawn by old men, women, and oxen, interspersed with screaming children and younger men. Crowded around him Amelia's men pounded Yuki on the back, waving him toward the pond, or shouting encouragement to the weary people who trudged behind the farmer. When he saw Amelia, Kenchi, and Haruto watching, Yuki broke out into a run.

"I hope you don't mind," he gasped, trying to regain his breath while bowing low before Amelia. "I have brought relatives from the hills."

"No, of course not," Amelia stuttered back, bemused by the assortment of people trailing Yuki. "These are all your relatives? Where did you find them all?"

"What happened to you?" Kenchi asked.

"Were you tracked by the warlord's soldiers?" demanded Haruto.

Amelia frowned. "Hold on," she said to Kenchi and Haruto, as the farmer's face twisted into a mask of confusion as the demands flew at him. "Let him answer one question at a time. Now Yuki," Amelia took him by the shoulders, "tell us in your own words what occurred after we lost sight of you at the raid. You were fighting a warrior and…?"

The little farmer took a deep breath. "I killed the soldier I fought," he said, "but tripped on a rock and hit my head." He snorted, remembering, and touched the top of his skull where a purple bruise still showed faintly on his skin. "I must have been unconscious for most of the morning. When I woke, the sun was up and everyone was gone. I walked back to the path but heard soldiers talking and hid in the bushes. Many patrols were searching the trails, so I stayed in the woods evading the men, and worked my way into the hills under cover." He took a deep breath and hooked his thumb over his shoulder at the carts. "I have clan in the mountains. I found a man, a farmer like myself, my uncle's youngest cousin, who hid me in his shed for the rest of the day in case the soldiers searched. He spread the word around I was there, and more of my relatives gathered to hear my story during the night. When I asked how my clan fared, all told the same tale. The warlord is conscripting men of fighting age for his army, stripping farms bare for food, stealing their daughters. Families live in terror, the young men taking cover every time the soldiers appear, farmers concealing food and women. All in the hills and mountains wished to flee, but had no place to go safe enough where the warlord would not find their hiding place." Yuki smiled brightly as the rest of the caravan caught up, parking the carts in the clearing around the pond. A low rumble filled the glade as the new arrivals gaped around in wonder. "I told my kin the Lady Amelia was raising an army to defeat the warlord, and she would protect all who rallied to her banner while riding her white unicorn." He waved a hand at the people crowding around the four, who stared in trepidation at Amelia. "So here we are."

Chapter Eight

"Now remember, when you see me signal, we attack. When the horn blows, we retreat. Sota, you take your men and go for the food wagons first. Haruto, your men seize the wagons containing the weapons." Amelia stared at each of her commanders to see if any held last minute questions. *They shouldn't. We've been over this a hundred times in the last two days. In and out. Simple—I hope.* She continued after receiving nods, "Kenchi and I will stay here watching for trouble, or to reinforce anyone who needs help." Amelia thought for a moment, racking her brain for any missed detail. "Oh, yes. Remember if you have a chance, grab a horse. Forget about the carts. We can't take them, and we brought enough wagons to carry back whatever we capture, but the horses we can always use— but only if you have the opportunity, understand? Don't take time from your assignments to go searching for one." Amelia fidgeted on the back of Lan Ying. "When you have all you can manage, return here and start loading the wagons, and hurry, we don't want to stick around if there's pursuit. I want this done fast. No fighting, understand? Or anyone hurt."

Amelia planned this attack for weeks. If there was pursuit, her people scouted all the trails and roads leading in and away from the village for escape routes. Three of Yuki's oldest relatives, two men and a woman, too ancient to fear conscription into the warlord's troops, spent a day roaming the village on the pretext of seeking work, while really gathering news about the strength of the company protecting the supplies for the army, roaming the hills, and the schedule when the soldiers left and returned.

Kenchi and Haruto devoted hours training the men, attempting to force the use of sword on farmers who'd never held a weapon in their lives, most old, and all scared. Repeatedly, Kenchi and Haruto argued about using old men and women in the new army. The older warrior claimed they wasted their time on teaching the ancients, while Kenchi pointed out this was all the army had, and farmers or not, the refugees better learn the handling of weapons or become killed in the first engagement. Amelia experienced a feeling of dread every day after inspecting the practice field where the men trained, and each time spoke a small prayer the unprepared troops would see no heavy fighting. For this reason, she'd chosen a small village, lightly guarded, well removed from the border where battles raged. A mere way stop to the front lines, a holding station for supplies to the army before the weapons and rice shipped to the main depot.

The sinking feeling returned to Amelia's stomach. She licked her dry lips. "Alright. Move down and take your places."

Haruto and Sota waved their men forward and along the hillside. Amelia said to Kenchi hoarsely, "You have the conch shell? You remember the signals we developed?"

"Of course he remembers the signals," Lan Ying's thoughts reverberated in Amelia's mind. *"The man has been practicing the same notes for two days in a row."* The unicorn's tail flicked in annoyance as she remembered the sound that had plagued her delicate ears from morning until dusk. *"When are we completed with this nonsense so I can return to my nice meadow and sweetgrass?"*

The girl patted Lan Ying on the neck. "Sorry honey, I'm nervous, that's all. We'll be home real soon and you can eat all the grass you want." *I hope.*

Lan Ying swung her head and nipped playfully at Amelia's fingers. *Do not worry about your safety. You ride a unicorn, brave and true. Nothing can happen to you while you are on me, I will not allow harm to come to you. I love you."*

Kenchi watched this exchange, his lips flickering upward at the corners. He said to Amelia, "Begging your permission and Lan Ying's, the time has arrived to unfurl your banner." He held a long pole and carefully unrolled the black flag revealing a white unicorn and girl outlined on the surface. He attached the banner to the rod and held the pole upright. "All the trappings of a real general now," he commented making a short bow to Amelia.

Amelia repressed a laugh. "Yeah. I hope not a general disaster, though. I'm scared out of my wits something will go wrong and the disaster will be my fault."

"Let us hope not," Kenchi replied drily. He raised the conch shell to his lips. "At your command Lady General Amelia."

Amelia carefully scanned the landscape below to assure herself the men were in position. From her vantage point, her warriors showed as small blotches concealed by brush and rocks scattered at the edge of the village. The small town was quiet, most of the residents still sleeping, or eating their morning rice before leaving for shops and fields. The warlord's soldiers guarding the supplies slumbered also, drowsing around fires, curled up on mats. Amelia took a deep breath, crossed her fingers, and whispered, *"Now."*

Kenchi blew a long, clear note reverberating through the air. At the signal, the men sprinted like silent ghosts into the village and spread out.

The scene unfolded as if in slow motion. Her men hastened to the wagons and storeroom, blades high. Screams of battle rage rang from the warriors as the startled guards sprang up still half asleep, groping for their weapons in panic. The two sides met and merged, yells echoing faintly to Amelia in the breaking dawn.

"Haruto's men have captured the weapons," Kenchi exclaimed tensely, waving his finger toward a ring of wagons. "I see him passing out bundles of arrows to his men."

Amelia followed the direction of Kenchi's hand. The soldiers guarding the weapon carts were down, trampled heaps of armor crushed under the weight of Haruto's men, as eager hands grasped the bows and arrows, spears and swords, their commander tossed from the interior of the wagon.

Amelia stretch upward, head swinging to the left and right, scanning the rest of the street. "Where's Sota? I don't see him," She bit her lower lip and shifted as if to ride into the village in search of the warrior and his men.

"There—there," Kenchi shouted, "by the end building! His men are kicking open the door to the storehouse." He jabbed the pole with Amelia's banner toward the building he was talking about.

Amelia halted, tensely, her vision sweeping up the street and centered on the structure, and then for some reason swung farther along the road. "Uh-oh. I see trouble approaching. Where did those warriors come from?"

A squad of soldiers marched up the street, sent from the front to bring provisions forward to the main supply depot. The commander expected no trouble in this sleepy village, but when he spied the battle raging, the warriors broke out into a run, drawing weapons.

"Those are trained soldiers," exclaimed Kenchi, "and I see samurai among the troops. I am going to blow the retreat." He raised the conch shell to his lips again.

The warlord's men sprinted forward. Haruto saw the troops approaching and shouted to his raiders, who looked wildly around in confusion. The old samurai struggled to leap out of the wagon and draw his sword.

Sota and his squad had entered the warehouse and not yet emerged. The lone man who'd been placed on guard as watch at the broken door stood paralyzed in fright.

"Too late. They'll be on our people before Haruto and Sota know what's happening to them." Amelia shouted to Lan Ying, "Quick. We must ride there and stop those soldiers before the men are slaughtered." Without waiting to see if Kenchi listened, Amelia dug her heels into the unicorn's sides and Lan Ying bolted down the hill into the town.

Dimly Amelia heard the bugle of retreat as Kenchi blew on the shell, mingled with the blare of the conch the pounding of the unicorn's hooves rang unnaturally loud. Lan Ying hit the main street of the village and galloped toward the approaching soldiers. Amelia raised her sword, murder in her eyes, as the filly approached the enemy. The soldiers halted, transformed into stone as a black-haired fury charged their ranks on a raging unicorn snorting hatred, shooting fire from their eyes. Her own men watched Amelia dash past and started a retreat into the hills loaded down totting provisions and arms. Still half stunned, the warlord's soldiers unfroze and released a volley of arrows along the street at Amelia and the men behind her. Lan Ying dodged, twisting her body left and right as she continued to gallop forward, head lowered, her murderous horn jutting as if a lance toward the lead soldier's bellies.

One arrow, better aimed than the rest, or anticipating the unicorn's frantic turns, grazed Amelia in the neck, leaving a deep gouge, as she swung her sword. Blood spurted, and specks of red splattered her kimono and Lan Ying's alabaster coat.

"Yeow, that hurt." Amelia touched her neck as she and the filly sped past the enemy soldiers, drawing away stained fingers.

"You are wounded?" Lan Ying dug her hooves into the earth, spraying dirt in the air, swinging around in a wide circle. *"Those beasts shall pay for their transgression."*

Half the soldiers ran toward the village. The remainder swung about and stood in a line, bracing for the return charge of Amelia. The unicorn's muscles gathered, and in a flash of speed she was upon the men in a raging fury. Amelia cut with her sword, bending low and caught one man between his body and thigh armor. Lan Ying's shoulder connected against a warrior's chest and he flew backward into one of his companions crying in pain. Both collapsed into a heap of arms and legs. The unicorn hooked her sharp horn, goring another warrior through the breast as she flew toward the remaining soldiers, who dashed toward the village.

Beyond the warriors Amelia raced toward, her white and black banner fluttered in the air, a lone monolith standing against the rushing tide of the oncoming warlord's men.

Kenchi held the staff in his left hand while he rode to Amelia, sword in his right, challenging the soldiers.

His horse reared, hooves flashing, screaming defiance at the enemy as Kenchi did himself. He swung his blade, and swung again. Soldiers dropped, but the rest of the warriors clustered about him, attempting to drag the young man out of his saddle to the ground. Kenchi beat at the men, swinging his sword and the butt of the staff, his horse kicking in a circle, hind legs crushing bone, front legs lashing out.

Her head lowered, Lan Ying struck this group, brushing aside soldiers as if the flesh were no more than leaves on the ground, trampling one underfoot with her iron hooves. The man's screams of pain rang in Amelia's ears before the cries cut off sharply. The unicorn kept running, shreds of the man's clothing tangled around one hoof, as

Lan Ying angled toward the hills behind Amelia's retreating warriors.

"Wait, we must go back and help Kenchi," Amelia pleaded when the unicorn showed no signs of slowing her headlong rush.

"If he stays and fight when he has no need to he is a greater fool than I thought he was," the testy reply floated back from the unicorn. *"I have made the way clear for him, our men retreat in good order, and you are wounded. I will not endanger your life for his sake or any man."*

Amelia twisted on Lan Ying's back, looking toward the rear. Seeing Amelia safe, Kenchi wheeled his mount around and galloped after the unicorn. His horse could not match the fleeing speed of Lan Ying, but no pursuit was offered as of yet by the soldiers, who were still stunned by the suddenness of the unicorn's attack. Instead, the confused and frightened men huddled around their wounded, screaming shouts to each other while frantically waving for help from those who held healing knowledge.

Lan Ying slowed enough while climbing into the hills for Kenchi to catch up on his lathered mount. "Our men are safe," Amelia gasped. For some reason she was crying. Her body shook as if wrapped in a blanket of ice. The trembling would not stop, and she swallowed uncontrollably to ease her dry throat.

"You are wounded," Kenchi rode close to her.

"Don't worry about me, I'm fine, but the men? Did all our people all escape? Are they unharmed?"

"Do not fear, we left no one behind," Kenchi assured her, "dead or alive." He rode close and bent over, examining her wound. A tight smile cut his face, pleased the gash was not worse, but still upset Amelia was hurt at all. "I will worry about you, however. You have a nasty cut."

Kenchi glanced down the hill. The remaining soldiers were in furious argument with the guards of the depot. The two hysterical fractions huddled in a frightened circle shouting at each other and casting terrified looks toward the hills, expecting Amelia's men to rush down and attempt another attack at any moment. Their wounded lay into the shade of a building. Two men crouched over their comrades attempting to staunch the flow of blood from the wounds.

Amelia and Kenchi galloped into the rallying point. Haruto and Sota busily supervised the loading of wagons. When the two saw the blood covering Amelia they leaped forward. "Amelia's hurt!" Haruto cried to the rest as she dismounted. Amelia wavered on her feet, and both Haruto and Sota grabbed her shoulders. Amelia shook the two off and pulled herself erect.

"I'm fine. Just wobbly from hard riding. Are we all set to leave?" She counted her men by eye, making sure all were present while dividing her attention between the warriors and the enemy soldiers below in the town.

"Yes, but we must attend to your wound first," insisted Kenchi, vaulting off his mount. "Let us bandage your neck." He placed a palm on her shoulder trying to make Amelia sit.

"No time. The soldiers...." Amelia struggled and threw off the hand, glaring in defiance.

"Plenty of time," Haruto said. "Right now the soldiers are afraid to track us here in case we plan an ambush or another attack. The warlord's troops have hurt men to attend to also."

Kenchi signaled to Haruto and Sota. "Haruto, you cover the point. Amelia is hurt and will ride in the middle of the formation. Sota, you stay with her. I will take your men and remain here in case there is pursuit from the soldiers."

"I was supposed to lead—"

"Hush. This is why we made back up plans." Kenchi said to the unicorn, "Tell her, Lan Ying. She is wounded and should not be placed in danger at the moment if there is fighting."

The unicorn looked surprised and snorted, swinging to Amelia. *"Although he is very presumptuous by addressing me by name, for once the man is right. You are wounded and should not put yourself in jeopardy where you can receive more injuries."*

"Oh, *all right.*" Amelia let herself be helped to a rock to rest on while Haruto fetched water and a cloth. He gently washed the dried blood away and studied the long gouge in her neck carefully. "You will live," he announced at last. "A flesh wound. Another inch to the left, though, and you would be dead." He took out a pouch of herbs, wet another cloth, and ground the powder into the cloth, making a moist poultice. "This will stop the bleeding and help the gash heal. I will change the dressing when we return to camp. This is something else we need, a healer who is versed in battle wounds."

Amelia touched the bandage gingerly. The gouge hadn't felt life threatening at all when she was nicked by the arrow, more like a bug bite. Too busy fighting the battle she supposed, but now the wound throbbed painfully. Amelia took a deep breath, gritted her teeth, and stood. "I'll survive. Let's go."

Completing the one raid, Amelia's army secured sufficient food to last their growing community for a month, and weapons to equip every man and woman, plus enough left over for new recruits. The new village need both. Men and women continued to trickle into their camp in small groups, drawn by the rumors of Amelia's attempt to defeat the warlord and the promise of safety. Nevertheless, most were old or crippled, run off their land by the warlord, who continued to rape the countryside for conscripts and supplies for his army.

Amelia settled these people as best possible. The exiles were her responsibility even though no one asked these refugees to enlist in her band. Small shacks and lean-to's sprang up among the cypress, pine and maple trees, and the meadow. Small children ran everywhere, brought by their grandparents after the soldiers hauled their mothers away to the army. The fear of detection was always on her mind concealing this many people. Amelia prayed daily to the Shinto gods and Buddha they would not be angered at this violation the Sea of Trees, or the demons who stalked the woods would not rise up and overwhelm the people of the new camp.

As the population of the small village grew, however, Haruto, Kenchi, and Sota trained the people as best possible in warfare. By slow degrees, Amelia saw her rag-tag army of women and old men turning into the semblance of a real army. The next step in the battle to free her mother became obvious—to Amelia, anyway.

"We need more horses," Amelia stated at a late night strategy session. As many people as possible jammed the cavern, listening in rapt attention or adding suggestions of their own as the plans for the next battle took shape. Kenchi, Haruto, Sota, and a few of the more prominent leaders of the growing army sat around the fire pit, hashing out the best way to proceed. "We have men and weapons for our troops to use. We need a cavalry, though. The samurai are mounted. We cannot fight the warlord without horses to ride into battle." Amelia slammed her right fist into her left palm to emphasis the point.

Murmurs of agreement arose from the people in the cavern. Amelia watched the faces of her commanders, anticipating the agreement she was sure would result.

Kenchi shook his head. "What good will horses do? Look around you. Who will ride the beasts? Old men and women? Children? Who will wield the weapons? True, these people learn, but so slowly. Now you ask these folks to do so while riding a horse? Individuals who have never held a sword or bow in their lives? We have been lucky in our last two raids and faced no determined resistance. The first time we cross hardened soldiers...." He left the sentence hanging, the facts speaking for themselves.

Haruto added, "For once the youngster is right. You yourself know it takes years of training to fight like a samurai. Even against young, untrained men, our warriors would not last a minute—and on horseback?" he snorted in derision, "they'd be lucky not to fall on their heads. Now if you ask me—"

"We can ride, we can fight," a wizened man raised a boney arm in the air, yelling from the back of the crowd, interrupting Haruto. The old samurai glared, craning his neck to see who shouted.

"And you will be slaughtered like pigs," Kenchi replied calmly, but loud enough for all to hear, especially Amelia. "You think you can battle against trained cavalrymen? Samurai? You would not swing your weapon once, on horse or foot." He glared at Amelia. "What we need are young men, maybe women, of fighting age. Untrained we can teach them, seasoned warriors would be better if we could find any who still exist."

Amelia bit her lower lip, but nodded in growing exasperation. "Great, but where would we locate young men and women of fighting age? The warlord has seized every able-bodied man in the province."

Kenchi lifted his hands in vexation. "I do not know. All I know is we cannot win battles using what we have here. Small raids, yes, as the one we accomplished, but anything larger? Horses or no horses, we would kill our own people for no purpose," he complained to Haruto in frustration. "You tell her, maybe she will believe you."

The old warrior nodded and waved at the people surround the fire pit. "As I have said, they have the temper, courage—yes, but not the skill or the strength. To take these into battle would be murder."

Someone from the crowd asked, "Can we hire mercenaries? I hear there are many such in China."

This brought a sour chuckle from Haruto. "And what would we pay these warriors? For that matter, how would we transport soldiers here? We have no boats, no money, and no time to negotiate with foreigners even if we sent someone to China to find mercenaries willing to battle for us."

Sota broke in. "Remember, fighters have a way of not leaving once the battle is won. If the mercenaries defeated the warlord's troops, we could well be trading one master for another. How would we get rid of these soldiers for hire?"

Grumbling arose from the crowd. Amelia gritted her teeth, suppressing the urge to shout, say her warriors were as good as the finest troops the warlord possessed, better than the best mercenaries money could buy in China. In her heart, however, Amelia knew what Kenchi and Haruto said was true. She balled her fists up at her side. "So you are saying we should do nothing at all? Curl up like sleeping curs in the road until the warlord decides we're a nuisance and destroys us all?"

A young man, one of the handful who was of fighting age, shouted, "I know where you can locate young men and women, and plenty, too, all eager to fight the warlord if given a chance."

Amelia searched over the heads of the people and picked the man out by eye, motioning him forward to stand in the circle. "Where? Come up here where all can see and hear you. This is important."

The man pushed through the crowd to the fire. Both Kenchi and Haruto said eagerly, "The people you speak of, how many, and why have we known nothing of them before this?"

"In the Buddhist and Shinto monasteries," he replied importantly, throwing out his chest. "The young men and girls go to become monks or nuns rather than fight in the warlord's army. The holy ones also give sanctuary to whoever asks and seeks the temples in goodwill. I myself was planning to do so until I heard about your army and decided to fight against the evil daimyo."

Amelia, Kenchi, and Haruto exchanged rapid glances. Haruto said, "The places of worship are full of priests and monks. Buddhist monks do not wish to fight, nor do Shinto monks. Clerics live by peace. Why would they fight with us?"

The young man bobbed his head knowingly. "The young men and women do not go there to become monks or nuns. The people do so because they do not wish to fight for the warlord. Given the chance, many would war against him. Like the rest of us, the soldiers drove the farmers off their land, families destroyed, or businesses confiscated. This is their last refugee against the tyranny plaguing the land."

At first, Amelia thought the suggestion was bitterly amusing. Go to the temples where the inhabitants lived by peace and harmony, and beg the priests to kill so her mother and the rest of the province would be free. The more she thought about the idea, however, the asking would not hurt, and if they received men and women of fighting age all the better.

Kenchi spoke up. "Now you have mentioned the fact, I heard rumors some of the warlord's own soldiers deserted at the beginnings of the war and became monks. I thought the reason was they were cowards, but perhaps.... I saw many men grumbling in the short time I joined the army complaining about the treatment of the people, both samurai and common soldier. Maybe they did not want to abduct members of their own clan or friends for the warlord troops."

Amelia asked the young man eagerly, "Do you know which monastery the men and women hide in?"

The young man shook his head in denial. "As far as I know, all monasteries. The people do not care as long as safety can be secured, and the monks are always searching for new recruits to train so the word about their religion can be spread."

"We must visit each one, then. A few men here, a couple there. We may recruit enough," Kenchi said, adding, "I will go. I know the countryside, and where many of these monasteries are located."

For a long moment silence hung over the circle of men, and then a chorus of *"Me too. Me too,"* rang out from the assembled people.

Amelia held up her hand for silence and said to Kenchi, "I don't think we can spare—"

"Nonsense. There is nothing here Haruto, Sota, and you cannot handle in my absence," Kenchi said, "and I do not need a crowd. Sorry, but some of these monasteries are in the towns occupied by soldiers. I will have enough problems sneaking in and out without guards stopping and questioning me, or taken prisoner. Extra people to worry about makes the job that much harder. I will meet patrols on the road, which I must evade also. The search will be safer and faster if I go alone."

A sudden chill swept over Amelia, and she didn't know why. "When would you leave?" she asked quietly.

Kenchi rubbed his chin. "Tomorrow, I expect. The sooner I go, the quicker I will return. My horse, enough rice to last me two days is all I need."

The hour was late. The meeting broke up. The crowd wandered off to their own huts to sleep and rest for the morrow's labors. Amelia and Kenchi lingered by the fire, enjoying the quiet having no one else around and talking in low voices.

"Do you really think you will recruit any men?" Amelia asked feeding small branches into the fire to keep the blaze alive. Red highlights flashed in her black hair.

Kenchi's dark eyes sparkled with the reflection of the flames. Amelia pushed out of her mind what tomorrow would bring, and wished this moment would last forever, just her and Kenchi, no worries for the moment, warm and safe.

Kenchi stretched his arms wide and yawned. "Who can tell? I will not know until I have looked. Let us hope the warlord's soldiers have not raided the monasteries first and taken the men and women by force. If so, you can be sure I will find nothing left."

Amelia studied his face. The flickering light made him appear like a specter in the shadows. "I fear you will never return." *Do not think of his death. He will return, he must.*

Kenchi reached out one hand and entwined his fingers with hers. "It will take more than a few soldiers to kill me, never fear. Remember when we were young and we hid from each other? You could never find me unless I wanted you too."

The corners of Amelia's mouth lifted. "Oh you are such a liar. I always found you."

Kenchi grinned back and squeezed her fingers gently before releasing her hand. "That's what I said, 'unless I wanted you too.'"

Afterwards, the two went to sleep. When Amelia woke, Kenchi was gone.

Even though surrounded by people, Amelia felt lost, abandoned as if no one else existed in the world. Haruto and Sota noticed her state of mind, but could not break her out of the mood she found herself. Lan Ying's only comment was, *"Well, one less male we have to worry about. Now if only we could rid ourselves of the rest of these men, I could graze in peace and finally smell the fresh air again."*

"Lan Ying, I miss him. You know I do."

Amelia and the unicorn stood by the pond while Amelia directed the men and women in the construction of new shacks for the people she hoped Kenchi would send. Lan Ying glanced at the people as the inhabitants hurried to collect wood and grass for the roofs. *"We have plenty more here. Why worry about one?"*

"Why? Because I, uh...." Amelia's face flushed pink. "He's my friend. I've known Kenchi since we were babies. We trained together as samurai and he is my closest advisor."

"Hmm...All I can say is all males are the same. If you have seen one, you have seen them all." Lan Ying twitched her long tail as if her statement settled everything. *"I am going to the meadow."* She watched the men and women hurrying about. *"This is becoming much too noisy for me. I will be glad when you mother is rescued and all this nonsense of people and Kenchi is over."*

Amelia threw her arms around the unicorn's neck and hugged her tight. "You will never desert me, will you?"

Lan Ying nickered softly and buried her soft muzzle into Amelia's armpit. *"Of course not. What do I look like, one of those love fillies and leave them stallions? I am yours forever."*

Head held high, the unicorn trotted away. Amelia tried to keep bursting out laughing as the unicorn wandered into the meadow, found a fresh clump of green grass and grazed, but a slow smirk broke over Amelia's lips. *I don't care what you think of Kenchi, I want the man.*

Chapter Nine

A week passed without word from Kenchi. Ten days later two men marched up the trail to the clearing, heads shaved, wearing yellow robes of Buddhist monks. Amelia happened to be lounging near the water, watching the minnows glide over the pond grass as she pondered the whereabouts of her friend. When the two spotted her, one of the strangers, a boy about seventeen, called out, "Are you Amelia? Are we in the right place?"

Amelia leaped to her feet, startled by the voice, wondering how the outsiders managed to evade detection by the scouts positioned throughout the woods. She spotted the intruders weaving their way up the tiny path and her fingers automatically reached for her sword. "Maybe," she conceded, keeping her hand placed casually on the hilt, but in plain sight so the two could see. "Who are you, and what do you want?"

The young men entered the clearing and paused, unsure of their next move. "We…we are from Daigo-ji temple. My name is Koki. This is Ritu," the older explained. "A soldier named Kenchi, a samurai warrior, sent us here. He said a woman called Amelia was raising a force to fight against the warlord of this domain. Are you she? We wish to join your army."

Yes! Recruits. Kenchi was successful! Our army grows. Soon we will possess the strength to march to victory.

"Uh-huh." Amelia dropped her hand and strode forward. "I am Amelia. You saw Kenchi? You spoke to him?"

The two bowed low. "We did. He approached our temple, seeking volunteers to fight for you. At first, the priests would send him away. The holy ones do not wish any part of the war happening in the country, but the more he spoke, the more some of us listened."

Amelia peered down the path. "Is he with you? Are there more recruits coming?" she asked eagerly.

Koki hung his head. "Maybe," the boy dodged. "Kenchi left to travel to the next monastery. After he departed, warriors appeared and the priests sent the troops away. We set off right after the soldiers did for fear the men would reappear and force us to join the warlord's army. Many of our brothers wished to go, but the monks urged the people to wait and see what happened. I feel sure many will leave soon also to journey here and join your army. The soldiers said troops would return if we did not enlist voluntarily."

Lan Ying trotted over from the meadow, head held high, sniffing the breeze, and eyeing the strangers suspiciously. She stood next to Amelia, nuzzled the girl, while pointing her horn at the boys.

The two young men gasped, their eyes growing large and round in wonder. "What Kenchi said is true. We would know you as the real warrior princess because a unicorn answering to your bidding."

Amelia giggled. "Kenchi called me a warrior princess? Well, I'm not a princess, and we have yet to see what type of a warrior I am. He was right though. This is Lan Ying." She threw her arm around the unicorn's neck in a hug. "She does not run to my call. We are friends, though."

"Who are these two? The humans smell funny." Lan Ying swished her tail and snorted.

"Hush. These boys are our new recruits." A stray breeze blew from the men toward Amelia. The odor of incense still clung to their robes even after days of travel.

More of Amelia's men wandered over to meet the strangers. Two of her scouts puffed up the trail. "We are sorry. We watched for strangers but did not see these intruders pass." Their faces burnt red with shame.

Ritu laughed. "We saw you, but do not be alarmed because you did not notice us. We were born and live in the mountains, brought up as hunters. Our fathers and uncles hammered into us at an early age stealth and patience while moving through fields and forests. We did not show ourselves because we did not know if you were friend or foe."

A rising excitement filled Amelia. "You are hunters? You know the use of a bow and arrow?"

Ritu drew back an imaginary cord and bolt, tracking across the azure sky as if he watched a bird in flight. "My father would hand me one arrow for my bow and tell me to bring back supper for the family." He licked his lips remembering. "We never starved."

"Good. You can train the rest of the men in archery and help provide food for the camp. Securing a company of bowmen such as you, we'd be in good shape to fight the warlord's troops. Now if we received horses for our men to ride we could form a cavalry too."

Koki slapped his forehead. "This was something else Kenchi wanted us to tell you. The warlord is buying horses from China for his army. The ships dock at the local seaports on a weekly basis."

Amelia's dark brown eyes lit up in joy. "Did he say which port?" *The cavalry I hoped to have. Yes. We can make this happen.*

"He mentioned Sakai or Nagoya on the Inland Sea," Koki gestured vaguely toward the coast, "but also said the ships arrive in many harbors at different times."

Amelia worried her lower lip between her teeth, thinking. *I should really wait for Kenchi to return before I raid, but.... I must send spies first, find out schedules, and scope the lay of the land before I do anything, but yes, this can all be done before he returns. I'll have everything planned and ready, then we will have our horses.*

She said to Koki and Ritu, "I am glad you brought me this information and have joined us." Amelia waved Haruto over. "Have these men settled and see to their needs, food if they are hungry and answer any questions which might arise. Our two new warriors are a valuable addition to the troops."

During the next month bands of young monks and nuns drifted into the camp, sometimes in groups of twos and threes, occasionally in larger parties of fives and tens, all sent by Kenchi as he visited the monasteries and temples in the region. All told the same tale—fear of the warlord's troops dragging the novice monks off as conscripts for his army, in some cases monasteries broken into, priests killed who tried to stop the soldiers, men hauled away bodily out of their beds in the middle of the night.

Amelia grew increasingly impatient for the return of Kenchi so she could start the raiding of the ships for horses. As time passed and he did not return, the urge to do something, anything, to strike back at the daimyo, became a burning fire in her chest, making her stalk the camp day and night like a tiger restraining pent up energy. Finally, she was unable to contain her passion and determined to do something.

Amelia decided to act alone.

***

"Are you sure no one is arriving for the horses today?" Amelia sat astride Lan Ying, Sota mounted by her side. Below, in the breaking early morning gloom, the small town of Nagoya still slumbered peacefully. Amelia barely made out a corral enclosing a herd of horses, the heads hanging low as the animals, too, slept.

"The mares will be left alone except for feeding and watering for at least another day," her lieutenant replied, broad grin revealing black, broken teeth. "Horses can't vomit, and they are seasick from the voyage from China. Their handlers insist the mares are given a week of rest to recuperate from the trip to regain their strength, before transferring the herd to the battlefront."

"We can move the horses, though, can't we?" Amelia said, distressed. "I have planned this too long to learn at the last minute I have a bunch of horses too sick to travel, especially if we are chased by the warlord's soldiers and must flee in a hurry."

Sota brushed this aside with a wave of his hand. "Oh, yes, the animals can be moved, not rode into battle, mind you, or herded hundreds of miles at a fast pace. They will be fine for the short distance we go, and once we reach the meadow, the horses will have plenty of time to rest."

Amelia nodded in understanding, licking her lips, a sense of excitement twisting her guts as she scanned the landscape below for signs of trouble. All was quiet. She bent over the unicorn's neck and whispered in Lan Ying's ear, "You know what you're supposed to do, right, baby? Do you want me to tell you one more time to make sure?"

"Humph. Five times is plenty, twice was too many. Of course I understand, but the humiliation of it all. Smelly men surround me again, and now I have to play lead mare to a bunch of sick nags who cannot even run for any distance if needed to. To think I have sunk so low. The embarrassment."

Amelia's eyes twinkled, but said uneasily as she patted the unicorn's neck, "You're doing this for a good cause, honey. Sure the herd will obey you? I mean you are a unicorn, but they're horses. How can...?"

"I speak horse quite fluently, thank you, and besides, if the mares do not do as I say, a nip on the rump or a prod from my horn is all I need to convey what I wish these nags to do. Even a man, as slow as males are, would understand my meaning."

Sota rode away to rejoin his men. Haruto waved to her, signaling his side of the line was ready any time Amelia issued the order to start the assault. The night sky gradually turned from dark grey to dim blue, red streaks of the rising sun painting the clouds. Amelia saw no reason to stall any longer. She waved her hand over her head and made a casting motion toward the corral. On either flank, Sota and Haruto did the same and the silent line of warriors weaved its way forward to the warehouse complex.

The two flanks comprised of the young men and women curled outward, encircling the compound and concealing themselves to repulse and possible attack from without. The center, led by Amelia, raced to the gate, each man a farmer or herder experienced in handling livestock. Each carried a halter for a horse.

The animals gazed back despairingly as the men opened the gate and crept into the corral. Amelia, astride Lan Ying, halted by the entrance to ensure there was no slowing down as the animals passed through the fence and left the enclosure.

Amelia divided her attention between the corral and the perimeter, her heart hammering, as she prayed no one approached and discover the company in the middle of the raid, while wishing the men would hurry up and collar the horses so the troop could be gone.

After an eternity, the warriors began leading the animals out of the gate, assisted by Lan Ying who bestowed sharps nips to the hind legs of any horse she decided was moving too slowly. A faint, *"What a herd of pathetic beasts these are. In all my days...."* rumbled in in Amelia's mind as the unicorn prodded one mare in the rump.

"Hey, what goes on here? Who are you people? Stop—Stop now. Do you hear me?"

Amelia whipped her head around. From the direction of a warehouse, one of the warlord's horse handlers strode rapidly toward the corral, waving his hands in the air. He shouted again, "Who are you people? I haven't been authorized to release those animals to anyone yet. Are you the daimyo's men? Where are your papers?"

Three of Amelia's archers drew back their bows and bolts zipped into the man's chest and stomach. He clutched at the shafts in surprise and dropped to the earth in a crumpled heap.

Nevertheless, his yells attracted the attention of others.

Questioning ricocheted back and forth from the buildings as more workers appeared, mingled with confused guards and soldiers.

"MOVE THESE HORSES, NOW!" Amelia shouted as the last of the animals passed through the corral gate. Lan-Ying released a bugling cry and the sick horses broke out into a shambling trot, the warriors leading the mares by the halters, loping alongside, attempting to keep up.

More archers rose, firing their arrows into the growing crowd approaching the corral, taking special aim at the guards, or soldiers if the archers spotted one among the rest of the men. In the confusion, Amelia's men started a retreat forming a line between the crowd and the escaping horses. Lan Ying made quick sprints between the herd and line of warriors, issuing impatient whinnies when the animals slowed. Amelia kept scanning the area to guarantee none of the soldiers managed to collect themselves and outflank her men.

Lan Ying darted back to the horses. One mare, slower than the rest lagged behind the herd. The unicorn jabbed sharply with her horn into a flank, drawing blood. *"Move it slow poke,"* Lan Ying commanded, snorting an impatient whinny. *"We do not have all day."*

"Lan Ying, don't hurt the poor creature," Amelia said when the horse screamed in pain. "We need her alive, not full of holes."

"This one is just being lazy," Lan Ying retorted with a shake of her mane. She threw an appraising glance at the mare followed by a menacing grunt. The mare quickened her pace and caught up to the rest of the herd. *"I have met her kind before. Ornery, but I will whip this group into shape before the day is out."*

Amelia kept casting glances behind her, positive at any time she'd see a company of soldiers in search of their trail, and the raiders would have to stop and fight for their lives, but by nightfall Amelia's band was well away from the coast, and the frantic pace slowed to a gently walk. The host made camp in a small field for the evening, ringing the perimeter with guards in case of attack.

"Shouldn't we keep moving?" Amelia asked Haruto and Sota. "We're still close to the town, if the soldiers have organized and track us things could go badly."

"We are far enough away," Haruto assured her, "and look." He waved to the herd. The horses stood with heads hanging low. "They still haven't fully recovered from their voyage across the sea. We must give the animals time to rest before we push on."

Sota nodded. "We are well protected here. I did not see many soldiers at the depot, and even if the commander added the guards to their number, there still would not be enough to give us a serious fight. I believe the officers will wait for reinforcements, which will take many days to arrive, before any set out to recover their lost mares."

Reluctantly Amelia agreed. The next morning, however, as they broke camp, Koki hurried to her, panting.

"Lady Amelia, I was scouting ahead as ordered," he gasped. "Soldiers—a whole company of warriors straight ahead in the woods. The men approach now." He jabbed his hand toward the dark trees half frightened, half excited.

I knew we should have kept marching last night.
Amelia thought quickly. "Okay, go back into the forest and
watch. Let me know when the soldiers approach close and
if the company deploys into a battle-line."

"Yes, Lady Amelia." Koki bowed low. He took a
deep breath. "I will return when the warriors are near." He
sprinted away.

Amelia waved Haruto and Sota over, holding a
whispered conversation. She pasted a forced smile on her
face so not panic the rest of the men, who drifted close to
overhear what was happening when Koki ran up in panic.
"What do we do? A company of soldiers? We can't elude
the warriors, not herding the horses, and it's too late to
move out of the way."

Haruto loosened the sword at his waist. "We fight.
What else? Fight and hope for the best."

Sota exclaimed, with a gleam in his eyes, "I will tell
the warriors to prepare for combat. I heard muttering
among the troop we didn't have much of a battle yesterday.
Our men want a fight to prove themselves. This will be
their chance." He left in a hurry.

*Oh, Buddha, let this end well. I don't want a battle,
not now. I haven't planned for this and the men are still
unprepared to stand against real soldiers.*

Warriors ran frantically about, extinguishing
campfires and snatching up weapons. Her body shaking,
Amelia mounted Lan Ying and drew her sword, nudging
the unicorn out before the line of men Haruto hastily
ordered assembled. "Soldiers of the warlord approach
through the forest," she shouted, jabbing her blade in the
direction of the woods. "We cannot run, and it is too late to
avoid the company undetected. We must fight." Growls of
assent greeted her. "If we die, we die upholding our honor."
Amelia galloped back and took her place in the center of
the line.

Haruto rode to her, his mouth bent in a scowl. "Amelia you must not take part in this fight."

"Huh? Why not?" Amelia exclaimed in surprise, shocked Haruto would say such a thing. "I am their leader. What kind of leader doesn't lead her troops into battle?"

"I know you want to, but think," the old warrior pleaded, "if you are killed, or even badly injured, what happens to the plan to rescue your mother?" He waved a hand left and right along the battle line. "What happens to these men? The old and young are here because of you, the woman who rides a unicorn. This small band you have collected will fall apart, the men caught one by one, and forced into the warlord's army. I will command our people. You must remain safe. If you want to lead, lead from the rear. Many generals do this."

Amelia ground her teeth so hard her jaw muscles hurt. She realized what Haruto said was true, but the idea galled her to think she couldn't direct the troops. "I will be like a paper tiger," she protested in frustration. "What will the men think if they don't see me in battle," she sputtered at last. "I am a coward? I will never deserve respect again."

"Your soldiers will believe you are a wise leader," the warrior contended calmly. "Those who follow know you are not a coward. They also understand the one leading has a dream. It is your vision of purpose we must preserve at all costs, which means keeping you safe."

"Oh, all right," Amelia spat out and swung Lan Ying around, shouting over her shoulder to Haruto, "If I see too much trouble, don't expect me to stand idly by and watch my army slaughtered without me."

Haruto took over her position in the center of the line, sword raised high. Koki ran out of the woods and raced back to his comrades, waving his hand over his head, and shouting, *"The soldiers come. The warriors form a battle line in the trees and approach."*

As the first ranks of the warlord's soldiers emerged from the forest Amelia's body tensed, as did her troops. Haruto ordered, "Archers forward."

The bowmen stepped to the front, holding their weapons and clutching bolts between their fingers.

"Ready." The men notched their arrows.

"Aim." The warriors drew back their cords, steel heads of bolts pointed at a forty-five degree angle into the air.

More of the warlord's soldiers scurried into view in a ragged line. Haruto gauged the distance and then dropped his sword.

"FIRE!"

Bowstrings snapped and arrows leaped into the sky. The shafts dropped on the enemy soldiers like a hail of death. The warriors crumbled, but more emerged from the forest with screams of rage as the men tore forward to the attack.

Haruto shouted, "Charge!" and the two lines surged at each other in a roar of hate.

The forces met in a clash of screaming men and flashing weapons. In the middle of the melee, Haruto chopped with his sword, twisting on the reins of his horse as the animal spun in a tight circle. Amelia watched, holding her hand to her mouth, barely breathing, as men dropped in bloody heaps on both sides.

Haruto raised his right arm to strike at a soldier charging him wielding a spear, and an arrow caught the old warrior in the shoulder. He slumped in the saddle.

"Oh, Buddha, no."

The men surrounding Haruto gasped as he collapsed with the bolt protruding from between his armor. One seized the reins of his horse and guided the beast to the rear. The rest of the warriors saw their leader led away and started a retreat toward the camp. Issuing howls of triumph, the enemy soldiers pressed their attack, attempting to turn the retreat into a rout.

"We're losing. We can't lose. I will not allow it." By reflex, Amelia drew her sword and kicked her heels hard into Lan Ying's sides.

"Ouch." The unicorn glared at Amelia. *"If you want me to charge, say so. You don't have to bruise my ribs."*

"Go. We can't lose this fight. We'll all be killed."

"Of course not. Order those useless men out of my way."

"Huh? What good will that do?" Amelia stared dumbly from Lan Ying to her warriors running backward toward her. She screamed, "MOVE OUT OF THE WAY!" Amelia frantically waved her hands over her head.

The confused, frightened men stared at Amelia. Slowly, a passage opened for her and the unicorn.

Lan Ying released a resounding bugle and leaped ahead. Amelia rocketed back, and then reached out, snatched Lan Ying's mane, and bounced herself forward as the unicorn's front legs hit the turf. Amelia settled firmly on Lan Ying, her heart pounding.

The herd of horses trailed behind, a thundering mass of snorting flesh and bone. Amelia's warriors saw the animals galloping toward the fighting and scrambled aside. The warlord's soldiers were not so fast. Most stood frozen in horror, unable to believe what was charging at their line. By the time the fighters realized what occurred, escape was too late.

The stampeding animals knocked aside everyone in their path. Sick, confused, and trailing their lead mare, the herd sprang to shadow Lan Ying, eyes rolling, froth flying from their mouths. Amelia hacked with her sword at any soldier in reach, spraying Lan Ying's coat crimson. Most of the enemy fled at her approach, leaping aside instead of facing the demented fury of unicorn, horses, and girl.

Behind, Amelia's men rallied, cheering, and charged at the remaining soldiers, screaming curses of rage. The stunned soldiers scrambling off the ground never stood a chance. With chops and thrusts, the warriors slaughtered the warlord's men before they could brace themselves, even the wounded who attempted to surrender. A handful escaped, hiding in the forest.

Amelia waved her bloody sword in the air. "Start collecting our wounded," she shouted to the men closest to her. "Bring the injured to the camp so the wounds can be treated. Once our people have been attended to, search for any weapons you can find." Amelia glanced around, spotted Sota, and beckoned to her lieutenant. "Take some men and pursue the soldiers who escaped. I don't care if you kill any or not. I want to guarantee their captain doesn't reform his troops and attack again. Understand?" She stopped, thinking. "I want prisoners, too. How did the commander locate us? We must know."

Sota bowed. "Yes Lady." He gathered a dozen warriors and loped into the forest.

Lan Ying lifted her head in the air and bugled. The exhausted mares gather around her, muscles shivering. She surveyed her charges for injuries. *"Well, the nags survived,"* she snorted. *"At least they turned out good for something, but I will be glad when we arrive at my meadow and I am shut of this herd."*

"Yes, the horses did," acknowledged Amelia, brushing hair out of her face, "and so did we. I'll be happy when our troop reaches the cave, also. We've experienced enough excitement for a while. C'mon," she nudged the unicorn. "I want to see how Haruto is doing."

Lan Ying neighed to the herd. The mares lifted their heads, ears cocked, and started cropping grass.

Amelia sat straight on the unicorn, letting her gaze sweep the field as she rode to the camp. As she passed her warriors, cheers rang out along with whispered, "Thunder goddess—*Kaminari*—Thunder goddess." Amelia's lips twitched but she refrained from correcting the men.

One of her warriors approached pushing an enemy soldier roughly before him. He stopped in front of Amelia and bowed low. "Lady, Captain Sota said you wished a prisoner. We found this one," he pushed the man to his knees, "hiding behind a tree. What should I do with him?"

"Imprison him and any others we catch, but I want to question him first." She scowled from Lan Ying's back. "You. How did you find us? There were not many soldiers in the town when we raided. Where did you march from?"

"Please do not kill me," the soldier begged. "I have a wife, children. I didn't want to fight. The warlord demands obedience."

"You will not be harmed if you answer," Amelia replied sternly. Lan Ying pawed the ground, snorting, and glared at the man. "How did you locate us?"

"Thank you Lady, thank you." The soldier took a deep breath. "The samurai who was in charge commanded us too. The Western Army destroyed our company in a battle. The warlord chose to send us to Nagoya to recruit more soldiers and bring the horses forward. We reached the town after you left, but the samurai decided we should track you down. We didn't want to. We were tired from the march, tired of battle. He marched us all night through these woods, following the tracks of the horses."

"Hmm…I hope you are telling the truth."

"*I can smell the fear on him,*" Lan Ying informed Amelia. *"He is not lying. He is too terrified to lie."*

"No one told you about our plans to raid beforehand? You are sure the samurai did not know?"

"I swear, Lady, by all the gods. The samurai was surprised himself, I heard him cursing about his luck."

Amelia said to her warrior. "Okay, release him." To the soldier she said, "You are free to go. Do not return to the warlord, for next time we meet you will surely be killed."

Amelia's warrior gaped at her. "Release him? Lady, he is the enemy. What if he reports to the enemy?"

"Tell Sota to release all the prisoners we captured," Amelia said. "We can't feed them all, and I don't want to bring the enemy to our camp so the warlord learns the location. Caution each man not to enlist with him again." She gave the enemy soldier a stern look and made a casting motion. Lan Ying prodded him. "Now go and consider yourself lucky."

The man bowed low, relief mirrored on his face. "Thank you, Lady. I will do as you say, and urge any of my comrades to do the same." He spun around and ran as fast as he could away into the forest.

As her warrior scurried off to find Sota and tell him the new command, Amelia battled her emotions. *So much butchery. In the heat of battle, my passion carries me away and all I want is to kill, destroy. I don't want these feelings—I don't, but I can see no way to rescue my mother without the slaughter.* She hugged Lan Ying. "C'mon, let's see Haruto and make sure he is okay."

A small hospital of sorts stood at the former camp where men boiled water for tea, and the single monk who acted as surgeon hurriedly ran from pallet to pallet attending to the wounded as best he could. Amelia located Haruto propped against a rock, a thick swathe of leaves pressed over his shoulder as a bandage. He gazed dreamily at Amelia with a weak grin as she rode up and leaped off Lan Ying.

"Are you going to live?" She surveyed the old warrior, hands on hips.

"Uh-huh," he mumbled back. "Surgeon tells me I will. Took the arrow out, cauterized the hole, and made me drink something." He blinked and yawned. "Tasted terrible and makes me feel dizzy." He attempted to push himself erect using his good arm, rose a scant inch off the ground and collapsed onto his pallet groaning. "Weak," he muttered to himself, "and I could'a sworn I head the men calling you Kaminari. Must have slept for a minute and dreamed."

The surgeon walked over. "He will live Lady, but we must construct a travois to carry him. He will not be able to sit astride a horse. I have three more like him also." He jabbed a finger at a pile of bodies laid out in a row. "I tried, but those I could not help. I do not have the knowledge and their wounds were severe."

Amelia bowed her head and released a sigh. "Gather men and construct your travois as quickly as possible. We can't remain here long. Even though I don't think so, soldiers may still be tracking us from the town and the ones we defeated could regroup and attack again." She swung back to Haruto. "You took my place at the head of the army so I would survive, and almost got yourself killed instead. For better or worse, from now I will lead the battles, riding in front of my troops, as a general should. I will not have anyone else endanger their lives to protect me. Do I make myself clear?"

Haruto's eyes fluttered shut. Amelia received a snore in return.

Chapter Ten

"What is that?" Lan Ying stretched out her neck and sniffed cautiously at the strange object Amelia set before her. The unicorn prodded the lumpy item, sniffed again, and lifted her head inquiringly. *"Smells like a dead animal left out in the sun too long."*

The unicorn and girl confronted each other in the small barn constructed to house hay and tack for the growing herd of horses and farm animals, mostly chickens, ducks, and geese. Soft sunlight filtered through the cracks of the walls and door, lighting up the dust motes dancing in the air.

"This is a saddle," Amelia informed the unicorn breezily, trying to make the information sound as if this was nothing remarkable. "A present from Kenchi for me and you. Wasn't the gift sweet of him?" She patted the arched front plate, letting her fingers caress the soft leather. "This is the pommel, see? I hold on so I don't fall off. Now I don't have to yank on your mane anymore." Amelia lifted the rings for the unicorn to see. Lan Ying bent closer and sniffed dubiously. "These are stirrups. I put my feet through the holes." She broke out in a grin, beaming at Lan Ying. "Isn't the seat pretty? Kenchi said he 'liberated' the saddle from a samurai officer during his travels."

"I suppose so, but it looks like a ridiculous contraption to me," Lan Ying replied. The unicorn nuzzled Amelia with a puzzled expression. *"What is the 'saddle' used for?"*

"Why, to sit on, silly. So I don't fall off your back."

Lan Ying shook her head, plainly mystified by the whole conversation. *"How could you fall off my back if you are squatting on a dead thing? The hide rests on the ground and does not move."*

"I place the saddle on your back and attach it with these." Amelia held up heavy leather thongs.

Lan Ying looked from the straps to Amelia and to the belts again. *"OH, NO."* The unicorn stepped backwards, shaking her head and snorting. *"I recognize the thing now. I see the horses wearing this type of clothing. You have never fallen off me while riding. I will not allow you too, nor will I permit dead animals attached to me, as if I were some nag who did not know how to carry a rider. No."* Lan Ying prodded the saddle with her horn to emphasis her point and took another step to the rear.

"Pleassse? The saddle is a present from Kenchi," Amelia coaxed. "He'd be terribly disappointed if I didn't use his present."

"So? Why should I care what a man thinks? If carrying a dead animal on one's back is so important to you and Kenchi, let him wear the saddle and bear you instead," the unicorn huffed in disgust. Lan Ying swung around until her rump faced Amelia. The unicorn's tail snapped back and forth angrily.

Amelia pictured the young warrior carrying her piggyback the way he used to when they played as children. She stifled a giggle so Lan Ying wouldn't hear. "I am not about to stand here and talk to your tail." Amelia stomped a foot in frustration and strode around the unicorn until she faced Lan Ying again. She placed her cheek against Lan Ying's soft muzzle and wrapped one arm around the unicorn's neck. "Using the saddle would mean so much to me," Amelia whispered into the filly's ear, stroking the long, white mane. "Remember how I was thrown around when we fought the soldiers in the raid for the horses? I *almost* fell off then and hurt myself. You don't want to see me injured, now do you?"

"You did not, however," Lan Ying countered. *"Next time hold on tighter."*

"Sometimes I can't when I'm clasping my sword or bow. Besides, you know how you complain when I pull your mane. I know the tugging is uncomfortable for you, but I have no choice. Using the saddle I wouldn't have to."

Lan Ying fell silent with a long pause, thinking Amelia's statement over, then, *"Well, alright. It is annoying when you clutch at my hair. No shoes on my hooves, or whatever else you force these stupid horses wear, though. You hear me? No bobbing of tails, or braids and ribbons in my mane. Carrying around a dead animal's skin is disgrace enough. I hope none of my friends catch me wearing that thing. The fillies would laugh me right out of the herd. I will never live the humiliation down."*

Kenchi returned three weeks after the raid for the horses, and presented Amelia with an ornate saddle he'd captured during a brief battle against a samurai he'd challenged to a fight on the road. Besides the saddle, fifty former soldiers from the warlord's army accompanied him, who abandoned the daimyo's side and sought to fight against him. Beside the saddle and the men, he also brought bad news. "I hear you defeated a company of the warlord's army," Kenchi said as he marched into camp with his volunteers. "The rumors are all over the domain. Every village and town in the han is talking about the battle."

Amelia threw her arms around his neck in a hug. "You heard? Yes, isn't our victory wonderful…and you're back and brought real warriors. Things keep getting better all the time." Amelia's face glowed with excitement as she made a quick count of the men. "So many new recruits. Our army is growing." She took his hand and tugged him toward the cavern. "Haruto was wounded in the battle, but I'm sure he's eager to hear the report you bring." Amelia prattled on about the other small raids she and her men made after the battle for the horses, leading Kenchi to where Haruto sat on a pallet of hay. The old warrior's lips raised when he spied the younger man, and he attempted to stand in greeting. His face was gaunt, and he winced as he shifted on the bed.

"Stay seated, old friend," Kenchi urged when he saw the expression on Haruto's face. He squatted next to the pallet, reached out, and patted the old man on his shoulder, the good one. "Got stuck by an arrow I hear. Feeling better? You are too mean to die."

"Better than I was," Haruto admitted sourly, "which isn't saying much. What news do you bring? I heard the men talking before you walked in. You brought samurai?"

"Yes, deserters from the warlord's army." Kenchi drew Amelia down beside Haruto and him, first checking to guarantee no one overheard their conversation. "Your raiding may have been too effective," he told Amelia. "The warlord has taken notice of us and is angry beyond words. He has vowed to stop the pilfering of his supplies at all costs, and has ordered troops out to locate our base and destroy the army."

Haruto squinted his eyes, scowling, and asked, "How many and when?"

"I do not know." Kenchi raised his hands, palms up in a sign of ignorance. "The warriors I brought say anywhere from one thousand to three thousand soldiers. These are not his frontline troops, but still…." He left the rest of the sentence hanging. What he'd said was worry enough.

"How soon?" Amelia asked quietly. "Will the samurai search here, in the Sea of Trees? I thought we were safe."

"The general has orders. He will have his captains search everywhere," Kenchi confirmed. "The soldiers may not want to enter the forest, but they will. The men have no choice. They will keep seeking us until battle is joined."

"We have no alternative, then," Amelia said with grim determination. "Whether the men are ready to clash against true warriors or not, our people must be prepared to fight." Her mind raced. Dread twisting her stomach. Amelia gave Kenchi and Haruto a smile to belie the nervousness. "We will devise a plan to defeat the warlord and his men," she said with assurance.

I hope my soldiers are ready. We have practiced, trained night and day. Gone on raids, all for this moment.

All this passed through Amelia's mind as she bent to place the saddle on Lan Ying's back. "Are you ready, baby," she cooed to the unicorn.

Lan Ying quivered and shrank in upon herself, her eyes closed. *"Go ahead. I am not afraid,"* the filly moaned as her legs shook.

Amelia tossed a blanket onto the back of the unicorn and picked up the saddle. "ONE—TWO— THREE." At three, she heaved the seat on top of Lan Ying. The unicorn winced, knees buckling, but made no outcry. "There, almost done." Amelia patted the long neck. "You're being a perfect angel about this. Let me buckle this underneath your belly and we'll be all set." Amelia bent over securing straps.

"You are tickling me," a giggle echoed in Amelia's mind as she ran fingers beneath the leather belts to make sure the bands weren't too tight. Lan Ying shifted and pawed the earth.

"All done," Amelia announced, straightening and dusting off her hands. She stood back, admiring. "You look the ideal mount now." She fitted her foot in a stirrup and took hold of the pommel, swinging herself onto the back of the unicorn. "How does your new wardrobe feel?"

Lan Ying took a few mincing steps and shook herself to settle the seat more comfortably on her back. *"Alright, I guess,"* the filly admitted dubiously, twisting and sniffing at the leather and Amelia's leg. *"Maybe once you use it more, this saddle of yours will not smell so much like a dead cow and more like you."*

Kenchi wandered in through the open door, stopped, hands on hips, and nodded approval of Amelia atop Lan Ying. "No more Lady Amelia. Now you look a proper samurai warrior princess. General Amelia astride her noble mount."

Lan Ying swung to face the young samurai. *"Hmm…. Well, at least he knows a noble mount when he sees one. Maybe he is not so slow after all."*

Amelia held her face stern. "What can I do for you peasant. Can't you see I am in consultation with my chief advisor?"

"Uhm…Yes." Kenchi shoved his hand over his mouth, coughing. "Ah, dusty in here. Good news and bad news. The ruse is working well. Our spies have spread the word to the warlord's commanders we are a rabble in arms. Old men and women totting pitchforks and hoes who argue all day. The army will think we will run at the first sign of battle and be easy rice for their eating."

A thrill of excitement ran up Amelia's spine. This was exactly what she and Kenchi desired: Make the soldiers feel overconfident. "What is the bad news?"

"We have spotted the warlord's army. The troops march this way as we speak. The host does not rush, but still approach with purpose."

The excitement Amelia felt melted away, replaced by a tightening in her belly. Leaping off Lan Ying's back, she breathed, "How many?"

Fifteen hundred," Kenchi guessed. "Mostly *ashigru*—common warriors, conscripts I suppose, and mercenaries. Green soldiers we might defeat, but the samurai who lead the troops?" He shrugged and shook his head in dismay.

"We will win," Amelia replied. "We may all die, but we will win."

"I will fight and die with you," Kenchi replied simply.

"I don't want you to die, but if samurai we need, we will have samurai," Amelia replied grimly.

Puzzled, Kenchi asked, "How? All swear to leaders holding clan affiliations. Even if we could locate some with no allegiance, the seeking would take months. True, we find a few, but we have little time before the army arrives, a week at the most."

Koki walked by checking tack, while pretending not to hear the conversation between Amelia and Kenchi. Amelia waved him over.

"Yes, Lady Amelia." He hurried to her and bowed low. "What do you wish?"

Instead of answering him, she asked Kenchi, "What makes a samurai?"

"Huh?" The young man thought for a moment. "He lives by the way of the warrior. The way of the bow and horse—Bushido. He is ready to die when he must and strike the enemy when he can."

Amelia turned to Koki and said, "Are you a warrior? Do you fight? Use a bow, sword, and ride a horse?"

"Of course Lady," the hunter replied, confused. He ran his fingers through his short black hair. "You know I have fought with bow and sword." He cracked a crooked grin. "You taught me how to ride a horse yourself."

Amelia swung back to Kenchi. "What else makes a samurai?"

"He has honor, bravery, loyalty. He is of good character, and shows mercy. He is not afraid to die for his cause, his lord, or his clan." Kenchi spread his hands wide. "All these things bring him honor in the memory of others when his clan and friends sing of his deeds, whether he lives or dies."

Amelia nodded as if she already knew the answer. "Koki, are you an honorable man? Would you die for me? Do you know the difference between what is right and what is wrong?"

The hunter's eyes widened and he drew himself erect. "Of course. Have I not conducted myself properly? You fight to save your mother. We must protect the weak, children, the old ones. This is right. When I sought you, I did so because I knew the warlord was wrong in his actions. I came here of my own free will, swore allegiance to you, and if I must, I will die for you," he barked, and threw a defiant glare at Kenchi as if daring the soldier to deny his words or deeds.

"You see," Amelia said to Kenchi as she laid her hand on Koki's shoulder, "this man obeys the way of the warrior, Bushido, whether he knows the fact or not. True, he can't read, write, or compute, recite lines of poetry, but in every other respect he observes the way of the bow and horse. He may not be able to express his thoughts, but his actions shout purer than words. Isn't he a samurai at heart?"

Koki gaped at her in surprise and threw his shoulders back. Kenchi nodded in understanding. "Yes, he is."

"Accompany me, all three of you." Amelia marched out of the barn with Lan Ying, Kenchi, and Koki in tow, hurrying along after her. Along the way, she snatched her bow and quiver. "Gather all the people together in the meadow," she commanded Kenchi and Koki, mounting Lan Ying. "We do not have enough room in the clearing for all to hear what I am about to say."

The two ran off in different directions shouting for everyone to hurry to the field. Amelia rode Lan Ying into the meadow and waited for the warriors to arrive.

Soon her force assembled, rushing out of the forest and tall grass of the meadow, excited queries fly back and forth as the men and women spied Amelia astride Lan Ying wearing the new saddle. When all had gathered, Amelia raised her hand for silence.

"I have received word a large force of the warlord's army march this way to do battle," she shouted so all could hear. "Most are common soldiers, but among the ranks are many samurai." Amelia paused to let her words sink in. She lifted a hand again for silence. "I have also been told we have few samurai among us, and we cannot defeat this force."

"I DENY THAT!"

Stunned silence greet her statement. Questions erupted.

"…where are samurai?"

"…do we receive reinforcements?"

"…how is this possible? I do not understand."

Amelia allowed the questions to rage and then shouted over the noise, "Who here is afraid to die in battle by honor for justice?"

"No one," a warrior shouted back.

"Are you all honorable men? Do you not wish to have your descendants think well of you, of your bravery and the deeds you accomplished in this life?"

"Yes," the people roared.

Amelia held up her hand again until the crowd settled. Once the warriors quieted down she yelled, "Do we not show mercy for the weak? Do what is right to cleanse this land of the evil plaguing our people?"

She heard a moment of silence. The answer was so obvious; the people did not know how to respond. An old woman stepped forward out of the crowd and yelled back, "This is why we have come to you, why we are here. What other reason would we fight?"

Amelia's heart pounded in her chest. Her eyes shone with pride. "Then I tell you, you all are *samurai.* In heart and soul as well as truth, you obey the way of the warrior and will fight as such. Is this not true?"

Swords and bows raised in the air. The warriors hammered each other on the back. A chant started *"Samurai—Samurai—Samurai."* The cry rose until the whole meadow rang with the words.

"Prepare yourselves for battle. Pray to Buddha and to your ancestors, the old gods of Shinto." Amelia raised herself in the stirrups, eyes flashing and head thrown back. She drew her sword, held her bow in the air and shook both. *"Glory—Glory—Glory."*

"Yes—Yes—Yes."

"Go."

The men and women ran off to their dwellings to prepare for the looming battle. Behind Amelia, Mount Fuji framed in the distance, snowcapped at the peak, soft white clouds floating overhead in a sapphire sky. Kenchi gazed at her in awe as her black hair twisted in the breeze. "She is truly a warrior princess," he breathed to Haruto who stood next to him. "A samurai warrior in every inch of her body and soul."

"Yes, she is," the old man retorted. "A worthy wife for a samurai warrior. The girl is young, though. Remember what I say. Her ideals of truth and justice are not what reality is."

Kenchi shook his head. "Her truth is the truth of the people, and will not be denied." He hurried over to Amelia, admiration in his eyes. "You have our soldiers all stirred up. Do you really believe everyone here thinks they are samurai now and can win a battle?"

"My men will believe they are warriors, every bit as good as samurai, and fight with bravery and honor whether they live or die. This is all that matters," Amelia retorted, eyes shining. "Do you have any doubt?"

Kenchi cocked his head, listening. Far off in the tents and hovels the warriors constructed, the shouts of excitement still rang out, drifting across the meadow. "No, our army will fight bravely. Let us hope your words are enough to defeat the warlord's soldiers."

Amelia nudged Lan Ying and the unicorn ambled toward the cavern. "If their courage and my words aren't enough," she breathed, "we don't have much else, do we?"

"Are you sure the warlord's scouts saw our cavalry? His army knows where we are?" Amelia asked Haruto anxiously a few days later. She leaped up on the boulder the two hid behind and scanned the slope and across the field to the dark forest beyond. "I see no sign of men approaching."

"It will take the army a while yet," the warrior assured her. "The force is large and unwieldy. The troops are undisciplined and march through heavy forest. Do not worry. The soldiers will appear and then the fun starts."

Amelia glanced to both sides. "Are you sure? Their force hasn't outflanked us, has it, climbing over those cliffs and through the woods to attack from our rear?"

Haruto and Amelia huddled at the apex of an inverted V. Bare rock rose on either side. Trees marched along the slopes to the field. "We have our own scouts out," Haruto said wearily. "Besides, unless the army has mountain goat blood, climbing down those hills is impossible anyway. Now stop fretting, Lady Amelia. You are making me as nervous as you are, and I'm nervous already." He checked their flanks. "I do not like the place you chose to have your battle. Yours is a good plan, but dangerous. No place to retreat to in case something goes wrong, but I suppose you have your reasons."

Amelia climbed off the rock and squatted beside him. "Of course I have a reason. If the warlord's soldiers outflank us, we're done for, we don't have enough troops. Our line is stretch too far as is, and the warlord's men would sweep through the holes."

"Uh-huh." Haruto studied the sky. Slate-grey clouds rolled in, more massing behind as he watched, changing the day into gloomily twilight. "Going to rain," he snarled, more to himself than to Amelia. "I hate to fight in the rain. Bad footing for both horse and soldiers."

"Works for me. The warlord's men will have to battle uphill through the mud. My warriors will have the advantage, most are farmers, use to walking in wet earth. In this case mud is our friend." Amelia added as an afterthought. "Everyone hates to fight in the rain." She leaped back up on the boulder and quickly surveyed the field of combat once more. "Kenchi is in place? He knows what to do?"

The old warrior sighed. "Yes, he should. You went over the plan five times, and he is the one who helped you develop the strategy—concealed in the trees leading the cavalry. If something goes wrong, the fault will not be because he has forgotten. I am sure he understands exactly what to do and when to attack."

Amelia scrambled off the rock and shifted among the boulders until she obtained a clear view of the field from a different angle, scanning in all directions. "I don't know why I'm so nervous. We will win, I am sure of victory. Our men face a choice. Fight and die, or fight and win. I'm betting they choose to live." She touched her sword, the bow strung over her back. Her fingers caressed the butts of the shafts in the quiver. "I'm going to stay with Lan Ying," she announced, "to be ready when the soldiers show themselves." Amelia hurried away to the unicorn, biting her lower lip in nervousness and shooting glances over her shoulder at the empty field. Lan Ying stood patiently, nibbling on the sparse scrubby brush and grass. "Anxious baby?" Amelia asked as she stroked the unicorn's nose.

"Anxious about what?" the unicorn inquired mildly. *"Except for the poor quality and quantity of the*

fodder hereabouts, everything seems to be quiet. It would be pleasant to finish this quickly so I could return to my nice pasture." Lan Ying cast her eyes skywards. A rumble of thunder reverberated in the distance and the dark clouds shimmered with a burst of light. *"The gods seem unhappy. Their brows knit in anger."*

"I hope not at us. We are doing nothing wrong, but yeah, everything is too quiet," Amelia replied darkly. "Don't you understand, though, soon we'll be riding into battle. A fight we may not survive. Aren't you frightened? I am." Amelia's mouth was dry, her stomach fluttered in knots at the thought of the approaching carnage. While discussing battle tactics she'd tried to remain calm, addressed the troops in a confident voice. Nevertheless, now, away from everyone else, fear overwhelmed her.

"I will let nothing happen to you," Lan Ying said softly. *"Why do you worry? Of course the gods would like what you do now. You fight to save a person you love. I love you and will protected you by my life if need be."* The unicorn nuzzled Amelia under her arm affectionately. *"Now as far as these smelly men go, the males can take care of their own selves. You cannot expect me to do everything."*

"I love you too." The girl buried her face in Lan Ying's mane and fiercely hugged the unicorn around the neck. *I hope you are right. Oh, Buddha, I'm so scared.*

A splattering of rain dripped on Amelia's head, more hitting the dry earth making tiny craters in the dust. She looked up. Black thunderheads massed overhead. "It's almost time," she announced. Amelia rattled her sword in the scabbard to assure herself the blade was loose, strung her bow, and mounted Lan Ying. Blanketing her mind, she pushed all fears aside. "Let's do this."

Spread out in concealment along the hillside, the troops waited tensely for Amelia's arrival. At her appearance, Haruto whispered loudly, "The enemy approaches."

The previous day, when Amelia decided this site was the perfect place to make her stand, she'd made Kenchi pace off the distance from their rock shelter one arrow's flight and pile stones as a marker, assuring herself and the bowmen they knew when the enemy was within target range. Amelia kept her vision on the rocks, switching to the approaching soldiers and back to the stones.

As the warlord's troops passed the marker, she raised her sword. *"Archers to the ready."*

The bowmen scrambled forward clasping their weapons, arrows notched.

"Fire."

A flight of arrows zipped upward like a hoard of angry hornets, descending on the advancing soldiers in a deadly swarm.

The men dropped. More took their places, rushing forward, howling bloodthirsty cries of rage, driven onward by mounted samurai behind who returned bow fire with bolts of their own.

Amelia swung her sword toward the approaching soldiers. *"CHARGE."* Her men boiled out of concealment uttering savage war cries and screams, Amelia riding Lan Ying in the forefront. She slipped her sword into the scabbard and jerked the bow from her back, drawing the cord to her cheek and firing arrows as fast as she could notch bolts and release. The two forces met in a wild melee of shrieking men and screaming horses, the din of clashing steel rising above all other noise.

Dirty hands reached up to rip Amelia from her saddle. She braced a foot against the stirrups and swung with her bow while Lan Ying bucked and kicked back legs. Amelia and Lan Ying broke free, flinging enemy soldiers in all directions. The unicorn skidded on her front hooves in the mud, dodged at the last second sideways as an arrow zipped past her breast. Amelia glanced up sharply. A samurai took another bead on her and let fly. Amelia ducked and the bolt whizzed over her head.

The two armies battled back and forth across the middle of the field. Amelia notched another arrow and shot at the samurai. The head of the bolt pierced the chest plate of his armor and a puzzled expression crossed his face. He toppled off his mount to the earth.

Lan Ying sprang into the air, leaping over a pile of dead warriors locked together, coated in bloody wounds. Amelia spied another samurai, released a bolt, but was unsure if the arrow hit the mark or not. Men wrestled on the ground, swinging at each other with knives as the battlefield changed into a gory tempest of seething bodies.

Where's Kenchi?

The rain pelted down harder, long, cold, sheets, stinging Amelia's cheeks like icy needles while obscuring her vision. Bolts of lightning ignited the sky and thunder shook the air. Amelia's long hair snapped in tangled strands about her face. She twisted in the saddle, searching for the cavalry, and a press of battling warriors slammed into Lan Ying's side. The unicorn flinched, bucked, attempting to leap sideways and lash out with her hind legs, while swinging around at the same time to confront the new menace. Amelia whipped about and the momentum flung her from the wet saddle.

Amelia landed on the ground hard, belly down, arms under her, the bow flying out of her hands. The air left her lungs in a *"whoosh,"* and she lay in the mud unable to breathe. Feet crushed her body, horses' hooves trampled inches from her face. Gasping to regain breath, Amelia shoved herself erect, grappling for the hilt of her bade at the same time.

Lan Ying stormed into the mass of fighting warriors still bucking and kicking. A common soldier wielding a sword rushed at Amelia. She squatted and jabbed upward with her blade using both hands. The sword caught the man between the ribs, ripping through his chest to the lungs. He crashed into Amelia shrieking of pain, driving the shaft deeper into his body until the point protruded from his back. Amelia landed on her bottom. All around bodies shuffled past, her men withdrawing toward the safety of the sheltering boulders.

No. We are losing. We can't lose. I will not allow us to lose.

A burning fire exploded in Amelia's soul. Fear of defeat appalled her senses. Her need for victory was absolute. Amelia kicked the dead man away, wiped mud from her eyes, and scrambled to her feet. She yanked the sword from the body, and in her fury raised the blade in the air. *"NEVER."*

The men closest stopped their retreat and stared at the sound of her voice. A soldier holding a *naginata* rushed Amelia. She kicked the weapon, squatted low and swept her blade at his shins. He fell sideways, screaming.

The passion within her rose to a fevered pitch. Amelia gripped her sword two-handed and sprang forward, a shriek of rage escaping her lips, swinging the blade as if chopping down trees as she drove into the enemy soldiers. Her men followed, rallied around her, a mailed fist driving into the warlord's army attempting to hold back the tide of onrushing soldiers. Tigers at bay fighting for their lives, as driven with desire to win as their leader was.

"Amelia."

"Amelia."

Chapter Eleven

Lan Ying surged through the warriors, eyes wild, goring friend and foe alike in her haste to rejoin her friend. Before her, Amelia saw the figure of Kenchi astride his black stallion, a dark scowl mirrored on his face as he plowed through the enemy soldiers, rocketing to her aid.

"Mount," Lan Ying snapped as the unicorn's side slammed into Amelia, knocking her off her feet again. The girl struggled upright, sprang into the saddle, clutching the pommel with her left hand while tightly clasping the hilt of her sword in the right.

Kenchi galloped up, his face red. "The cavalry has divided their army in two. The lesser part swept away. The greater retreats," he announced in a hoarse voice, face red.

"Give them no quarter," Amelia gasped, attempting to regain her composure as her heart hammered madly in her chest. "Keep forcing the troops backward until they scatter."

Amelia drove her heels into Lan Ying's side and the unicorn leaped into the battle once more. Amelia slashed at the remaining enemy as her men threw themselves at the soldiers from the front of the battlefield, while Kenchi and his cavalry assaulted from the rear and sides. The remaining samurai of the warlord fought valiantly and died. The conscripts turned and fled. Amelia continued to strike at the enemy soldiers in a blind fury, crisscrossing the field seeking anyone who remained standing until Kenchi rode up to her. "Amelia—*stop*. They are all dead."

"Huh?" In a daze, she gazed about. A flash of lightning illuminated the field and through the sheets of rain Amelia saw dark lumps, bodies of men, some on top of each other heaped in piles. Nothing stirred. "We won?" she breathed, taking a shuddering gasp of air, not believing what was before her eyes. "The battle is over?"

The rain pelted down harder, washing the mud from Amelia's face and clothes, plastering her black hair over her shoulders. She wiped the wetness from her face and peered through the gloom. "How many men did we lose? Was it bad?" The thought of friends spoken to the day before lying in broken heaps on the earth sent a shiver through her wet body, as the realization of the carnage they'd wrought struck her.

"We will not know until we walk the battlefield," Kenchi sighed wearily. He withdrew a heavy blanket from a saddlebag, shook it out and tossed the covering to Amelia. "Wrap this around your shoulders. You are shaking." He surveyed her critically. "You are a mess."

Amelia draped the blanket around her. The shivering did not stop. "Thanks. You don't appear so good yourself." The legs of Kenchi's horse dripped red mud. So did Kenchi's boots. She looked again, harder. Why was the mud red? It dawned on her. The red was blood from the dead. The whole field held a crimson tint. Amelia glanced down at herself. The stain coated Lan Ying hooves and her feet. *Will I ever feel clean again?* She obliterated the thought from her mind. "Count quickly. I want to know who died so their families can honor their spirits."

Kenchi scanned the field, squinting. "I do not think we lost too many men," he commented. "Riding back here, most of the bodies I saw wore the insignia of the warlord. Your plan worked out well."

Amelia took the comment with a silent nod. "Nevertheless, I want to know who we lost." A wave of weariness swept over her. Amelia's shoulders slumped. Her whole body ached, and her sword arm refused to rise. "I'm tired," she said in a small voice. "I'm riding back to the boulders and wait for reports."

Amelia found an overhang, a mere ledge jutting from the rock where a few of the returning warriors started a fire out of the rain and huddled, trying to draw warmth from the blaze. Amelia slide off Lan Ying and crouched close to the heat, drawing the blanket closer around her slim body and hoping the shaking would stop.

One of the men next to Amelia, a person she knew by sight but not by name, turned to her. "Did we win? I saw no more enemies to kill so I walked up here." Before she could answer, he continued in a hollow voice, "I slashed like *this*," he made a chopping motion, "and like *this*." He swung his hand again. "Blood was everywhere. The screams of the dying hurt my ears." The warrior showed Amelia his fingers covered in blood. They still curled as if holding the hilt of a sword. "I must pry my blade from my hand afterwards. I couldn't let go...."

Amelia gulped, remembering the soldiers she'd killed. She ordered her rebellious flesh to remain calm. "Yes, we won," Amelia replied in a low voice, "this time."

In the end, Haruto and Sota counted only fifty of their men dead. *Only fifty,* Amelia sighed to herself. *Could have been worse, but, oh Buddha, I am so sorry my men and women died. My fault, all my fault.* The body count for the warlord's soldiers was close to five hundred. Amelia's people took their fallen to bury the men. The enemy dead lay where they fell, for either their relatives to find and take away, or for scavengers to dispose of the corpses.

That evening, Amelia and Kenchi hunted game. "I should send an ultimatum to the warlord." A coven of quail sprang into the air from their hiding place in the tall amber grass. Amelia and Kenchi drew back their arrows and let fly. Two birds dropped to the earth. "Now we have defeated his army he may release my mother if I agree not to fight him anymore." Amelia looked at Kenchi for confirmation of her idea. The notion seemed obvious. What could the warlord possibly gain by holding her mother and continuing to lose troops and supplies? The two strolled to the spots where their prizes lay in the grass.

"You have a good thought," Kenchi replied, stooping to pick up his quail and arrow. "However defeating a handful of conscripts will not make the warlord cave in to any of our demands. If anything, his defeat will anger him beyond all measure, and if he realizes he holds your mother, in his rage he might kill her for revenge of what you have done."

Amelia never considered the possibility of the warlord taking his wrath out on her mother. She bent to retrieve her bird. "You think so? He will send more troops to confront us?"

Kenchi waved a finger North and West. "Maybe, maybe not. In the Great War brewing, his is the last stronghold of the East in the territory the Western army controls. If he withdraws troops from the battlefront, the Western army is sure to overrun his domain, but he will not give in to your demands. To do so would show weakness."

"I read the philosophy of warfare," Amelia said. "My father kept books and scrolls, but I never understood what I saw, and he died before he could explain the meaning to me." She shook her head, remembering her father's library, destroyed when the warlord's troops put her home to the torch.

"We studied the books together," Kenchi reminded her as they sauntered through the meadow to the cave. "I did not understand the characters either, at the time. Since then other samurai have explained the significance of the accounts."

The contrast between the brightly lit meadow and the soft greens of the clearing made Amelia blink hard, her eyes having difficulty adjusting to the change in light level. "You know how to force him to deliver my mother?" Amelia stopped short of entering the glade and grabbed his sleeve. "How? If he does not send more troops to defeat us, do we seek his soldiers out and battle again, conduct more raids on his supplies?"

"Raids, yes, but we must take control of the villages and towns, one by one. This is where his wealth originates from to buy arms and rice to feed the soldiers. Once we rule the towns and have domination over the surrounding countryside, the crops produced, taxes from trade, the resources will be ours. Deprived of money and food for the troops the warlord cannot wage war."

"You're right. I never thought of the towns," Amelia said as surprise transformed her face, and a completely new aspect of her fight took shape in her mind. "I always believed if I led an army I could compel the warlord to release my mother." She stopped by the pond and shook her head as a distressing thought crossed her mind. "How does one go about conquering a village?"

This brought a chuckle from the young warrior. "The same way the warlord did when he defeated the old daimyo. You ride in, say, 'This village is now under my protection,' kick out the old magistrate, and appoint your own. Whoever disagrees we banish or kill. There will be enemy troops stationed in the towns, yes, but not many, more of a police force to maintain law and order. We hand the soldiers a choice, swear allegiance to us or depart—quick, and then we leave our own troops in their place."

"Just ride in," Amelia said, incredulously. "You think riding in will work? The idea seems so—simple."

"Unless the warlord dispatches troops to drive us out, who will stop us? Yours is the only other army in the province." Kenchi reached out a hand and wrapped his arm around Amelia's shoulder in a hug. "He cannot withdraw his good troops from battle, and we have defeated his second best."

Amelia broke into a grin and started laughing. "Simple. All we have to do is capture all the towns."

Kenchi laughed along with her. "Yes, simple."

They kept giggling until both were red in the face and gasping for breath, joking phrases such as, "No problem," and, "As easy as eating rice from a bowl."

Lan Ying wandered out of the barn and approached the two cautiously as Amelia and Kenchi clung to each other for support. *"What is so funny?"* the filly inquired mildly glancing between Amelia and Kenchi.

"Oh, baby, we're going to town." Amelia released Kenchi and threw her arms around the unicorn's neck in a tight embrace.

"Really? We rode to a town once and you wanted to leave in a hurry. Why go back, did you forget something?"

"In a manner, yes, but this time we won't have to run away," Amelia said. She shot a look at Kenchi. "I hope."

"I did not suppose you would want me to take you back there after you wanted to leave so quickly," snorted Lan Ying in disgust. *"I wish you would make up your mind."* She glared at Kenchi. *"Probably all his idea. Anything to make the unicorn work. Remember, I am not a donkey. I do not even associate with donkeys. As for mules—ugh."*

Amelia shoved her fist in her mouth to stop from laughing. When she was able to, she said, "The town was both our idea, and yes, my mind is made up, and no, he doesn't think you're a donkey. You are the most beautiful, precious unicorn in the whole world."

Kenchi watched this one-sided debate with amusement, heard the uncertainty in Amelia's voice and saw the glare Lan Ying threw his way. "Wait, I'll be right back." He sprinted into the cave.

Amelia threw Lan Ying a startled glance and shrugged. The unicorn pawed the earth. *"Men."*

Kenchi was back in a moment, out of breath, and holding a folded piece of paper. He thrust his hand out to Amelia. "Here. I wrote this after you addressed the men before the battle. I knew then nothing would stand in our way."

"What is it?" Amelia unfolded the note and read aloud, Lan Ying hanging her head over the girl's shoulder, staring at the letter.

"Clouds in air,
Snow Capped mountain tip reaches high.
Goddess with bow."

Lan Ying gave a snort of disgust and walked away.

Amelia read the paper twice, and then stared up at Kenchi. "You wrote this about me? How sweet.' She glanced down at her body. "I'm hardly a goddess, though."

"Well, at the moment you looked like one," Kenchi hedged, shading to pink. "I've been practicing my poetry. Not very good, I admit, but, well, I tried."

"You did perfect," Amelia exclaimed.

"I recall reading your father's poetry. He was much better."

"My father wrote poetry?" Amelia said. "I don't remember ever hearing him recite any. Other people's yes, but never anything he composed."

"I do not know how much he wrote, but I found one tucked in the side of his writing box when I asked to borrow ink and paper." Kenchi closed his eyes. "Ah, must have been after you took that trip with him to the coast."

"Wind blows strong.
Waves crash on the beach.
Amelia walks alone."

Amelia's face shone as she thought back. "I remember. I searched for seashells along the shore." Her eyes clouded over. "The wind was blowing so hard, my hair flew all over."

"Your father loved you very much," Kenchi said. "Your mother, too." He added softly, "You will never have to walk alone again."

Amelia's heart took a little leap. "Thank you." She reached out to hand his poem back.

"No. No, you keep the poem," Kenchi insisted. "I wrote it for you. When we ride into town, remember, you are a goddess and everything will go all right. You have your whole army behind you."

"Okay." Amelia folded up the paper and tucked the haiku away. "We still haven't decided which village we'll take over first. I don't know....Does it make any difference?"

"Why not our town," Kenchi suggested. "The village is close. We know who our supporters are, and which are against us."

Amelia's eyes grew wide and her lips twitched. "I wonder what Chikako will say when I march into the village at the head of an army, riding a unicorn having you by my side. Oh, I can't wait to see the expression on her face." She was at the point of telling Kenchi how Chikako treated her and the names the girl said by the river, but thought better of it. *I will make the slut squirm, though. I surely will. I'm a little mouse, a rodent, huh? I'll show her.*

Kenchi read Amelia's expression and said quickly, "This will not be the time to redress old grievances. We need the people of the village to be for us, not angry at you."

The girl wagged her head up and down solemnly. "Of course. I am purity and truth. A goddess. I wouldn't want the villagers to think anything less of me. I am above petty revenge." *I will gaze at her from the back of Lan Ying. Not say a word, and then smile. The smile will be enough. She will see, remember her words, and fear retribution.*

At the nightly meeting under the bright stars in the glen, Amelia chose one hundred of her best warriors to accompany her and Kenchi the next day. Haruto was to stay in charge of the rest of the army, but Sota would act as Kenchi's second in command. The old farmer, Yuki, begged to accompany the troop also. "I have distant relatives in the village," he explained, keenly aware of the importance of this new chapter in the war. "When my family sees me, they will know I am on your side and spread the word you are an honorable and just ruler, who must be obeyed."

"You have clan in the village?" Amelia said. "I didn't know. Who are your kin?"

"Oh, yes. My third cousin owns three vegetable stalls in the market," the farmer explained proudly. "Many of my relatives who farm in the area bring him their produce to sell. He is an honest man." Yuki stretched his lips in a toothless grin. "Well, fairly honest, anyway."

"Okay," Amelia replied. "You come too. We can use every friend on our side we can find."

A deep silence filled the troops the next morning. Amelia rode at the head of her men through the Sea of Trees, under a brilliant lit sky sprinkled by soft clouds drifting overhead. At the last moment, Amelia decided to have Haruto accompany her, reasoning the advice of the old warrior would be invaluable in case of trouble. Even Lan Ying was unusually quiet, whether unwilling to break the peace of the dawn, or disgruntled by the men marching behind her. Amelia did not know which. Once she caught a thought, *"I should be in my nice meadow, grazing on sweet green grass and dancing with the butterflies."* Another time, *"I hope no other unicorn's see me being trailed by a herd of men and horses. Oh, what shame. My age mates will think I have gone out of my mind."* A quick flick of her head in Amelia's direction let the girl know Lan Ying blamed the circumstances entirely on her and Kenchi.

The troop hit the dirt road. They passed the blackened remains of Amelia's home. She refused to look. Instead, Amelia kept her vision squarely fixed on the town in the distance and announced, "We are almost there. Everyone be sharp. First impressions count, you know," remembering what her mother always told her when meeting someone new for the first time.

The farmers working their fields stopped and watched as the troop rode by, and then dropped their hoes and rakes, calling into their homes for their wives and children to hurry and come out. Before long, a crowd of people trailed Amelia's small army talking loudly, but at a safe distance to the rear.

The streets of the village already bustled. People hurried about their early morning business. Just as the farmers, the inhabitants of the town halted in amazement when they spied Amelia on the back of Lan Ying, her warriors riding sternly behind in silence. The warlord's soldiers on the street gaped at the warriors carrying quivers of arrows and bows draped over their backs, and blades hanging at their sides. The men scampered away in panic and barricaded themselves in the magistrate's ornate house.

To the men and women Amelia knew to be friendly toward her or her parents, she nodded and smiled. Others, who were so quick to denounce her father and family when the new daimyo rose to power and captured the town, received a scowl instead. Amelia ignored the rest she was unsure of, hoping to keep any animosity at a minimum. In either case, she said not a word, maintaining a stern silence until the army reached the middle of the town where the temple stood. Amelia raised a hand and halted her men. As the Buddhist and Shinto priests emerged to see what all the commotion was about, she said, "This town is now under my rule. You shall pay all taxes to me. My laws will be obeyed." Amelia gazed, first at the priests, and then let her vision sweep over the gathering crowd. "Is there anyone here who would deny my word?"

Kenchi placed his hand on the cap of his sword. The rest of the warriors pulled their bows off their backs and notched arrows. Lan Ying lowered her horn, snorted, and pawed the ground. No one in the mob contradicted her.

The Shinto priest raised a trembling hand and pointed a finger at Lan Ying. The old priestess hovered behind him, whispering. "You ride a mythical beast, a unicorn. Are you a *miko,* trafficking among the spirits and the world beyond?"

A low rumbling swept through the people. The thought never crossed their minds, so awed were they by the sight of the unicorn and the warriors. Many knew this girl, her parents. She'd lived on the outskirts of the town all her life, some watched her growing up. How could Amelia come to possess a unicorn, or become one who strove with ghosts?

The idea never entered Amelia's thoughts either, but she decided having a connection to the other world wouldn't hurt, and she was riding a unicorn. *Buddha forgive me.* "Yes," Amelia said solemnly. "I talk to the ancient gods of our people and the deities have appointed me as the guardian of the land. This town and all the people are under my protection now." She eyed the Shinto miko standing near the priest, as if daring the hag to deny what was said, and patted the side of Lan Ying's neck for good measure. "So you know this is real, they sent me a unicorn to ride, so all may know I speak for the gods and tell the truth."

"They did? I do not remember anyone sending me to you. In fact, I was in such a panic....It was those warriors chasing me—"

"Hush. I'll explain later."

More babble erupted throughout the villagers. Amelia swept the mob with her vision, her sight resting on the clothier shop, the black hair and one eye of Chikako peeked around the door jam, watching. Amelia allowed her gaze to linger on the door. Her eyes wandered to Kenchi sitting astride his black stallion, beside her. Amelia stared back at the door jam, a slow smirk flitting over her lips. *Yeah, that's right. He's mine. Hide. Don't you dare step out here, you....*Instead of saying anything aloud to Chikako, Amelia straightened in her saddle and yelled, "Bring the magistrate and the warlord's soldiers to me—*now.*"

A group of villagers hurried away. Amelia heard shouting and the splintering of wood. Moments later a disheveled man in a bright yellow silken kimono and frightened soldiers were hustled before her.

The magistrate, a short fat man who had a tendency to lift the corner of his lip in a half-snarl when he spoke to people, dropped to his knees, head bowed. Amelia knew him of old. The man fawned on her father when the old daimyo ruled, and hustled out to greet him whenever her father rode into town, but after the new warlord rose to power, the magistrate was the first to denounce him. Amelia never liked the man in the first place. His chins hung down in folds, reminding her of a pig, and from the whispered conversations she'd heard between her mother and father about the young girls entering his home, Amelia knew she held good reason to.

Amelia hated the killing she caused. At night, drifting off to the nether regions between true slumber and wakefulness, she saw the faces of the dead on the battlefield, heard the screams of pain from the dying ringing in her ears. Sometimes she smelled the odor of the blood. If she could possibly keep the slaughter to a minimum, she would.

"You," Amelia stabbed a grubby forefinger at the magistrate, "should be killed for how you behaved without honor or mercy to these people. Nevertheless, because I am a kind and benevolent ruler, I shall permit you to live. Pack

your trunks, I will allow you two. I banish you from this village and domain, never to return upon pain of death. Do I make myself clear?"

The magistrate lifted his head. His pitiful blubbering tapered off and he rubbed his eyes with the sleeve of his kimono, a sickly smirk covering his oily face. "Oh, thank you, Great Lady. Your father was always a kind and generous man, great in my eyes. Full of honor as you are. If it wasn't for the evil warlord and his men," he cast a despairing glance at the soldiers next to him, "I would never—"

Amelia heard enough. *"Go.* I give you two hours to leave. After which you forfeit your life and your family's."

The man scrambled to his feet, bobbing his head in respect and scurrying away amidst the whoops and jeers of the villagers. Three small boys tailed him, throwing rocks and calling names.

Amelia switched her attention to the soldiers. "My father was a warrior, a samurai. The warlord gave him a choice. Swear allegiance to your new daimyo or die. He chose to die with honor. I will allow you the same choice offered to him. Pledge your support and loyalty to me as your new daimyo, or die by the blade."

The crowd held their breath. So did Amelia. These weren't ashigaru; most were older warriors long pledged to the warlord, handed this job as a reward for long service.

The soldiers glanced at each other, and then held a whispered conversation. Finally, a grizzled warrior stepped forward and spoke up. "I am the captain of this band, a samurai, as was your father. I knew him by reputation as a brave soldier. My men choose to live. I do not blame the people for all have years left, families containing small children." He drew himself erect and said proudly, "But I am samurai, and have served my daimyo loyally all my life. I choose *seppuku.*"

Amelia nodded. This was better than expected. Only one would die. The warrior's next statement startled her.

"I see your father's sword by your side. Has the blade been kept sharp as a samurai's sword should be?"

Amelia glanced down at her hip in surprise. "Yes, of course. Sharpened and cleaned every day. This sword is the only thing I have left from my father, except the knowledge he gave me, and I treasure the weapon highly. Why do you ask?"

The old warrior drew a short bladed knife, a *ranto,* from within his armor. "I have no one to assist me. I wish you to do the honor. You know what you must do?" He kept his gaze steady on Amelia.

Amelia gulped. Yes, she knew what he wanted, and what must occur. She'd heard her father speak of the process. Kenchi glanced at her quickly and said to the warrior, "I am samurai. I will help you. The act is no t—"

Amelia put her hand up. "No. I will do as he requests. He honors me by the asking, and I shall respect him as well by doing what is required." She slipped off Lan Ying's back and drew her father's sword. "Here? Now?"

The warrior nodded. "In these times of war what does ritual matter? We shall do the custom fast so you may go on your way." He made a short bow to Amelia's soldiers. "I see you are busy and have much to do." He fell to his knees.

Amelia took a step forward, sword raised.

The samurai plunged his knife into his stomach slashing both ways.

The blade of the sword flashed in the sunlight. Amelia chopped down, slicing halfway through the samurai's neck so the head still attached to the body. Blood splattered everywhere.

Amelia released a shuddering breath she hadn't realized she held, and refused to look at the remains. She said to his comrades, "He was a brave and courageous warrior. Bury his body with honor."

Chapter Twelve

As the men covered the body and lifted the dead samurai away, Kenchi asked, "The magistrate has run off also. We saw his carriage leave bearing him, his wife, and family. Who do we assign to take his place as your official of the town now?"

Whom to station in charge of the village? The idea was to seize the town and occupy the area with people of her own. The thought never entered Amelia's head the person she would appoint afterwards. The notion was completely alien to her life. She ran through her mind the members of the town, and dismissed the names as quickly. Amelia knew none well, most through her parent's business dealings. Her parents stayed aloof from the rest of the townspeople, except when buying or selling the harvest from the farm, concentrating on the tilling of their lands and the training of Amelia and Kenchi.

She switched her speculation to her warriors. Was there one among the army she was willing to lose, and capable of handling the administrative responsibilities? Kenchi certainly could do the job, and well. He lived in this town, knew the inhabitants, and had his parents to advise him on whom to trust. He commanded respect, could read, write, and compute, but she needed him by her side. Haruto? Sota? All three were her top lieutenants and Amelia didn't want to lose any to the mundane job of overseeing a village. One of the Buddhist priests turned warrior? She didn't know the newer recruits well enough to make a hasty choice.

Everyone was staring at Amelia, even Kenchi, waiting for the decision on who she would appoint. In desperation, Amelia whispered to Lan Ying, "What do you think? Who would be a good magistrate for the town? Any ideas?" Asking the unicorn was a long shot, and probably the craziest idea she'd thought to date. Lan Ying knew nothing about running a village, didn't like humans in general, and the men in her army in particular, but she didn't want to appear before the townspeople and her own troops as if she were ignorant and hadn't planned this well in advance of taking over the village.

Lan Ying snorted, swiveling in a circle on her hooves until the filly surveyed the soldiers lined up in ranks behind her. *"Does who you choose matter? They are all foolish men. Pick anyone of those standing here. Oh, do not look so confused, I will do it for you."* The unicorn lowered her head and took a few steps forward, sniffed the breeze as the wind blew her way, and jabbed Yuki the farmer gently in the stomach. *"This one will do. I can feel the admiration for you and me flowing from inside him. He smells of the earth, too, and green growing plants. Also the odor of sweat, but what can you expect from a male. You cannot have everything."*

Amelia viewed the man in a new light. He was one of her original warriors, brave, too. He'd taken on a soldier during their first disastrous battle, and brought back volunteers. Not the brightest, but loyal.

Yuki? Why not. At least temporality until I can figure out whom to appoint for real. He is loyal anyway. How much can he mess up? All he has to do is collect taxes and make sure there's no riot. He'll have soldiers in case there is trouble.

As if this was her decision all along, Amelia said promptly, "Yuki, step forward."

The old man's head jerked backward in surprise and he stepped out of line. "Yes, Lady, what is your wish?"

"Until I decide otherwise, you will act as my eyes and ears in the town, collect taxes, maintain order, and make sure my commands are—"

"Amelia," both Kenchi and Haruto exclaimed at once, gaping at her as if she'd gone out of her mind. Kenchi continued in a rush, "You are not serious. He is a simple farmer. Brave yes, loyal of course, but he can neither read nor write. How will he be able to administer a whole village? You must select someone else."

Haruto spoke up. "Lady Amelia, I know this is strange to you. I will appoint someone. I know of several men in our ranks who can perform the duties of a magistrate."

Amelia thought quickly and replied, "Above all I want someone who is honorable and honest. Who has the character to know right from wrong. This man," she swung a finger at Yuki, "is both. I have chosen." Haruto started to say something, thought better of it, and made a short bow. Amelia said to Yuki, "You said you have a cousin in the village? He owns vegetable stands. He can read and compute I assume if he runs a business, no? He must if he doesn't want to be robbed by his employees." She glanced over the crowd. "Is he here now? Fetch him and bring the man forth so I can meet him."

"Yes, lady," the farmer replied swiftly, "right there." Yuki waved to a portly man standing in front of the villagers. He gestured and his cousin hurried over, bowing deeply to Amelia.

"You are Yuki's cousin?" Amelia tried to remember the face, recalling her mother and her selling produce to the man. He gave honest payment; his weights balanced true, as well as soft spoken when he addressed her mother.

"Yes, Lady. We are of the same clan."

"You read, write, and compute numbers?" Amelia asked.

He bowed again. A modest smirk crossed his lips. "Of course, Lady. I am a business owner. I keep my own records, both of sales and purchases, and of what I pay my employees. This is part of my job."

Amelia nodded again. "I appoint you as Yuki's assistant to help him carry out my orders. I let Yuki decide what your compensation will be for this task. Do you agree?"

Yuki's cousin shot Yuki a sideways glance. The famer nodded back silently. "Of course, Lady, if this be your will, I will do as you command," the man replied with another dignified bow.

"Good. We are done here for now, I think," Amelia announced. She picked out a half dozen of her men by eye. "You will stay here for now under Yuki's command to act as his soldiers alongside the old guard." A peal of thunder rolled across the sky. Grey clouds raced overhead, darker ones mounting behind, blotting out the light from the sun and changing day into dusk. "Kenchi, it is time we leave; a storm is brewing." Amelia swept her vision over the townspeople one last time, allowing her gaze to center on Chikako briefly, who still peeked fearfully from her father's shop, afraid to show herself openly. "My words will be obeyed by all who live and work here. Do not let my wrath fall upon you, for I am merciful to those who submit to my will, but to those who don't.... " Amelia left the sentence unfinished, instead, gazing at the red earth where the old samurai fell, allowing the people to fill in with their own minds what her punishment would be.

The crowd hurried to bow issuing many mutterings of, "Yes, Lady. Of course, Lady." Chikako's head vanished from the door.

You'd better run. Hide in the deepest root cellar you can find. You....

Without saying another word, Amelia wheeled Lan Ying about, back stiffly erect, and marched her company from town. The army entered the countryside and struck out overland to the Sea of Trees. Kenchi rode beside her, his lips flickering upward, his eyes twinkling. "You were magnificent," he exclaimed. "I thought you would faint when you chopped into the samurai's head, but were brave."

"Ugh. Don't remind me." Amelia shuddered, remembering the gore. She never realized how much blood was in a human body. "I hope I never have to do that again." She twisted in saddle, checking to make sure none of the townspeople watched from a distance, and slumped, exhaling a groan of pleasure. "This becomes more difficult all the time. First, I must become a general, and then I am a priestess and communicate to the gods. From now on, no more executions. If we must kill someone again, I'll let Haruto or Sota deal with the slaying. This is too much for any one person to handle by herself. All I set out to do was save my mother."

"He was only a man," Lan Ying's thought floated to her. *"Why should you care how many of their heads you cut off? One more or less does not matter. There are plenty more around, and males never use their thick skulls anyway. At least not for thinking, I mean."*

"I don't care if he was a man or a woman," Amelia snapped back, appalled at the unicorn's callous remark. "The gentleman still acted with integrity and should be respected. He showed the true spirit of a samurai warrior."

"Humph."

Kenchi listened to Amelia's partial discussion; saw the expression on Amelia's face. He leaned over and whispered in Amelia's ear so Lan Ying wouldn't hear, *"You did the right thing, and he did act as a samurai warrior should displaying character."*

Haruto cantered up on his horse and fell into step beside the young warrior. He said to Kenchi, "I'm glad I wasn't picked to stay at the town and ride herd on a bunch of complaining civilians bringing all their petty problems, but I felt the choice would fall on me, you, or Sota." He leaned forward and said past Kenchi to Amelia, "Are you positive Yuki can handle the job? If need be, I can always return and teach him for a few days to see he knows what must be done. Or, as I said, I know others who can oversee a village."

Before Amelia could reply, Kenchi said, "Never question the warlord on her decision. I may be wrong, and you might be wrong, but our Amelia is never wrong." For once, Lan Ying neighed in agreement.

Amelia tossed her head back and laughed. "You place too much confidence in me. I've been mistaken more times than right so far. I'm surprised we all haven't been killed yet. Me least of all."

"How did you dream up Yuki as the new magistrate?" Kenchi asked. "At first I could not believe you actually thought he would be good pick, but now I think, given the help of his cousin, we could leave him there permanently. Of course, we will have to wait and see how they do but...."

"A wild idea I had," Amelia answered.

"Your idea? I thought I was the one who selected the man. In fact, I distinctly remember you asking me—"

Amelia bent forward and whispered in the unicorn's ear, "Oh, hush. I asked you because you are my most trusted advisor. So selecting Yuki was my idea originally."

"But...."

Amelia ignored Lan Ying and said to Kenchi, "Now if I could figure out a way of rescuing my mother without any more deaths...I hate all this killing. If only I could think. Haruto is right. This is all new and strange to me, and I never have time to stand still and plan except for the next battle."

"So do I," Kenchi replied. "Let us hope the fighting is coming to an end."

With a sinking feeling, Amelia knew the killing just started. She closed her eyes, and in the darkness saw a long road of death and destruction in her wake. She didn't know any way to halt what she knew must be done in order to obtain the release of her mother, and save the people a life of terrorism.

Buddha, show me a way.

"Kenchi, take the men and ride ahead. I want to be alone and think by myself for a while. I will meet you at camp," Amelia said.

"Are you sure?" the young samurai asked, throwing a fast look at the darkening sky as more clouds rolled in. "The heavens will start to rain soon, and who knows what other dangers might lurk about—bandits, homeless warriors from the war. I know you fear nothing, but still, you are a woman. The countryside is in disarray and traveling alone is not safe for you or anyone. Remember, I told you, you would never have to walk by yourself again. This is one of those times when it is better to be safe."

Amelia reached out and patted his thigh. "Oh, posh. I have my sword, bow, and most important, Lan Ying. Nothing can hurt me. Certainly a little rain won't either. I've been rained on before and I've never melted away into a puddle. Besides, I'll get wet whether the army is protecting me or not. Go. I wish to think by myself. I'll be fine."

"If you really need to," Kenchi said slowly. Lan Ying halted while the rest of the troop rode on, the young warrior throwing worried glances over his shoulder until the soldiers faded from view into the gloomy hills. Amelia nudged Lan Ying forward.

"Something is troubling you?" The unicorn shot a worried glance at Amelia as she ambled along, picking her way through the tall grass. *"What is your worry? You can tell me anything. Unicorns are very wise, you know, and we like to help."*

"All this killing and talk of slaughter," Amelia confessed. "I know I shouldn't let the deaths upset me. I am the daughter of a great samurai warrior, whose father was a samurai before him. Still...." Her voice petered out and she threw an anxious glance at the clouds.

"Death is part of nature," Lan Ying replied at last. *"All things must pass away in time."* The unicorn tossed her horn skyward. *"Even these clouds above us will disappear. The men you kill will depart from the earth one day also, whether by your hand, or the gods, as each are called to their ancestors."*

Thunder rippled across the sky again, a clashing of explosions shaking the air. Splattering of raindrops hit the earth like a flight of arrows. "I know," Amelia admitted sadly, "but still, I wish I could devise some way of freeing my mother without causing bloodshed."

Even though night had not set in, an ominous darkness descended as the thunderheads obliterated the light of the sun. Lan Ying plodded on, Amelia deep in thought as she worried the problem in her mind.

Lan Ying raised her head sniffing the breeze. *"Men up ahead,"* the filly announced, her ears twitching, alert for noise. *"I sense five on horseback riding this way."*

"Let's hide behind those boulders." Amelia swept her hand at a dimly seen projection of rock to their left. "We'll stay silent until the riders pass."

The unicorn dutifully swung toward the ledge. Through the grey darkness Amelia detected the "Clop—Clop—Clop," of horse's hooves thudding on the dirt, the rumble of men talking, growing closer each second. Amelia strained forward, trying to hear what the voices said.

"You are a great daimyo. Surely, the Western Army cannot stand against you forever. They will retreat and we shall be victorious as always," one man said. "Your triumph is only a matter of time."

"Perhaps you speak the truth," a deep voice grumbled, "but I am not in charge of the whole force. Katsumoto wastes my strength and of my men by ordering our troops anywhere he pleases. I suspect he has an ulterior motive, perhaps he fears I will overthrow him. Now these continual raids on my supplies slow us even further. How can I accomplish what is needed when no one allows me the time to construct a well-organized campaign into place?"

Amelia froze drawing a sharp intake of breath. The warlord. He must be returning from a visit to his castle. He could not possibly know about the village taken over yet, and no one would dare inform him. His rages were notorious and the bearer of such news would feel the wrath of his anger. If she'd met him and her troops an hour ago all the problems would be solved, with him captured or dead and her mother free at last. Amelia cursed her luck silently and trembled in anger.

The horsemen drew closer. A wild idea erupted in Amelia's mind. She knew what she must do.

Too dark for a good bowshot and I don't know which is the warlord until I ride close. My sword? Yes, if I can attack swiftly enough. There's five but I only have to kill one, but who should I kill first?

The riders were close enough now so Amelia could make out distinct shapes in the gloom. One in front, two in the middle, and two behind. Rain pelted down, obscuring her vision, and plastering her hair to her head. *Guards front and back. One of the two in the middle must be the warlord.*

Amelia drew her sword, hunched low over Lan Ying's back, and swept her hair out of her face. Tension crept along her spine as she whispered in the unicorn's ear, "Ready baby? Gallop straight through the center of the two in the middle." They must be quick. The soldier in front was no problem. She must take the two in the middle by surprise before the guards reacted. Swing at one, and then the other. Given luck, she'd catch the men unaware and kill both before either could react. The riders in the rear would attack her, but if Lan Ying ran swiftly, she'd pass the escort, and the suddenness of the attack would throw the guards into confusion.

"If you say so," the unicorn replied cautiously, *"but I do not think this is a goo—"*

"GO."

Lan Ying leaped forward, head lowered, spiral horn jabbing ahead through the murk. Amelia released a whooping war cry of hate, sword drawn back for a hard chop at a throat.

"What the...."

Lan Ying galloped at the first rider, leaping aside at the last moment as the horse reared. The unicorn sped toward the two warriors in the middle. Their mounts halted in fright, the men fumbling in haste at their sides for swords. Then Amelia was upon the band, slashing first right and left. Her sword connected against the man on her right and felt steel slicing flesh. Her second swing missed the neck of the warrior on the left by inches. A bolt of lightning illuminated the sky, changing the stygian darkness into brilliant light. Amelia saw the face of the man on her right clearly, that of an old wizened warrior. He toppled off his mount with a gurgling scream.

A crushing pain laced through Amelia's side. She twisted in fear and shock, glimpsed the warlord glaring at her, his face contorted in rage as he drew back his sword for another stroke. Lan Ying burst past him, galloping between the two rear guards as their mounts rose on their hind legs, pawing the air. "Turn around," Amelia gasped, the pain in her side making breathing hard. "I can still kill him." She gulped a deep breath, grasping her sword in two hands, and gritted her teeth against the agony along her ribs.

An arrow flashed by Amelia's head. Another zipped lower down. *"Owww. That hurt."* Lan Ying stumbled, regained her footing in the mud, and continued to run into the gloom.

"No—you're going the wrong way. Turn around," Amelia panted. "We must...we must kill the warlord." It ached to talk, but she knew if she could get in one good swing....

"No. you are wounded. I am hurt. To return means death." Lan Ying steadily hobbled into the darkness, blood flowing down her hindquarter.

"After her, she's wounded."

"You see?" Lan Ying dodged left and right through the sheets of rain as arrows laced the air. *"They pursue us. We must hide."*

"No, do not bother," A cold reply came from the warlord to his men. "I saw her. Some crazed peasant woman. No doubt a farmer's wife whose land was confiscated. We do not have time to search the bush for her. Not in this weather." He issued an evil laugh. "After I have dispatched the Western Army we will have plenty of opportunity to deal with the likes of her and her kin. Handed the cut in the ribs I gave her, she'll be dead in a few hours anyway."

One of the rear soldiers called out, "What was the creature riding, a goat? I swear the beast wore horns."

The lead guard called back, "More like a white donkey dressed in oversized ears, if you ask me."

A chorus of chuckles arose from the party and they rode on.

Amelia and Lan Ying did not hear the warlord or the words of the soldiers. Amelia only caught the laughter and the thudding of the unicorn's hooves mingled with peals of thunder as she pounded away through the rain. Lan Ying tripped again, explosions detonating around the two from the sky. Amelia pressed her hand to her side, grimacing at the throbbing lacing through her body. In the dim light, she saw her kimono was soaked in blood. "We must hide," she gasped to the unicorn, "before the guards find us. Oh, Buddha, why was I so slow and stupid."

The pair found refuge in a copse of trees, partially protected from the wind and freezing rain by a jumble of boulders. Amelia half slid, half-collapsed off Lan Ying's back and struggled to stand upright. *"Let me look at your wound,"* The unicorn pleaded, nudging Amelia on her good side. *"I can—"*

"LEAVE ME ALONE!" Amelia cried. "Let me die in peace. I am so stupid. I should have known. I should have, should have..." She grimaced at the pain, and doubled over, dragged herself closer into the shelter of the rocks and trees, pressing her hand over the wound attempting to stop the flow of blood soaking her side. Her heart raced, huge gasps of air blowing in and out of her mouth and nostrils. Amelia remembered the sight of the warlord's face and squeezed her eyes shut to blot out the memory.

She was beaten, defeated. All the scheming, all the planning, all gone, and for nothing because of one stupid mistake. She would die alone, only Lan Ying to see her last panting breaths. Her strength ripped away as the agony in her ribs radiated along her side to encompass shoulder and hip, and Amelia could do nothing to halt the ache.

Lan Ying stepped over to her, whinnying softly in pain as she walked. Amelia reached out in the darkness, found the unicorn's nose, and stroked her warm muzzle softly. Lan Ying blew soft heat into her palm. *"This isn't your fault. It's mine. I am a unicorn, sworn to protect you and I failed."*

Amelia tried to reply, say the unicorn was not to blame, but every time Amelia took a breath, her ribs hurt so bad nothing came out. She had no way of stopping the bleeding from the slash. Amelia balled her kimono up as best as possible into a wad, hand-held the fabric in place against her side. *So stupid. One against five? If only I struck the right man.* Rage mounted replacing the anguish in her body. She would find him again one day. Fight the fight and win this time. "It's okay, baby," Amelia croaked weakly to Lan Ying as the unicorn nuzzled her and whinnied. "We'll bring down the whole kingdom around his head. We will not suffer him to live."

"Yes, we will, but you must rest now. You are hurt and so am I. I will stand here and protect you." The unicorn placed her body between the icy bullets of rain and boulders, until she straddled Amelia. *"I will not permit you to die. You will live, Amelia. You must."*

Amelia's rage drained as fast as the hatred filled her, replaced by a freezing numbness creeping through arms and legs into her chest. "Must be the rain," she muttered, shivering, as she drew the wet kimono tighter around her thin body. "I feel so cold."

***

"You are alright now. Everything is okay."

"Huh?" Amelia gazed up, focusing on Kenchi's face hovering over her with concern. "Did I fall asleep?" she murmured. "Such a terrible nightmare." Amelia attempted to push herself erect, discovered she didn't have the strength in her arms to do so.

"You should be glad I started worrying about you, disobeyed your orders and sent riders back to check and make sure you were okay," Kenchi said. He placed the palm of his hand on Amelia's forehead. "Your fever is down, which is good, but you would have bled to death if the men did not find you in time. You are fortunate." He chuckled lightly, but Amelia saw the worry clouding his eyes. Kenchi sat on a stool next to her pallet of straw. "Even your unicorn was glad to see our men for a change. What happened? Run into bandits? I told you riding by yourself was dangerous."

The battle during the rainstorm rushed back to Amelia in stark clarity. "The warlord, I met him while riding to the camp. I tried—I tried to kill him." Her head thrashed back and forth recalling the failure and the humiliation of the disastrous attack. "He escaped, and I was wounded and...." Amelia struggled to sit up again. Kenchi held her down with one hand on her shoulder.

"You what?" Kenchi froze, mouth open. "How many men did he have?"

"Uh, four men. I killed one, I think, but the warlord managed to draw his blade and slice me before I brought my sword around. I don't know what I was thinking."

"You are lucky to escape with your life," the warrior replied. "No matter how good you think you are wielding a sword, attacking five armed men is a foolish thing to do. You know better."

Amelia's face burnt red. "I realized afterwards, but by then it was too late. Lan Ying received a wound too. Is she alive? Okay?" Her face was wet. "She was hit by an arrow, I think, in the leg. Please say Lan Ying is all right. I'll never forgive myself if she isn't and the injury is my fault."

"Your unicorn is fine," the warrior assured her, "and already healed, which is more than we can say for you. When the men finally discovered where you were hiding, you were unconscious and half-frozen from the rain, and then the fever set in. For a week, we did not know if you would live or die."

A week? "How long was I out?"

"Ten days," Kenchi replied, his mouth drooping. "Ten days of worry, priests, healers, and monks hovering over you. At first, you were unconscious, then delirious from the fever. You kept cursing Chikako, begging your mother and father to forgive you. Your wound is healing well, though, and you are cool for the moment. Let us hope you stay this way. You have two broken ribs also, I guess from the sword stroke, but the healers say you will be back to your own self soon."

Amelia reached over and touched her side gingerly, wincing in pain. A thick wad of bandages covered her ribs from armpit to hips. "I was a fool," she muttered, balling her fist and striking the pallet feebly. "All this time wasted. I must get up." Amelia attempted once more to push erect, grinding her teeth against the hurt with the effort. Kenchi held her down again as her body failed.

"Keep trying to sit up before you can and you will open your wound again," Kenchi cautioned. "Even the great Lady Amelia cannot eat rice before the kernels are cooked."

Amelia glanced up at the warrior and saw his eyes traveling to the bandage on her side. She couldn't help herself. Amelia smiled, her face lighting up like the sun. "I guess the *great* Lady Amelia will have to wait for the water to boil, huh?"

The young warrior bent over, reached out, and brushed the hair off her face. "You are so adorable." He kissed her swiftly on the lips, his dark eyes gazing into hers.

An electric shock of thrill shot through Amelia's chest. She blushed pink, trying hard not to giggle. "Is—is this your code of honor," she stammered at last, "taking advantage of a woman when she is wounded and defenseless?"

It was Kenchi's turn to shade red. "I could not help myself. You are so beautiful when you smile. Your whole face lights up like the moon and the stars in the heavens."

An awkward silence followed. Amelia said suddenly to break the stillness, "How does our battle go? I don't suppose much has happened since I was wounded. As soon as I'm up and well again—"

"We have occupied two more villages in the last week," Kenchi replied, glad for the change of subject. "Small ones to be sure, adjacent to the first town we conquered, but the warlord's grasp on the countryside is disintegrating."

"What? You have? It is?" Amelia exclaimed in astonishment.

"Yes. You are not the only one who can plan a battle or head an army. We have also heard from deserting soldiers the Eastern Army fails badly in in the north. If this continues, the warlord will lose his whole domain. Already, some towns refuse to pay taxes to him and have driven his soldiers out. The land is ours for the taking as soon as we march."

"Good," Amelia lay back on her pallet staring at the rocky ceiling of the cave. "His destruction can't happen fast enough for me. I want him defeated, dead or captured, and my mother returned!"

Her last outburst left Amelia wheezing for breath. Her exhaustion rested heavy on her chest, squeezing the strength from her body, and prodding her mind into peaceful oblivion. Amelia drifted off to sleep, and a curtain of blackness overwhelmed her as the warlord's face drifting in and out of focus. Words, like fierce red flames streaked across her mind's eye in bright letters.

Buddha, make it so.

Chapter Thirteen

Amelia recuperated slowly. While she waited for her wound to heal and strength to return, Kenchi continued to make raids on the small villages and hamlets in the surrounding countryside, adding to the territory Amelia's army controlled directly or by proxy. Each time the men marched away Amelia fretted, fighting the urge to mount Lan Ying and lead the soldiers to victory. The thought galled her with success so close to hand, she was no more than a bystander watching the action.

Much of her lagging recovery was due to Amelia herself.

"Lady Amelia," the Buddhist priest who acted as surgeon and physician pleaded, "this is necessary. Too much movement will open your wound again. You have done so once already." He held the odd shaped bowl out to her, two husky warriors flanking him. "This is the way it is always done."

Amelia looked at the vessel in horror, and then at the men, her gaze returning to the healer. "I will not. I will walk to the latrines like everyone else." She struggled to rise, winced as a flash of hurting laced from her ribs and the gash in her side opened again, staining the bandage crimson. The priest gasped and applied pressure to the wound while Amelia sank onto her pallet helplessly.

The priest fussed at her, unwrapping the bandages to see what damage Amelia did to herself. Kenchi watched this exchange from the entrance to the cave, a mute witness trying hard not to burst out laughing. "We lift you here, or we carry you to the latrine, and stand there watching until you are done," he called out. "Your choice."

Amelia glared back at Kenchi.

The physician looked helplessly at Kenchi.

"I have an idea." The young man waved one of the warriors over and held a hurried conversation. The man bolted away, returning with four old women, farmer's wives, whose job was to cook and do laundry for the camp. "Here." He strolled over, scooped up the bowl and handed the vessel to one of the women. "Uh, Lady Amelia needs a hand," he muttered, nodding slightly toward the girl. The woman bobbed her head knowingly. Kenchi said softly to Amelia, "Best we can do. You'll survive." He picked out the men by eye and motioned the embarrassed soldiers to leave. From then on, two of the women attended to Amelia at all times, to do her running, fetching, and whatever else needed for her personal comfort. Afterwards, Amelia decided if she wished to recover, it was best to listen to the healer, even though the thought of laying uselessly on the pallet caused her to grind her teeth in frustration.

Kenchi carved a walking stick, and when Amelia was able to, hobbled around the camp, first in short jaunts inspecting and issuing orders until exhaustion set in, and then farther, gradually increasing her speed, distance, and stamina each time, pushing herself to regain strength and endurance. Lan Ying accompanied her on these walks, constantly watching and making solicitous comments when Amelia's energy faded and she needed to rest. The unicorn still blamed herself for Amelia's injuries, and whenever the girl halted to regain her breath, apologized with embarrassment, until the abject pleas for forgiveness grated on Amelia's nerves.

The two paused by a stone ledge, Mount Fuji looming tall, snowcapped, behind Amelia and Lan Ying like a giant black cone topped in ice, while emerald valleys and saffron plains stretched below to sink into the haze of the distance.

"The gash is not your fault at all," Amelia exclaimed in exasperation for the third time during the morning, as she rested on the rock to catch her breath. Amelia pressed her fingers to her ribs. "My injuries are my own stupidity. If I wasn't so eager to kill the warlord and thought the idea through, I would have realized I didn't stand a chance." She studied the unicorn's rear leg. The wound inflicted by the arrow was gone, the hair a glossy alabaster. "I wish I could heal as fast as you. My side still hurts everytime I bend over to put on my sandals or twist."

"I am a unicorn. We always heal quickly." Lan Ying muzzled Amelia in the neck. *"This is our nature. The instinct to protect the one we choose to ride us is in our nature too. I failed and did not protect you as I should have. Unicorns are smarter than humans are. I should have known better and prevented you from making a mistake."*

Amelia decided to drop the subject, Instead, gazed at Mount Fuji's snow covered peak. "I wonder if the gods still reside within the mountain," she said to Lan Ying. "Unicorns are mythical creatures. I've been told you have existed since the birth of the world when deities walked the earth. Have you ever met a god?"

Lan Ying snorted in surprise. *"Not face-to-face. Gods are fearsome beings and do not reveal their presence to just anyone, not even unicorns. Nevertheless, when I have a need I speak to spirits and the deities reply back sometimes."*

"Really?" She regarded Lan Ying in a new way. "Do they impart words of wisdom? What do they say?"

Lan Ying snorted in humor. *"Many things. Mostly the gods say to solve my own problems in my own way, but one told me I would meet a descendant of Uzume, and she would ride upon my back. Then I met you."*

For a minute, Amelia was stunned with surprise. She blurted out, "Me? Descendent from the goddess of joy and dance? Don't be ridiculous. The spirit must have been joking." Amelia tittered and slapped a hand over her mouth when she saw the expression of the unicorn's face. If the gods were listening, Amelia didn't want the creators thinking she was disrespectful and laughing at them or Lan Ying.

"Did you not tell the Shinto priest you are a miko? I know you did. I heard you."

"Yes, but...."

"All miko's are descendent from Uzome." Lan Ying flicked her tail as if this settled the matter.

Amelia leaped up, winced at the stab in her side, and threw her arms around the unicorn in a fierce embrace. "I can never win an argument against you, can I?"

"Of course not," Lan Ying replied smugly. *"I am a unicorn. Unicorns are never wrong."*

"Well, maybe you are right, I might be a goddess of dance, but I don't feel up to prancing around right now. Soon, but not right now." Amelia checked the sun, gauging the time. "C'mon. We'd better start heading back to the cave. It's late and I don't want people out hunting for me. I've caused enough problems already." She eased herself off the ledge.

"You could ride on my back," Lan Ying complained as Amelia took up the cane and hobbled her way through the forest. *"You do not have to walk all the time, you know, especially using the silly stick you carry. What would the other unicorns say if my fillies saw you with me walking instead of on my back?"*

"Well, I don't see any other unicorns around here at the moment, and I need the exercise. This is the whole point in taking these walks," Amelia made an exaggerated production of scanning the forest. "Besides, I hurt when I have to scramble onto your back. I don't turn as well as I did before."

"You are being stubborn," the unicorn whined, batting her brown eyes at Amelia. *"I could kneel. You would not have to leap at all. You have mounted like that before. I remember."*

"I still need the exercise," Amelia said exasperated, with an obvious effort to keep her temper.

Lan Ying snorted and pointed her horn at Amelia's side. *"I asked before, but if you want, I could—"*

"Hush." Amelia held her palm up, listening. "I hear someone calling my name." She cupped her hands around her mouth and shouted back, "OVER HERE."

In way of a reply, the sound of a crashing body through the brush greeted her, and Sota appeared clambering over a rock out of breath. "There you are," he exclaimed, pleased, as he straightened his kimono. "I was sent to locate you. You are needed at the cavern. There is trouble."

"What kind?" Amelia asked as she hobbled faster.

"I do not know." Sota danced around in excitement and worry. "One of our soldiers rode from Yuki's village and sought out Kenchi with a message. Haruto was there also. The group talked in whispers for a minute and then Haruto shouted to me to locate you." The warrior ran ahead of Amelia, waving for her to hurry.

Wild scenarios of the warlord invading the town with his army, or armed insurrection by the townspeople holding Yuki and his men prisoner, ran through Amelia's mind trying to move faster. A sudden throbbing ran up her side. She gasped, forcing herself to walk at a slower pace.

"You could always ride." Lan Ying shot Amelia a bland look. *"Here, I will kneel."* The unicorn stopped and folded her legs beneath her, laying down.

"You were waiting for something like this to happen, weren't you?" Amelia accused. Nevertheless, she eased herself onto Lan Ying. The unicorn stood and began trotting. *"Unicorns are never wrong."*

"Oh, be quiet, smarty," Amelia grated between clenched teeth. As gentle as the unicorn was while trotting, still, the bouncing sent shocks of agony along Amelia's ribs. She clamped her jaws shut, and instead, concentrated on dodging branches whipping at her face as Lan Ying hurried past the trees.

The camp was a-buzz with excitement as Amelia rode in. Men ran in every direction fetching bows and swords, or strapping sword belts around their waists. Young boys gathered the horses, throwing blankets and saddles across their back for the warriors. Haruto stood outside the waterfall on the ledge, pointing and shouting orders to the soldiers who raced by. When he saw Amelia, he waved frantically. "Over here."

Lan Ying halted beside the warrior and carefully folded her legs again so Amelia could dismount. "What's the matter?" Amelia asked breathlessly as the two hurried into the cave. "Sota said something about a rider from Yuki's village. Is there problems in the town?"

The fire inside the cavern was built up, illuminating the stone walls, red shadows flickering like dancing ghosts. Kenchi sat by one of the soldiers left with Yuki. They both looked up at Amelia's arrival and the messenger sprang to his feet bowing. "We were waiting for you." Kenchi stood. "We have trouble."

Amelia slipped herself between the rider and Kenchi. The warrior sat as did Haruto. "What happened?" Amelia asked.

"The warlord has learned of the loss of the village," the rider started, "and those of the rest of the towns you have taken. He loses on the battlefield, too, and pulls his army back this way from the front. We hear rumors he has vowed to recapture the villages lost and finally destroy our army. Some of the townspeople, headed by the cloth seller, have started talking rebellion. Yuki and his cousin put a halt to the talk, but the grumbling still remains and we believe the conspirators secretly collect weapons, and try to recruit others to their cause. Yuki thought it was best to inform you of what is happening at once before fighting breaks out."

Amelia snorted hard through her nostrils and nodded, digesting this information, while trying to think of what to do. "Any word when the warlord and his troops will be upon us?"

"No." The messenger shook his head in denial. "The rumors do not say. We only hear talk from those fleeing before the warlord and his soldiers as the army withdraws. The refugees also say, during the battles, the fighting armies destroyed the imperial capital of Kyoto. The shogun has turned his back on the war. Everything is in chaos, the city looted by vandals and honest citizens murdered in their homes."

An inner peace swept over Amelia. She felt as if her father's hand rested on her shoulder, calming with the soothing voice he'd used when she attempted a new weapon. Her mind saw clearly at last what she must do. The end was drawing near. "Yuki did right, so did you by bringing us this news." Amelia made a command decision. Her voice took on power she never knew she possessed, and said without a tremor, "We march. Gather our forces. We leave at daybreak tomorrow, first to confront the townspeople, and then the warlord in a final battle."

Kenchi laid his hand on Amelia's arm. "Have no fear. I will lead our men, quell the dissents, and defeat the warlord once and for all in your name."

"Nonsense." Amelia swept her hair back, eyes blazing. She thrust her chin out. "I will command our troops. This has been my war since the beginning. I will see the battles through to the end, or die trying."

Haruto's mouth twisted in surprise. "How can you ride at the head of an army when you are wounded and barely able to walk? You are committing suicide, Lady. It would be better to plunge a ranto into your belly and save the warlord the trouble of killing you."

Kenchi said nothing. He kept his gaze fixed on Amelia.

Amelia hesitated. She knew Haruto spoke true words, but was not about to lay back and watch everything she'd worked for unravel. If this was the end, so be it, the finish for better or worse. Amelia sought Kenchi's dark eyes and touched his fingers, speaking hardly above a whisper. "We live or die together?"

The warrior nodded back silently.

"I will not wear protection." Amelia glared in distaste at the scale armor Sota held up the next morning. "Even the chest and shoulder plates alone weigh too much and slows me down." Her side sent a twitch through her body. "I am sluggish enough already. I don't need the help of extra baggage to make me waddle like a turtle."

Sota struggled vainly attempting to wrestle with the new dilemma, torn between Kenchi's orders that Amelia must wear the strongest armor possible for her own protection, and the willful girl's stubborn refusal to don any sort of defense against bolts or blades. He retorted weakly, "But Lady, *please*. What of the arrows? Blade thrusts? Your side," he said fiercely, gesturing at the bulge of bandages under her kimono, "needs shielding. A sword stroke has already injured you once. Without this armor, you will die as soon as the two armies clash together in battle. You may not conceive of your own death, but the killing can happen."

Amelia disregarded the obvious fact. "Lan Ying will dodge arrows, or I can duck. Katana thrusts I can parry with my own blade. No." She threw her hand up, palm out. "Take the armor away. I won't use protection."

In desperation, Sota played his last card. "Lady Amelia, I will be in great trouble if you do not wear this." He held up the helmet. "Kenchi ordered me—"

"He did, huh?" Amelia huffed. "You can tell Kenchi…no just a moment." She tapped one foot. "I will tell him myself what he can do with his armor and orders." Turning her back to the man, she strapped on her sword belt, strung bow and quiver over her shoulder. From a pouch, she pulled a black leather band and tied the strap across her forehead to hold the hair out of her face. "There," Amelia said, some of her rage abating, "this is all I need. Let's find *Lord* Kenchi." She tried stomping out of the cavern, winced, and tread more softly.

A blood sun rose over the mountains, painting the clearing in scarlet light and streaking the clouds with pink fingers. Lan Ying stood patiently by the pool, browsing on a pile of hay. The unicorn looked up at her approach woefully and issued an inquiring snort. *"Good morning. Why are we awake so early?"* Lan Ying stretched like a cat and a shiver rolled along her back from mane to tail. *"At least I should have been allowed to eat my breakfast in the meadow as I usually do where the food is fresh and sweet."* The filly nudged the dry grass with her horn. *"This fodder is nasty, stale, and boring."*

Amelia kissed the unicorn on the cheek. "It's okay, baby. After today you'll graze in green pastures drinking sweet water," she assured the grumbling unicorn.

Either with the gods and Buddha, or on Earth. I don't know which.

Kenchi rode up on his black stallion, wearing black scale armor, a white unicorn enameled on his chest and back. "You are not clothed for battle," he said sharply, leveling his gaze at Amelia in her kimono and headband. "We were to leave at daybreak. The troops are ready to depart at your order." Her warriors lined up in rows, clad in what armor they owned. The cavalry assembled in front, decked out in unicorns emblems as Kenchi wore.

"I am as dressed as I will be." Amelia stared back at him defiantly. Her tone left no room for argument. She heard a scuffling noise behind her and glanced to the rear. Sota raised his hands in defeat and shrugged his shoulders. Amelia's face battled between a smile and frown. The smile won—barely. "Lan Ying. If you please, kneel so I can mount."

Kenchi's lips tightened, but he kept his mouth firmly closed, biting back a remark. With a savage jerk on his reins, he wheeled his horse around and rode to the head of the army.

Amelia made herself comfortable on the unicorn's back and Lan Ying trotted to the front of troops, horn raised in the air, long tail flicking from side to side and mane fluttering in the breeze. Amelia waved her hand forward and the column set off, a long line of men, horses, and wagons, winding its way through the Sea of Trees like a giant serpent out onto the open plain. Amelia and Kenchi rode before the army, right behind the two followed Haruto and Sota. The latter carried Amelia's new Battle Flag made from silk, embroidered with the image of a unicorn and a girl. As they neared the town, Yuki himself galloped out to greet the troops, relief etched on his weather-beaten face.

"I am glad you arrived so fast at my message," he said, falling in line beside Amelia and Kenchi. "As the warlord draws nearer, the muttering of dissent grows louder and more violent. Masked men attacked one of my soldiers last night. I do not know how much longer our troops can maintain control before active rebellion breaks out among the people."

"Should have rounded up the ringleaders and executed the whole bunch at the first sign of trouble," Haruto grumbled, overhearing what Yuki said as he rode up. He spat on the ground. "Would have settled the problem right from the start. Now that the warlord approaches, we do not have time for this nonsense."

"At first all we heard was mere complaining," Yuki hurried to explain, sighing as the four neared the town. Farmers in the fields halted their work and gaped as the army marched by, "but there is always criticism for those in power, and I thought nothing of the talk. Then my cousin brought me word people were hiding swords. He thought the ringleader was the cloth seller, but was not sure. Of course, I brought the man in for questioning as soon as I was told. He denied any knowledge of rebellion or weapons, and I could not find anyone else willing to confirm my cousin's suspicions. I was afraid if I pressed the matter I would start the very rebellion I was trying to suppress, without enough soldiers to put the fighting down if need be."

Chikako's father. I should have known. A troublemaker like his daughter, and blames me for the alliance between his family and Kenchi's falling apart. "You did right to call me," Amelia said. "We can't go beheading everyone in the village on rumors. If the rebels want to become angry at someone, let their frustration fall on me, not you."

The villagers ran out of their shops as the army marched up the main street, and stopped in front of the temple. To the right of the building stood the cloth shop: Tanaka-san's business. He hurried to the road with the rest of the townspeople, Chikako and her mother scurried out a second later, hiding behind him fearfully. The man thrust his lower lip out, glaring insolently first at Yuki, and then at Amelia.

Amelia smiled to herself. *He knows. I hope he decides to confess his crime. As much as I despise Chikako, I do not wish to kill her father.*

Lan Ying wheeled about until Amelia confronted the man, Kenchi on one side, Haruto and Yuki on the other. "Tanaka-san, I understand you have grievances about me and my rule? If so, say your criticism to my face. Do not whisper behind my back like an old woman complaining about the cost of rice." She raised her voice and called out over the crowd "If you have friends who feel the same way, let those men and women speak now and air their protests. I stand before you. I am here to listen."

All eyes shifted to Tanaka, his hands balled up at his sides in rage. Finally he spat out, "I have told all I know to your dog Yuki. It matters not what my friends or I think about you. Soon the warlord will return and liberate this town, destroy your puny army, and you will be gone. You will be less than dust beneath our sandals."

"He is, huh? I will be, huh?" Amelia took a deep breath to quell the rising anger inside her before speaking again. "Yuki, take this man into custody. Use as many soldiers as you wish. In addition, detain anyone else suspected of being a traitor. I will have no more of rebellion and treason talk."

Yuki nodded, rode forward, waving to his men who stood on the perimeter of the crowd. They shoved forward, surrounding Tanaka and five other men who stood near him.

"Take your hands from me! I can walk by myself," Tanaka shouted, shaking the arms off. He straightened his kimono, and plastering an expression of utter contempt on his face, walked away with the men. He shouted over his shoulder to Amelia, "Remember what I said. Your end comes when the warlord returns."

Amelia watched him go without retort, and then raised her voice so her words drown out the clambering of the assembly, "If I hear any more talk of rebellion from this town, I will burn the village to the ground until not one stick rises above the earth."

A hush fell over the people. All but one bowed their heads in respect. Amelia said to Kenchi and Haruto, "I think we have cleared this matter up for the time being. We should—"

"Slut. Coward. You are a weakling who needs an army behind you to do your dirty work."

Yuki and his men paused and swung around, searching over the heads of the crowd for the source of this new outburst.

Chikako stalked forward to the edge of the circle, red in the face, eyes blazing. "If Kenchi and your men knew what a little mouse you really are these peasants would never follow you anywhere."

Amelia turned Lan Ying around slowly, grinding her teeth together, eyes narrowing to mere slits. She appraised Chikako in cold fury as she would an annoying dog and snapped back, "If people knew what a sniveling conniver you are, deceitful and a liar, you'd be tossed out of this village on your ear, and you'd deserved the exile." Her body shook and Amelia balled her hands until the knuckles shone white, fingernails digging into palms and drew blood. Amelia attempted to slide off Lan Ying and a stab of hurt laced up her side. "Oh, let me down, Lan Ying. I want to tell this one what I really think to her ugly face."

"Is confrontation wise? The female appears angry and unstable. You have men. Let the males handle the girl. They must be good for something. This is one of those times."

"LET. ME. DOWN. *NOW!*"

The unicorn dutifully dropped to her knees and Amelia clambered to the pavement. "What do you think you're doing," Kenchi said as he vaulted off his horse to restrain her. "We have no time for arguments. Get back on—"

Amelia threw her hand up in the air and shoved him aside. "This will only take a minute." She drew a deep breath and strode forward to within arm's-length of Chikako. The people surrounding the girl quickly backed away, leaving her standing in a large empty space.

Amelia stabbed a finger at Chikako's chest. "From the first you were a lying pig, pretending to be my friend to get close to Kenchi, currying my favor to make my mother and father like you, and to promote your own family's interest. Have you ever told the truth in your life?" Amelia hooked a thumb over her shoulder toward Yuki, his men, and Chikako's father. "See what you and your scheming has brought? *Nothing.* Exactly what you deserved from the first."

Chikako's mouth dropped open, but she did not back away. Instead, the girl leaned forward as if to bow and lower her eyes. "Amelia," she said in such a small voice that Amelia could hardly hear her, "I am sorry. Sometimes I speak without thinking. The words I spoke at the river, well, I guess—I guess I was being mean, but I never tried to use you." Her head dropped lower and Chikako took a step forward. "The gifts I presented to you were real and from the heart."

Some of the anger swelling up inside Amelia flowed out. *Perhaps I have judged Chikako too harshly. Any girl would desire Kenchi, he is kind and handsome, and of course, she wished to promote her family's concerns. Who wouldn't? If I was in her position, I might have done the same thing myself.*

"Well, we can never be friends, again," Amelia said, hesitantly, relaxing her stance, "but I understand what you mean."

"I have one more gift for you," Chikako replied softly. "Here." She reached inside her kimono, withdrew a kitchen knife, and lunged. *"This."*

The attack took Amelia off guard. The knife descended toward her chest and she threw her hands up in reflex to catch the blade. Chikako's lunge drove Amelia stumbling backward. Kenchi dove forward to catch Amelia before she fell to the ground, and then stepped between the two girls, grabbing the knife hand as Chikako attempted to plunge the blade into Amelia's chest. "Let her go," grunted Amelia. With a deep breath, she ignored the ache in her side, dropping her bow and quiver to the ground and flexing her fingers. "I'm going to end this once and for all."

"Are you crazy?" Kenchi gasped. "She's trying to kill you. You're bleeding!" Amelia's white kimono was already staining red on one side.

"I don't care," Amelia said. Her sight focused on Chikako, until all she saw was the girl's face. "That's an order."

Kenchi said to Chikako in a low voice, "If Amelia dies, so do you," and released the girl's arm.

Chikako lunged forward again, blade jabbing at Amelia's chest, reaching out the other hand to claw Amelia's face like a crazed tiger with long nails. Amelia grasped the knife hand again while fingers slipped into her mouth, in response she bit down hard, feeling iron wetness flood her mouth. Chikako howled in pain, snatching a bloody hand away. She stopped her assault for a moment to gaze dumbly at her red-soaked fingers. *"Pig,"* she shrieked. "You fight like an animal."

Amelia took a chance and freed the girl's knife arm, and grappled for her sword, while keeping her vision lock on Chikako.

Chikako saw the movement, spread her legs wide, and leaped again at Amelia's throat with a snarl of rage.

Amelia released the hilt of her sword and gripped the girl's bloody fingers in her own. The two girls struggled back and forth, maddened beasts locked in battle. The wound in Amelia's side screamed, breath snorting in and out of her nose in short gasps, sweat dripped down her forehead to sting her eyes. She felt her strength ebbing as the taller, heavier girl bore her over backward, while the knife Chikako held inched closer to her chest. The girl's face loomed before Amelia, a look of hate and triumph in her eyes, her hot breath blowing in passion against Amelia's cheek.

Summoning her last remaining dregs of strength, Amelia kicked sharply into Chikako's groin.

Chikako kneeled over clutching herself and howling in pain, dropping her knife and falling to the ground into a tight ball, rolling in agony. Gasping, blood streaming down her side through the bandage, Amelia booted the weapon away from the girl and drew her sword. Through a haze of sweat smarting her eyes, Amelia hovered over Chikako preparing to plunge the blade into her back.

"*No.*"

Lan Ying thrust her head and horn between the two girls. *"Females are for breeding, not killing,"* admonished the unicorn sternly. *"It is wrong to kill one of your own; no matter how much you despise her, or what the girl has done. First the females, then the foals. Do not travel along this path."*

Amelia faltered, drew herself erect, attempting to hide the grimace of torture running up her ribs. Her heart hammered, hands trembling. She released a long shuddering breath and swept a loose tangle of hair from her face, which escaped the band and hung between her eyes. Willing herself to calm, she breathed through her nose, drawing air into her lungs, and blowing it out softly through her lips. When she felt relaxed enough to speak without a tremble in her voice, Amelia stared down at the girl in loathing who still curled up in pain. The whole fight lasted no more than thirty seconds. "Well, this one better stop thinking of breeding with Kenchi." She shot a quick glance at the young warrior. He shaded pink and studied the clouds in the sky. "The *girl* is not one of mine, never was, never will be," Amelia muttered to Lan Ying. She wavered again, and felt a strong arm around her shoulder. "Kenchi?"

"Are you all right? I told you not to fight her. There is blood everywhere." Kenchi eased his hand across the side of Amelia's kimono. His fingers drew away scarlet. "Your wound has opened up again. Let me take you to the doctor."

Haruto stood there also, a scowl etched on his face while he shook his head. "This was foolishness, Lady Amelia. A child throwing a tantrum, and for what? Pride? A wise general and ruler must put aside pride for the greater good. What would have happened if you'd been killed?"

Barely able to walk for the pain, Kenchi led Amelia away. She murmured to the old warrior, "I am not dead, and have no plans to die anytime soon. Have Chikako locked up alongside her father and the rest. Best to take the mother, too. See they don't escape. I will deal with the rebels after the warlord."

Haruto made a low bow, his scowl still marking his lips. "Yes, Lady. As you order."

As the physician tended to Amelia's side, Kenchi said, "You are lucky Chikako did not split you in two. Why did you confront her in the first place? What foolishness to try to fight. Haruto spoke true words. This is why you have an army."

"I...." Amelia winced as the physician applied a poultice to her wound. Why had she stood there and argued with Chikako, and then wanted to fight her? What Haruto said was right. What Kenchi said was right. She'd been foolish and let rage carry her away. Maybe she was too young to control her emotions like an adult, but even adults grew angry at times, and the girl made her so *mad*. "I lost my temper," Amelia admitted. "I know I shouldn't have, and yes, I was stupid. I will not allow my emotions to run out of control again in the upcoming battle."

"Huh? Your wound will keep you out of the struggle. You are in no shape to fight," Kenchi replied as the doctor wrapped cotton cloth around Amelia's waist and bound the bandage tight. As if to confirm Kenchi's statement, the doctor looked up from his work and shook his head sadly. "You cannot ride, let alone do battle like this."

"Who says I can't," Amelia flared. Her old stubbornness returned and she told the physician, "Put another wrap of the cloth around my ribs." The doctor appeared startled but dutifully bound her again. Amelia stretched her arms over her head. The bandages appeared too tight about the middle, but she supposed the doctor knew what he was doing. She ignored the stabbing ache in her side. "See, all better." Amelia knew she lied to herself and Kenchi. The throbbing was worse and she needed to concentrate not to let the ache overwhelm her to the point of screaming aloud. Amelia gave the young warrior a tight smile and gritted out, "I haven't fought all this way to stop now because of a cut."

"How are you going to stay on the unicorn's back? You cannot stand."

Lan Ying ambled over, sniffed curiously at Amelia's bandage and then nuzzled the girl affectionately on the good side. *"I will not let you fall. You may even hang onto my mane if you wish for this once."*

Amelia smirked at Kenchi. "I ride a unicorn, Kenchi. I cannot fall."

Chapter Fourteen

"Are you sure the warlord marches this way?" Amelia peered into the growing gloom, fidgeting and picking at her nails. The sensation of impending battle howled in her mind, grating on her nerves, and scaling upward past the point of her understanding. Her whole life centered on this moment, this night, and the coming dawn when she and the warlord would join in life or death struggle. Amelia felt like a penned animal, prowling along the bars, ready to leap as soon as her keeper unlocked the cage.

"Yes, I am sure," Kenchi replied. He rose from the campfire and waved at the barely visible horizon fading into a purple haze in the twilight. "We have scouted for the last day. See those lights along the skyline? If you look hard, you can spot a line marching along the hills. Those are the cooking fires from the leading edge of the army approaching us. The rest of the warlord's soldiers will arrive shortly, and more during the balance of the night. Tomorrow we fight."

Amelia rose and stood next to Kenchi, hanging onto his arm to support her weight. Indeed, one by one, small light appeared on the hillside, twinkling like excited fireflies in the dark. "Why can't they all reach here at once? We could have started combat at noon," she complained. "I was ready to, why wasn't the warlord? I did not believe he fears us so much."

Kenchi tenderly squeezed her shoulder. "Savage little warrior, huh? We should have sent him a note saying the lady is impatient. Please hurry your army so the slaughter can begin."

Amelia swatted at him in peevishness. "You know what I mean. The warlord acts as if we were no more than mosquitos he could brush aside at his leisure. I've always been told he is one eager for a battle handed any chance to fight."

Kenchi cupped his chin in his hand and nodded thoughtfully. "True, but he moves a large army loaded down with wagons, supplies, and siege machines, not to mention cooks, camp followers and wounded. An army so large does not travel swiftly as our smaller force does."

"He plans to run over us in a frontal assault, doesn't he?" Amelia said, her mouth straightening to a bitter line. She squatted back down on her haunches and studied the flames in the campfire, hoping to see a vision of how the battle would go. "Do you think my plan in a good one? We will win?" In her brief studies with her father, Amelia read books on former battles. Most without understanding, and her father died before he explained the words. Kenchi studied too, perhaps absorbing a better knowledge, but neither could grasp the fine details, which made one plan win and the second lose. After hours of talking, sketching out tactics on the dirt, and speculation, Amelia hammered together a scheme she hoped would succeed, on condition, of course, the warlord cooperated.

"If the strategy works, yes." Kenchi continued to stare into the night as more fires sprang up in the distance. "Provided everything goes as planned. We make no mistakes, and, as we hope," he sighed heavily and sat next to Amelia again, "the warlord attacks as we believe he will. I would, so would you if you outnumbered your enemy five to one, but neither you, nor I, know how the warlord thinks."

"It means after his allies have deserted him and the defeat against the Western Army, he'll be anxious for somebody to smash and smash quickly, to show he is still in command of his province, and his might is powerful enough to crush upstarts like us," Amelia said grimly. "He won't want to try anything fancy. A headlong attack to roll over our men like a tsunami."

"You still insist on fighting in this battle, as weak as you are and not wearing armor?" Kenchi made it a point to study the bulge beneath Amelia's kimono. The doctors stopped the bleeding again, but made no promises the slit in her side would not open and become worse. The physicians urged rest—rest which Amelia would not take.

"I considered armor after the run-in with Chikako," Amelia admitted, "but then I thought about the fight itself—if I wore protection I'd be too sluggish, too clumsy. Right now this wound slows me. The extra weight would bring me to a halt. They'd find an opening in the armor and I'd be dead meat. No," Amelia continued, "for better or worse I fight as I am. Buddha, the Shinto gods, and Lan Ying will protect me. The doctors have promised a potion to kill the pain for tomorrow. I will be fine, and after the battle is won, I'll have plenty of time to recuperate and heal."

The hillside flickered with lights from one end to the other. Kenchi rubbed Amelia's back gently and said, "The time is late and we rise early tomorrow for battle. Go rest. I will stay up for a while, watch the enemy, and do your worrying for you."

Amelia suppressed a yawn with the back of her hand. Between the fight yesterday with Chikako, the hurried night march to this spot right after, and the interment pacing and fretting throughout the day, she *was* exhausted. "Don't stay up too late yourself," she said to Kenchi, "and if anything happens during the night wake me at once. We can both fret together tomorrow when the sun rises."

Amelia walked to her pavilion and lay down, but sleep refused to come. She kept running over the plans for the battle in her mind, agonizing over each detail, tracing the line of troops in her mind's eye to catch miscalculations in their arrangement. Groaning, she rose, dressed, and stalked the camp with her cane, checking on the sentries, attempting to count the campfires on the horizon and estimate how many warriors gathered. The more she counted, however, the faster new blazes sprang to life, until the hillside and horizon shone with a brilliance of fire, as the warlord's army continued to halt and settle down for the night. Amelia found cooks preparing pots of tea, ready for any who wished it, and rested, drinking cup after cup to keep herself awake. She kept staring into the cooking fire, twisting the bowl in her fingers, wondering if her troops still had time to beat a retreat, rethink their battle strategy, and fight at another time in a different location. She was still speculating on their chances of survival when a hand shook her roughly awake.

"Amelia, Kenchi has me searching the whole camp looking for you. I thought he said you were in your tent sleeping. Have you been here all night?"

Amelia's eyes fluttered open. Sota towered over her dressed in his armor. "Huh? Yeah, I guess so. I was inspecting the camp, stopped to drink tea, and—"

"It is time. Soon dawn will break and the troops prepare to march into battle. The cooks make rice if you are hungry, but hurry, Kenchi and Haruto expect you." He strode away, shouting at men to make haste and finish eating.

"I'll be there in a minute," she muttered still only half-wake. Amelia stretched, accepted a bowl of rice from one of the cooks, and wolfed down the contents hungrily. After finishing, she was still famished, but decided to find Kenchi first. Around her, men rushed in all directions in the predawn darkness collecting their gear. Shouted commands rang through the air, calls from captains to their troops. Campfires blazed as the soldiers ate a hasty breakfast, gulping tea before running off to mount their horses or fall in line alongside their companies. Amelia hobbled as fast as possible, gritting at the throbbing in her side through the warriors, in the direction Sota disappeared, scanning right and left for her commanders.

"Amelia—*over here.*" Kenchi waved from a cooking fire along with Haruto and Sota. "Rice, fish, and vegetables," he announced, rising and handing her a steaming bowl.

The doctor anxiously stood by also. After accepting the rice, he poured a clear liquid into a cup of tea and handed the potion to her. "For pain, Lady Amelia," he said.

Amelia took a cautious sip. The tea was slightly bitter, but not bad at all. She hurriedly gulped the rest down. "Thank you." The ache in her side faded and for once in a long time, Amelia felt pain free.

Kenchi poured her another cup of tea. "I hope the drug makes you feel better, now hurry and eat."

Between mouthfuls of the potage, Amelia ran through the plan once again, more for her sake to calm her nerves than theirs. "Haruto you have the right flank, Sota the left...Kenchi you control the cavalry. Make sure everyone knows the flag signals. They'll have to see them waving on the other side of the battlefield."

"I have rockets as well," Kenchi said. "If my riders cannot see the flags, they will see the rockets. I will use both at the same time when I order the cavalry to move."

Amelia took a sip of tea as the soldiers continued to line up. "Do you think the warlord will use rockets against us? Fire spears? Exploding arrows maybe? I know we've been through this before, but we cannot be too cautious."

Haruto spoke up. "I do not think so. The warlord has no intention of sitting back and firing anything, and I have seen none deployed yet. He means to make a quick rush, roll over our army, and finish us off once and for all."

Amelia emptied her bowls of rice and tea. "Okay, then. I take the middle. When I fall back, the flanks swing in. Kenchi, when you see the enemy line drawn into the center of the battlefield to break my troops, you take the cavalry around the perimeter and attack from the rear. Any last minute questions?"

Sota spoke up. "Lady, what do we do if you cannot hold the enemy in the middle after you have begun your retreat?"

This question plagued Amelia since she first devised her plan, and was the one uncertainty about the tactic. The center of the line would give ground, pulling the enemy into the middle of the battleground attempting to split her force in two, but the assault on the flanks would lessen, allowing Sota and Haruto to swing their men inward. With Kenchi attacking from the rear the warlord's army was encircled, most of the men trapped in the center unable to fight. What would happen though if she couldn't hold the line?

"Run," Amelia said softly. "Run and try to save your lives. If the center breaks, or the cavalry does not attack from the rear, our plan has failed and we are all dead."

The somber men looked back at her, saying nothing.

Amelia studied each face. She saw no fear, only grim determination. When she stopped at Kenchi's, he silently mouthed the words, "We live together, or die together."

An unknown sensation overwhelmed her chest.

Amelia shook her head, blanked her mind, and announced, "Someone fetch my weapons and let us mount."

Lan Ying whinnied softly at Amelia's approach. *"Another early morning?"* the unicorn inquired glumly. If a unicorn could yawn, Lan Ying did so. *"And this time not even a bale of dry, tasteless hay."* Her head swung back and forth in despair, staring at the bare earth and she pawed the ground. *"I am tired and hungry. Let us ride to the nice meadow, clear water from the pond, sweet grass in the field."* The filly nickered plaintively, but knelt so Amelia could mount her, a hopeful expression in her eyes.

"You are fat and lazy," the girl responded patting Lan Ying's neck, "but I love you so dearly. When all this is over I promise you a long rest in your field." Amelia bent low and kissed the unicorn on the top of her head, and then nudged her gently with her knees. "C'mon. I want to address my troops before the battle starts."

Kenchi, Haruto, and Sota had the soldiers lined up in companies when Amelia and Lan Ying approached. She drew her father's sword, trotted along the ranks, her dark eyes boring into those of the men as she passed each troop. She had yet to tie her hair back and the long black threads streamed in the air behind her like a banner, as did Lan Ying's alabaster tail. Finally, Amelia stopped and yelled, "Today we fight for honor and glory. Your ancestors and descendants will remember what you do on the battlefield this morning, whether you died bravely or survived, so mark your actions well. I have named you all samurai. You act by the code of horse and bow, whether your fight holding a sword and draw a shaft on a horse, or battle on two feet striking with a blade."

"Yes. Yes. Yes."

In a lower, kinder voice, Amelia said, "You all make me proud. Today we fight for freedom, also justice and a release from oppression, not only for our families and us, but for all the people of this province. I know you will not fail me in this hour." She raised her voice again, and stabbed her sword to the sky. "We will win or die trying. *Glory. Glory. Glory."*

Her soldiers shouted back to her, raising their weapons in their right hands, *"Yes. Yes. Yes."*

Amelia nodded to Kenchi. "Let's move out."

The warlord's army already lined up, a long, black string of men stretching across the landscape, Mount Fuji slowly revealed in the fog. The Alp rested white capped and immense in the background, like a silent referee waiting to judge the conflict, as the sun rose. On a lone hilltop, a solitary pavilion sat with the emblem of the warlord fluttering overhead. The man stood outside, surrounded by riders who he dispatched bearing last minute messages to his commanders, aligning his troops as he observed the configuration of Amelia's. Amelia never realized how immense the warlord's force was until observed in the daylight, battle flags fluttering in the wind, and the light reflecting off the samurai's armor like shimmering stars. Amelia tried to make sense of what she saw, but the hillside kept drawing her attention with the man she hated. Even at this distance, Amelia saw him laughing, hands on hips, as he gazed at her small army.

She surveyed her own troops, seeing how tiny they were in comparison, how poorly equipped.

Her body trembled.

Amelia waved her sword and rode forward.

The two lines crept together gathering increased speed. Men howled and screamed with bestial battle cries as the forces race onward. Amelia yelled too, bending forward along Lan Ying's neck as the unicorn galloped at the enemy, the pounding of her mount hammering overly loud in her hearing. She plunged the sword back into the scabbard, pulled the bow off her back and notched a bolt. As the soldiers drew within arrow rang she fired.

The armies clashed, two opposing waves surging back and forth for survival. Amelia shot another arrow, and then another, drawing back the bowstring and releasing so fast her hand was a blur. Lan Ying bucked, lashing out with sharp front hooves, powerful rear legs kicking at any who drew too near, and trumpeting a sound of rage that reverberated off Mount Fuji itself.

A screaming soldier leaped high in the air, two hands clutching a sword over his head to spit Amelia in half. Lan Ying caught the man on her horn, tossing him over her head. His death howls rang in Amelia's ears as his blood splattered her face and body. The unicorn whirled to catch another in the belly as he prepared to swing a blade. Amelia bent low, sweeping out her bow, knocking the sword from his hand. A third soldier rushed their way clutching a *naginata* like a lance. With a kick, Amelia deflected the tip and Lan Ying lashed out her front hooves, hurling the man backward into a warrior.

Oh, Buddha, I never realized. Make it stop—please, make it stop.

A soldier staggered against Amelia, one of her own. He gazed up with pleading eyes and reached out an arm. His hand was missing at the wrist, the severed stump pumping blood. As he collapsed, he painted Lan Ying's side and Amelia's leg in a stream of red.

Amelia fumbled for another arrow, the two armies fully engaged, and found her quiver empty. She yanked her sword out and withdrew a conch shell from a pouch, blowing three long notes. The men surrounding her looked her way and started a slow, measured retreat, yielding ground by inches to the warlord's soldiers as they fell back. Amelia watched in satisfaction. This was the most important part of the plan. Too fast a retreat would change into a route from which her army would never recover.

The enemy soldiers yelled in triumph and pressed their advantage, hoping to split Amelia's line in the middle. Warriors and commanders on the flanks saw their comrades advancing in the center and shifted to join their comrades.

Hold. Hold. Not too fast. Please don't break.

Amelia glanced left and right. Battle flags carrying a white unicorn waved in the air. Haruto and Sota signaled their men to swing the flanks in.

The sides of Amelia's line moved forward, starting to fold inward into a U.

The plan is working. A few minutes more and Kenchi can sweep around with the cavalry and close the trap. Her warriors in the center were hard pressed, cut and bleeding, but held on grimly in desperation, their faith in Amelia unshaken. Lan Ying surged along the line, goring enemies while Amelia swept her sword in a circle chopping through armor and flesh alike. *Don't break, please don't break. We're almost there.* She hacked again and searched the sky, praying for the rocket signal indicating Kenchi moved the cavalry around the perimeter.

"Beware."

Lan Ying twisted and kicked at a samurai riding at the two at full tilt, sword raised high in the air, a savage scream on his lips. Her iron feet connected to the horse's chest. The animal screeched in pain, collapsing to its knees. The warrior flew forward over the neck of the beast and Lan Ying trampled him with a crunching of bone. The unicorn braced herself on her front legs and swerved again in a wild leap. Amelia felt an arrow zip by her hair, missing her head by inches. She reached out, swinging her sword, and chopped into the soldier who shot the bolt as Lan Ying galloped past.

All around men dropped, the dead heaped in piles. Sweat ran into Amelia's eyes, stinging and making her ride half-blind. She wiped her forehead on the sleeve of her kimono to clear her vision. What was taking Kenchi so long to send up his rockets?

Yells of triumph rang out from the flanks. *Finally. Kenchi rides to close the trap. We could not have held out much longer.* Taking a chance, Amelia rose as far in the saddle as she could and exposed herself, presenting a perfect target for any bowman in range. Amelia looked sharply to her right, sure to see Kenchi's battle flag speeding to the open end of the U.

Amelia froze in horror.

Fresh enemy troops dashed in to reinforce the flanks. More poured into the center of the battle line. The warlord cunningly concealed reserves out of sighed behind the hills and now dispatched his troops to annihilate Amelia's army.

A rocket flared into the air. Kenchi's banner moved forward, stopped, as more enemy soldiers rode out of cover on horseback to challenge the cavalry and push the riders backward.

All around Amelia her soldiers died, or fell back in disarray as the warlord's army stormed forward, trampling over the bodies of the fallen with murderous cries of victory. The clatter of horse's hooves and the ringing of steel upon steel filled the air joining the wails of the dying. Amelia swung her sword in desperation, hoping for a miracle to change the tide of battle, but knowing the attempt was useless and the finish drew near.

The men retreat. The center of my line is collapsing. My army trapped against the wagons and everyone slaughtered. Great Buddha, what do we do? This is the end.

"Pray."

"Huh?"

Lan Ying tossed her horn, catching a foot soldier in the ribs, casting him aside like a rag doll, while kicking another in the belly. *"You are a meko, a descendant of the goddess Uzume. There lies Mount Fuji in front of you, the holy mountain of the gods. Pray to the ancient spirits for salvation."*

"You're mad," Amelia gasped, stabbing her sword at another foot soldier, catching him in the shoulder. "I only said I was to appease you."

"You are miko." Certainty filled Lan Ying's reply. *"Your power lies inside. Pray to the gods and I shall pray with you."*

In desperation, not knowing what else to do, Amelia clenched her eyes, drowning out the clashing of steel and the cries of the wounded. She drew up a picture of the white tip of Mount Fuji in her mind and started to pray.

Gods of my ancestors, Lord God Kuninotokotachi, hear my plea. I am Amelia, miko, descendant of Uzume who danced in joy and brought happiness back to the world. Help me in this struggle to free this land, so light, glee, and contentment can return to the people. I beseech you Lord, help me win.

Time and space melted away. The clatter of battle vanished. Amelia stood before a throne. A massive figure sat facing her, thighs as thick as oxen and arms knotted with oaken muscles. The head clouded in mist, beams of light shooting in all directions like stars. Unimaginable power emanated from the body, pulsing in hot waves, searing her eyeballs. The shrouded head turned to regard her, but no answer to her prayers appeared. The being did not speak. Amelia never knew how long she stayed in that place. A second? An eternity?

Then she was back on the battlefield. Amelia heard Lan Ying echoing her thought. She opened her eyes still in a daze. White birds like doves flew swiftly through the air to the mountaintop.

The noise of battle returned to her.

"We must retreat, try and save our men." Kenchi was by her side astride his black stallion, blood seeping between the scales of his armor and dripping onto his saddle. His mouth twisted as he sunk his blade into an enemy warrior. "I could not break through…too many….we shall all perish," he gasped.

A blanket of calmness enveloped Amelia. She felt as if she looked through another person's eyes, and the cares of the world no longer bothered her. In an otherworld voice Amelia said, "We wait. Something will happen."

Kenchi's lips squeezed into a thin, hard line.

A bolt of lightning flashed across the sky from the tip of Mount Fuji, brightening the heavens, like a hundred blazing suns exploding all at once. A blast of thunder ripped the air, shaking the battlefield with a detonation of passion as the earth trembled. The two armies stopped fighting, stunned by the magnitude of the discharge, and turned as one to stare at the mountain in awe and fear.

Kenchi whispered, "Fuji is erupting." A torrid haze filled the atmosphere. Diamonds of alabaster swirled skyward.

An enemy soldier, transfixed by the mountain, shouted, "It is an avalanche!"

The mist descended to the earth and covered the ground like a sheet of ice. The pearly tip of the mountain flowed down the slope, long ashen fingers creeping along the side to the plain below. A pale fog rose into the sky at the passing, and the rumbling of the whiteness hurtling over the ground roared through the air.

The white drew closer, reflecting sunlight in shimmering beams to rent the sky. Individual shapes appeared through the fog and brilliance, took form as the mist dissolved into a thousand alabaster unicorns at full gallop charging into the rear of the enemy line.

Amelia shook herself out of her trance. Lan Ying reared, pawing the air with her front hooves and bugling a ringing welcome of joy. Amelia raised her sword high in the air. *"CHARGE!"*

Her men, at first as paralyzed as the enemy soldiers, cheered and raced forward, attacking the enemy soldiers with renewed fury, Kenchi and Amelia leading the troops shouting frenzied screams of wrath. The pair fought side by side, opening a gap in the enemy lines, hacking their way through the troops toward the lone pavilion on the hilltop where the warlord's battle flag waved in defiance.

The herd of unicorns galloped past Amelia and Kenchi, separated around the two, a river of death bypassing an island to hurl themselves on the enemy warriors, a savage plague of death and destruction.

Ahead of Amelia, standing outside his pavilion, stood the warlord. Rage mirrored on his face as his army crumbled under the berserk onslaught of Amelia's troops, and the trampling hooves and horns of the unicorns. The samurai held bow and notched arrow in his hands. Around the tent lay the scattered remains of his staff, crushed by the passing of the unicorns. A maniacal grin crossed his face as he took careful aim at the two approaching him.

He released his arrow.

"Kenchi, *watch out!*"

Before the young warrior could react, the bolt slapped into his shoulder. Kenchi slumped in the saddle, grimacing with a cry of pain. His mount slowed, and then stopped.

The warlord fixed another arrow into his bow, this time taking a bead on Amelia as she drew near. Amelia ducked low against Lan Ying, pulling her sword arm back for a killing stroke, dark eyes narrowed in concentration. Her vision locked onto the man's head and shoulders.

The samurai released his arrow, not at Amelia, but at the unicorn's chest. Flipping her horn, Lan Ying deflected the shaft, bellowing in contempt and the next moment her powerful shoulder smashed into the warlord, spinning him sideways while Amelia chopped down between helmet and shoulder pads. As the two flew past a keening wail exploded and stopped.

Lan Ying slowed to a fast walk and made a wide circle. Before Amelia, the battlefield stretched out in panoramic view. Black lumps, the corpses of enemy soldiers, littered the earth. The unicorns trotted between the dead, finishing the remains of the warlord's army, their spiral horns stained red in blood. A low drone filled the air, the groans of the wounded pleading for help and mercy. Amelia's men wandered the field of combat, too, dazed, searching for their injured comrades among the dying.

"Kenchi?"

He sat in the saddle, a bemused expression on his face as he gazed at the arrow protruding from his armor.

Amelia hurried to him. "Don't worry; I'll bring you to the surgeon. You will survive," she exclaimed, bending over to snatch the reins of his mount.

"Do not bother." His mouth set in a grimace as he reached across his chest. With a tug, he yanked the arrow out, studied the head, and dropped the bolt to the earth, wincing. "Ha—barely penetrated the armor," he commented. "A scratch, nothing more, but for a moment I thought I was dead. Hurts like a wasp sting." He gazed over the battlefield. "What is happening? Have we won?"

The unicorns were rising on their hind legs, long trumpets ringing the air. Lan Ying reared, pawing the air, returning their call adding a bugle of her own.

A pure white unicorn stallion trotted up to Amelia, Lan Ying, and Kenchi, his tail held high, head lifted, his long, flowing mane draped in curling tresses over his shoulders. He stopped before Amelia and Lan Ying, and snorted at the latter. Lan Ying whinnied in answer. Glaring at the filly, the stallion switched his attention to Amelia, dropped to one knee in a bow of deep respect, and then rose.

"What's he doing," Amelia asked Lan Ying in a whisper.

"He wishes to see your wound."

"Huh?" Amelia looked at her kimono stained crimson with her blood and the enemy. Even though she felt no pain, Amelia knew the gash was open again and bleeding "Uh, okay." She lifted the kimono up, revealing a blood-soaked bandage. Amelia forgot about the slice once she drank the potion given by the doctor. Now, at the sight of the gory dressing, the cut commenced to ache. Clamping her teeth, she carefully unwrapped the cloth holding the bandage in place, revealing the slash oozing scarlet. Snorting disgust at Lan Ying, the stallion laid his horn along the wound. The whiteness of the spike transformed to red, while the gash puckered closed, the black and blue bruise fading until only satin smooth skin showed. The stain from the horn dissipated and the spiral spike gleamed white again.

The stallion reared, trumpeting to the rest of the unicorns. The creatures lifted on their hind legs in answer as did Lan Ying. One by one, they turned translucent, melting back into sparkling mist, which glimmered in the sky until this too, evaporated from sight as the breeze whisked the vapor away.

"The gods sent unicorns in answer to Lan Ying's and my prayers," whispered Amelia.

"The herd saluted you before leaving," Lan Ying commented, dropping onto her front hooves. *"They paid homage to the daughter of Uzume. I thanked the stallions and mares."*

"We won." Amelia wrapped her arms around Lan Ying's neck. "You did it. You are the one who told me to pray. You wonderful, wonderful, unicorn. I love you forever."

"Of course. Unicorns are very loveable. I love you too."

"I never saw a unicorn stallion, before," Amelia said. "Males are very impressive. Why did he appear so angry with you?"

Lan Ying pawed the ground, nervous. *"Well, if you must know, he was angry because I did not heal your hurt. He thought I was being lazy in my duty to you."*

"You mean you could have healed me any time you wanted to?" Amelia replied, shocked. In reflex, she ran her hand over the smooth skin. "Why didn't you?"

"I tried, twice," Lan Ying replied with a whine in her voice. The unicorn nudged Amelia's fingers by the spot where the gash was. *"Once when you received the slash. You told me to leave you alone. The next time when we were in the forest. When I started to suggest I heal you, you*

told me to hush. I thought the remark was very rude because I was only trying to help."

Amelia started to say she'd told Lan Ying no such things and then fell quiet. She thought back. She told the unicorn to leave her alone, and to hush, but hadn't meant to refuse her help. "I'm so sorry," Amelia replied, aghast. "Did I get you into trouble? I promise I will always listen to you."

"No. Stallions like to show off, makes the males feel big and strong as if they know everything there is to know. He will brag to the other stallions how fillies cannot do anything correct, and it was necessary for him to set things right and heal you himself, but what can you expect. He is a male."

Kenchi was a silent onlooker to the exchange, changing back and forth between Amelia and the unicorn as he tried to puzzle out what both discussed. He coughed abruptly. "Do not become too carried away, you two," he cautioned finally. "We still have to take the castle and rescue your mother. Even though the warlord is dead this will not be an easy task."

"The war is over? Does that mean we can go home to my nice quiet meadow?" Lan Ying asked hopefully, disregarding Kenchi. *"You said we would after we won."*

A pang of guilt shot through Amelia. "I know, honey. I promise, we're almost done. Okay? Kenchi is right, we still have to assault the fortress and free my mother. That is why we started this whole thing, remember?"

Lan Ying issued a long-suffering sigh and glared at Kenchi. *"Men."*

Kenchi tugged his reins out of Amelia's hands and wheeled his horse around. "We must gather what is left of our army and march, before the castle is evacuated and the soldiers take you mother away again. If the defenders go into hiding for fear of their lives we may never find her."

"You're right." Amelia cupped her hand and screamed, "*Haruto—Sota,* where are you?"

Answering cries issued from the battlefield and two horses galloped her way.

"A good fight," Haruto exclaimed, riding up. "I didn't think we would win, especially when the warlord sent in his reserves, but, I never would have believed it if I had not seen this myself." He said in wonder, "Where did all those unicorns come from?"

"Sometimes prayers can work miracles." Amelia stroked Lan Ying along the neck. "Especially when someone believes in you."

"What do we do now?" Sota asked. Amelia's men busily attended to their wounded; more walked the field, stripping the dead of their armor and weapons. Still others saw the leaders of the army in conference and wanders over to learn the new orders.

"Kenchi, do you know how to conquer a castle?" Amelia asked.

"I have read accounts," he said, scratching his chin. He said to Haruto and Sota, "Do either of you know?"

Sota spoke up. "We storm the walls. The warlord can't have many soldiers guarding the fortress. We will lose men, sure but if we move fast enough, the loss will not be great."

Haruto held his hand up. "Your father needed to take a castle once," he said. "I was with him. First, he encircled the fortifications so none could escape. He hurled flaming balls of hay over the battlements operating a trebuchet day and night. After a while, the defenders grew weary of extinguishing the flames. They ran out of food eventually. The siege took three months, but the soldiers finally surrendered without a fight."

"*What?*" Amelia shook her head so hard her long hair snapped angrily back and forth. "I am not going to wait three more months to rescue my mother, nor risk anymore of our men assaulting the castle. I will not have anyone else die. There must be another way. We should think and devise a better plan."

"I keep telling you, but you never listen to me," sighed Lan Ying. *"Did not listen when I wanted to heal your wound, or tell you how to rescue your mother. I do not know why I keep trying to make suggestions. Humans can be so stubborn at times."*

"I don't remember you telling me how to rescue my mother." Amelia squinted her eyes, trying to recall everything the unicorn said. "Tell me again."

"Knock on the gate and ask politely. It is really very simple."

Chapter Fifteen

"You can't be serious" Amelia stopped as an idea swelled in her mind and her face lit up. "Maybe you're right. Can't hurt to try acting reasonably."

"You have an idea?" Haruto said, watching Amelia's expression.

"I was thinking—"

"Uh-hum."

"Lan Ying and I have a thought," Amelia amended. "I'll have to work out the details in my mind, but let's start moving. Kenchi is right. I don't want the castle abandoned before we arrive. Whoever escaped from the warlord's army is sure to run straight there and tell the soldiers what happened."

Amelia issued orders for their dead buried, wounded transported to the camp in the Forest of Trees. The weary host was quickly reformed, the warlord's wagon train ransacked for trebuchets, and anything else useful to bring along. The sun set over the mountains when they stopped at a lone, rocky hill on top of which perched the warlord's castle controlling a commanding view of the countryside. Along the way, the troop passed cartloads of peasants escaping the area for fear a battle would soon be raging. Amelia ordered each person questioned and the wagons search in case her mother hid among the fleeing.

The fortress blazed with lights when the army reached the fortifications. Warriors poised on the battlements, bows in hand, anticipating an attack each were positive would start at the arrival of Amelia and her soldiers.

"Encircle the castle," Amelia commanded, "and set up the trebuchets on all four sides." She measured by eye the slope leading to the walls rising at a steep angle. "Make sure we have ample crews on each siege machines—and be certain those defenders on the battlements see you doing so. I want the warriors to understand there is no way of escaping unless they depart on my own terms."

Sota gave a cheery waved to the enemy watching, and said to Amelia, "Are we going to walk into the tiger's den and capture its cub?" He glared at the warriors, made a rude gesture in their direction, and loosened his sword in the scabbard.

"First I will try to entice the cub to step out on his own." Once she positioned the men as she wished, Amelia got an idea. "Sota, erect a scaffolding by a trebuchet so I can drop one of the slaughtered cows on the arm. Haruto, we have no bales of hay such as my father used, but a rock, covered in cotton cloth and then soaked in pig's fat, and secured by wire will work as well." The old warrior nodded wisely and hurried away, yelling for a few of the men to accompany him.

The warriors on the battlements watched the commotion, calling others until the whole complement of the castle packed the wall shoulder-to-shoulder. When Amelia assembled everything, she nodded to Haruto. "Okay, load the rock into the sling and light the cloth. Release the carcass of the cow and fling the rock over the wall."

Haruto waved his hand above his head and shouted to the trebuchet crew. The dead cow dropped on the short end of the trebuchet, the long arm swung in a slow arc, and the flaming cloth wrapped stone soared through the air, dripping pieces of burning cotton along the way. The rock sailed over the castle fortifications and disappeared.

Shouts rang out from inside the fortress accompanied by hoarse commands. A shimmering red glow appeared over the wall reflected off the castle, quickly extinguished. "Hit a pile of hay?" Kenchi said, "Or maybe a stack of wood for cooking and heating?"

"Who cares," Amelia replied. "The rock could have hit nothing for all I know. I want the people inside to realize what is in store tomorrow if we start a bombardment. Now they'll stay awake fearing an assault tonight, jumping at the slightest noise. By morning the whole lot will be nervous wrecks." She suppressed a yawn. "I'm going to sleep. Wake me if the warriors try a sneak attack during the evening. At first light, we will begin negotiations. If I wasn't so tired, I'd say have men beat on drums to keep those soldiers on alert and thinking, but I want a good night's rest." Amelia staggered off to her tent. Even though the wound had fully healed, her ribs ached. Amelia stretched out on the pallet, laying on her good side, released a shuddering groan and fell asleep at once.

"We will die before we surrender," the old samurai yelled from the castle walls the next morning. He drew his sword and shook the katana over his head, as if he were ready to jump from the stone throwing shelf and duel Amelia in person. "Go away before we emerge and chase you away like a pack of rabid curs."

Amelia smiled to herself. It was an empty threat. From quizzing the fleeing farmers, she'd learned long ago the warlord stripped the castle of all capable warriors to fight the war in the north. The old and wounded remained, but they posed no threat to her men. Amelia waved to one of the trebuchets. "You saw what I did last night. I will send Chinese fire spears and exploding arrows over your palisades as well as firepots and burn the fortress around your ears." This was an idle boast. When the men searched the supply wagons of the defeated army, they found no missiles or explosives of any type. Amelia wasn't about to admit the fact, though, and this warrior didn't know she lied. "I will rip the stones down around your ears one by one, or you can surrender to me. Your daimyo is dead. I killed him myself in battle. Even monkeys fall from trees, but you do not have to fall with him. You have my word of honor as a samurai no harm will come to you or the people of the castle. My sole wish is to rescue my mother and see her once more."

"Never."

Lan Ying pranced under Amelia. *"You have not tried please, yet."*

"I do not think that would work, baby." Amelia said to Kenchi, "I don't want to fire the castle. My mother is in there; nor do I want to attack the fortifications. Too many of our people have died already. I am sick of all this death."

"We can bide our time. Eventually the defenders will have to surrender from hunger. "

From the top of the battlement, a shriek blasted. Amelia looked up as the old warrior tumbled over the wall to fall in a grotesque heap on the rocks below. The body rolled down the slope and lay still.

Another soldier stood on the shelf, a bloody knife clutched in his hand. He was missing one arm at the elbow. "What are your demands?"

Murmurs of astonishment and disgust circulated between her men. Surprisingly, no such outcry issued from the garrison on the palisades who stood watching their comrade silently. The warrior called down to Amelia again, "You say you want your mother? Who is this woman? How do you know she is held here by us?"

Kenchi called out, "Who are you? You have murdered your commander. How can we trust you? You are without honor."

"I am Captain Goto, second in command, now first. He," the captain waved his sole hand to the corpse, "was hated by all. He only commanded here because he was a favorite of the warlord, his brother-in-law in fact. The man acted as steward of the castle and bookkeeper, but no one ever saw him fight in a combat, and I do not believe the warlord expected him to direct men in battle if need be. He was miserly and cruel, never true samurai."

Amelia studied the man's features, trying to decide if he spoke the truth. She swept her gaze along the battlement, scrutinizing the other warrior's faces to see if anyone would naysay him. Amelia saw nods of agreement and heard muffled words of support as the majority inched toward him in proof of his decision.

Kenchi said, "What do you think? Do we trust him?"

Amelia shrugged. "Why not, if he gives me what I want. The rest of the warriors up there agree with him." She called out to Captain Goto, "The castle personnel may leave safely with whatever each can carry on their backs, including horses and personal weapons. You have my word no harm will come from my army as long as you offer no threat to us. My mother's name is Mochitoyo-san, you'll probably find her in the kitchen if she still lives. Mother was captured months ago and brought here by the warlord's men when the soldiers learned I harbored this unicorn." She patted Lan Ying on the neck.

Captain Goto paused, considering. "I believe I remember her, but I am not sure. We have heard rumors of the girl who rides a unicorn and of her honesty when dealing with others. I have your word we will not be harmed?"

Amelia drew herself erect and said proudly, "On my word of honor. I am a daughter of samurai born and bred. My father was samurai, as well as was his father before him. I live by bushido, horse and bow. I lead this army as the commander. Upon my vow, no harm shall befall you. Send my mother out and the rest of you may leave peacefully. Your master is dead. The war between us is over."

"I will take your pledge, Lady. Wait." The captain left. After a half an hour delay two figures emerged onto the battlement, Goto and a woman. A hurried conversation occurred between the couple with pointing fingers and they departed again. Ten minutes later, the fortress gate opened and the pair stepped out, crossing the drawbridge, Captain Goto and Mochitoyo-san.

"Mother." Amelia leaped off Lan Ying and rushed forward, embracing the old woman in a fierce hug while Captain Goto looked on.

"Amelia?" Tears of joy streamed down Mochitoyo-san's face.

Captain Goto's lips flickered upward. "We were not positive if we held the right lady," he explained. "Your mother was not certain herself if she was the one you sought when she saw you astride the unicorn from the castle walls." His eyes flicked to Lan Ying in disbelief, still was not sure what stood before his eyes.

Mochitoyo-san peered past her daughter at the soldiers lined up behind Amelia. "All these men obey you? How? How is this possible?" Her gaze drifted to Lan Ying and the woman shook her head in bewilderment, and then she looked at Kenchi who sat on his black stallion beside the unicorn. "Kenchi? You are here, too? You fight against your own family? Clan? I do not understand all that is happening here. Is this a dream while I sleep?"

"I fight with your daughter to protect her and to bring you to safety," he replied. The pride and love in his tone as he grinned broadly at the two left no doubt what he said was true.

Mochitoyo-san bobbed her head up and down in understanding. "I am an old woman," she muttered, peering long into Kenchi's face as he gazed adoring at Amelia. "I know not how all this has come about, but I can see this much is true."

Her arm still around her mother's waist, Amelia said to Captain Goto, "You may depart the fortress. No harm shall descend on you unless swords are raise against us." She waved Haruto and Sota forward and said to her mother, "These are my two lieutenants. You must be tired. They will take you to my tent, fetch anything you want and answer all your questions. I must remain here with my men and see to the evacuation. I will join you when I can. The next two day will be busy, after the castle is emptied, the rooms must be searched for assassins and booby-traps before I take possession."

Mochitoyo-san nodded and embraced Amelia. "Daughter, I missed you so."

Wetness ran down Amelia's cheeks. "I missed you too, Mother."

Captain Goto asked, "I have one favor to ask of you. Can the people take as much food as each can carry? The stores of the castle are slim, but I do not want my men to go hungry."

Amelia waved her hand in dismissal. "Let your personnel take as much as necessary. I would rather they empty the storerooms and starve myself, then have soldiers turn bandit and rob the farmers in the countryside, and rape the places of business. This goes for the servants inside as well. I will not see anyone in this domain go hungry."

"Thank you." Goto bowed deeply. "You show mercy and character: the mark of a true samurai warrior."

The emptying of the fortress defenders took a surprisingly short time, even with the servants, who Amelia insisted leave also for fear of spies or assassins. A few grumbled they had no place to go, and Amelia assured the helpers anyone could return later if desired. Most were happy to leave for the captive workers possessed families they wished to return to. After her men swept the lower levels of the castle and made a cautious search of the bedrooms above, Amelia, Kenchi, and Mochitoyo-san sat in the spacious dining room of the castle, a view of the landscape beyond, enjoying a cup of green tea and talking.

"I can't believe the fighting is over," Amelia breathed, gazing at her mother. "It seemed impossible to rescue you from the start. I never really thought we would win. I still can't."

"I always feared I would never see you again," Mochitoyo-san replied. She stared around the dining room, taking in the walls, rafters, and table. "I do not remember how many meals I helped serve in here. I thought my life would be an eternity of labor and servitude until I died. I always prayed I would see you one last time."

Kenchi reached across the table and took Amelia's hand in his. "I never doubted. When a samurai daughter puts her mind to a task, all things are possible. We wake from death and return to life, right?"

Amelia giggled and blushed. "Well, be as it may, we have finished the battles, night marches, and constant worry of oblivion. We have nothing left to do."

"Besides ruling this han as the new daimyos? Oh, yes there is." Kenchi took Amelia's other hand also and gazed into her eyes. "Will you marry me?" He said to Mochitoyo-san, "If I have your permission, of course."

Amelia's mother laughed. "Who am I to tell the new daimyos what to do? Daughter? This is your choice. What say you?"

Amelia froze. Her heart hammered in her chest and the first impulse was to say yes. Then her thoughts drifted to Lan Ying. *Only a virgin may ride a unicorn.*

"I'm not sure."

Mochitoyo-san's mouth opened in surprise. Kenchi clamped his jaws shut, hurt mirrored on his face. Amelia rose, keeping her gaze averted from the two. "I'll be back." She hurried from the castle to the courtyard where Lan Ying stood. "Let's take a ride."

The unicorn's eyes lit up. *"To the meadow? Finally?"*

"Anywhere you want to go," Amelia choked out, leaping on the unicorn and hugging her neck in a fierce grip. "As fast and as far as you want to. I need to feel the breeze in my hair and see your mane flash in the air, smell the odor of your coat, and the strength of your muscles beneath me."

"I have not had a good run in a long time," Lan Ying admitted. *"Hold on tight. This will be fun."* The unicorn cantered out of the courtyard tossing her head for joy, through the castle gate bugling in happiness, and across the moat, turning her nose westward. She galloped; at first the land sped below the two, and then faster until the ground was a greenish-beige blur beneath Lan Ying's hooves. The sea appeared. They barely touched the water, leaving a grey spray of foam behind, then more land— China with bustling crowds of noisy people, ornate temples and stores, pungent odors of incense, food, and bodies packed tightly together. Lan Ying did not stop. They traveled over endless amber plains and dense emerald forests. The sun exploded in a bust of pinks, reds, and orange, only to reappear in all its glory. Rain fell and stopped in a blink of an eye as thunderclouds evaporated giving way to blue skies. People in strange clothes emerged and disappeared in a kaleidoscope of flowing colors. Spiral onion-shaped domes rose up surround my men and women wearing robes, replaced by massive stone cathedrals in the centers of bustling cities.

More water appeared, land filled forests, pyramids and saffron prairies, and then an ocean. The filly flew over islands, dodged mountains erupting in bursts of red fire and smoke, burrowed through dense jungles holding screeching animal life. Amelia squinted as the sun reflected off the sea, and Lan Ying slowed to a gallop over land once more, with Mount Fuji rising like a beacon of home in the distance to greet her.

Amelia's eyes shone. Lan Ying's great chest heaved from exertion. The filly shook her mane and released a long neigh. *"I have not done that in a long time,"* the unicorn huffed, reentering the courtyard of the castle. *"I must get into the pasture more. I need exercise. All this army life is making me soft."*

"It was wonderful," exclaimed Amelia. She brushed her hair back and exhaled deeply. "I always dreamed of distance lands, but I never thought I would see them all."

"I am glad I made you happy." The unicorn nuzzled Amelia and nipped at her leg gently. *"I love you."*

The girl leaped off the unicorn and threw her arms around Lan Ying's neck. "Oh, I love you too, baby. I love you so much."

*** *

"See, I told you we would return." Amelia viewed the clearing by the waterfall, the crystal-clear water cascading from above, and the meadow filled by wildflowers beyond. She slid off Lan Ying's back, knelt at the pond, and scooped up a drink of fresh water. "Ahhh. Cool." Amelia stood, placed her hands on hips, and glanced around with joy and regret at the place they'd so recently schemed and plotted for her mother's release. She sighed.

"About time. I thought we would never be back." Lan Ying stood beside Amelia and dipped her muzzle in the water. *"Just as I remember."*

With a small part of the army settled at the fortress and the rest dispatched throughout the territory Amelia controlled, all that remained of the former camp were empty shacks, burnt out fires, and broken furniture. Clothing and personal items not worth saving littered the sod.

Lan Ying surveyed the mess and snorted in disgust, pawing at the ground as if she could bury the refuge in dirt. *"Nature will clean, but the cleansing of this place will take years."* The unicorn gazed at Amelia with her brown eyes. *"I see you are troubled. I have felt your sorrow all the way here while we rode. I will leave you to your thoughts until you are ready to talk. If you want me I will be in the meadow grazing on the sweet grass, smelling the odors of the flowers, and taking a well-deserved rest."*

"Wait, don't go." Amelia reached out and hugged the unicorn. "I always wondered. Are there more male unicorns? You've never mentioned the males. I saw one at the battle, but don't remember seeing any more, or even hearing about stallions in tales and legends."

"Male unicorns?" Lan Ying tossed her head and snorted. *"Of course there are more male unicorns. How do you think we get unicorn foals?"*

"Oh, I guess so. You never talk about the rest though."

"I have told you about my fillies, my age mates. Males? They are such silly creatures, really. Come mating time the stallions prance around so fierce, tossing their horns in the air, bugling and rearing, as if anyone cared what they did. Of course, we all watch," Lan Ying confided, giggling. *"You really cannot help seeing the antics. All of us mares go, 'Ohh' and 'Ahh' to make the males feel good. So much nonsense, but the stallions eat our comments up. Besides parading about, males do not do much. Ask a stallion what he does all day and he will reply, 'Busy with herd business.'"* The unicorn snorted. *"As if the lead mare does not do all the real work of running the herd. Humph."* Lan Ying watched Amelia curiously. *"Is this what is bothering you? You want to see male unicorns?"*

"No, I was curious." The girl threw her arms around Lan Ying again. "I love you," Amelia whispered in one furry ear, her heart aching.

"Of course. I love you too." Lan Ying turned and wandered to the meadow, clumped through the tall grass,

and chased a butterfly in joyous abandonment before settling down to graze.

Amelia watched the filly go, her lips lifting as the unicorn's tail swayed contently back and forth. Her shoulders slumped and she strolled into the cave.

The cavern felt cold and empty. The odor of old wood smoke clung to the dirt floor and walls. Memories all that remained clutched to the stone exhibiting no sign of leaving. Amelia left and walked through the silent forest deep in thought.

She located the spot where she'd rested while recuperating from her gash, with the view of Mount Fuji on one side and the village on the other. Amelia sat on the ledge, leaned back on her arms, swinging her feet over the edge as imagines of the future zipped through her mind. If she cocked her neck, Amelia could make out the castle on the hill.

Funny, I use to be able to see the black dot, which was my home. It's not there anymore. Amelia searched harder, assuming she was searching in the wrong place, and realized the green of new growth replaced the black earth. *It's been months. Everything went so quick. Time. Everything changes with time.*

What do I do? Kenchi or Lan Ying? I love both. Need both. I don't want to hurt either one.

The majestic tip of Mount Fuji drew her vision. *I prayed once and received an answered. I wonder if the gods will answer me again.* Amelia closed her eyes, pictured the words in her mind, shot her thoughts like flaming arrows at the mountain peak. *Gods of my ancestors, Kuninotokotachi—Uzume, the new god who's come to the land—Buddha. Help me decide. What do I do?*

Amelia waited for an answer.

She received none.

She didn't expect any.

With a grunt of determination and frustration, Amelia slipped off the ledge and strode to the clearing. Lan Ying trotted up to greet her from the meadow. *"You are still upset. What is the matter; new battles?"*

Amelia shook her head fiercely. "No. No more fighting, no more wars. Battles have passed, for better or worse. It's time to return to the castle. I have a lot of preparations to make."

When she arrived at the fortress, Amelia left Lan Ying in the courtyard and entered the castle, asking a guard, "Where are Kenchi, Haruto, and Sota?"

The man hesitated, and then said, "Haruto and Sota are in the main hall celebrating our victory and peace."

Amelia nodded and strolled inside, walking along the corridor and entered the main hall where Sota and Haruto reclined at a long, oaken table talking and drinking sake out of small porcelain cups.

"Enjoying yourselves?" Amelia asked, taking a seat also. "I don't blame you. You both deserve to relax after all we've been through. Where is Kenchi? I would suppose he'd be here."

Haruto stared at his cup, turning the small mug in a slow circle in his hand. "Celebrating, yes, but Kenchi will not be here." He looked up, staring into Amelia's eyes. "You see, there has been a change of plans."

"Huh? What's happened now?" Amelia's heart raced. Could a new warlord have invaded their territory already? The relative of the old warlord started a rebellion against her leadership?

"Sota and I have decided it would be best for the people and the land if we ruled over this domain. You must understand, you and Kenchi are still young, not even out of your teens yet. How could you possibly–"

"WHAT?" Amelia sprang to her feet, disbelief and anger in her voice. "You are betraying me? My two most loyal advisors? How could you? Where is Kenchi? What

have you done to him?" Her hand drifted to the pommel of her sword, her body shaking in rage.

Sota waved his hand and a troop of guards marched in. Amelia did not recognize any of the soldiers. "Kenchi is okay, so is your mother," he assured her in a placating voice. "You will join both soon."

Haruto smiled benignly at her. "You should be glad we take this burden from you and the boy. You accomplished what you set out to do—free your mother. This is all you really wanted, right? Not the extra responsibility of ruling over farmers and merchants who forever squabble and cause problems."

"You will free Kenchi and my mother then," Amelia countered quickly, "or am I exchanging one evil daimyo for another?"

Haruto twisted his cup, making circles on the top of the table while he stared at the liquid within. "We cannot have you wandering about, now can we? You will have every consideration, but release you? I cannot afford to have you roaming free where you might start a rebellion." He raised his head, smiling. "You are a very resourceful young woman. You overthrew one warlord; I do not want to be another."

Amelia glanced left and right as the guards surrounded her. She thought about fighting, decided against it. "You will never get away with this. The army is loyal to me. The men will never obey you."

"Of course they will," Haruto said, suppressing a bored yawn. "Who do you think the soldiers take directions from now? Your orders, of course, but handed out by Sota and me. How will the army know you are still not issuing the commands we send to the troops?" He said to the guards with an air of dismissal, "Take her to the others and lock her up."

Before Amelia could react, a soldier plucked her sword from the scabbard and bound her hands with leather straps. "Both of you are lack honor or loyalty," she hissed, lips curling into a snarl, face red. "Is this how you repay my father? Myself? Neither of you are samurai, nothing more than thieves in the night stealing rice. Not only do you disgrace yourselves, you disgrace your ancestors and descendants."

Sota stared at his cup and said nothing. Haruto replied, "Perhaps, but we do this for the good of the people and the land." He said to the guards, "Let her complain to Kenchi and her mother. This one is starting to become annoying."

Amelia's guards led her to a staircase, climbing to the highest portion of the keep where the sleeping chambers were located. The steps were narrow. Only one soldier could stand behind her at a time. She tried twisting her hands, hoping to loosen the bonds. If she could free one arm, it might be possible to spin around, snatch the sword from the guard, and somehow escape. Amelia felt the leather strap on her left hand stretch from her sweat, but before Amelia could release herself, they reached the top of the staircase. Two soldiers stood in front of a door, guarding the entrance. At their approach, the men drew swords, standing at the ready. The warrior behind her shoved Amelia forward, and banged his hand roughly on the door. "Stand back," he shouted. One of the soldiers produced a key, opening the entrance wide enough for Amelia to enter.

"In you go, Lady," The guard gave Amelia a shove and she stumbled inside. The door slammed roughly behind her.

The chamber was spacious, one of the bedrooms for high-ranking guests of the castle. Kenchi and Mochitoyao-san sat at a table by an open window. As Amelia entered, both turned in surprise.

"*Amelia.*" Kenchi leaped to his feet.

"Daughter." Mochitoyao-san hurried to Amelia. "Are you all right? Have the soldiers hurt you?"

"Yes, Mother, I'm fine, but when I get loose Haruto and Sota won't be." She stamped a foot and turned her back to Kenchi, "Get these straps off and tell me what happened."

The young samurai struggled untying the knots, picking at the throngs slowly. Giving a final twist, Amelia pulled her hands free. While she rubbed her wrists, Kenchi shook his head ruefully. "Haruto and Sota must have planned this for a long time, way before we defeated the warlord. We were too busy laying out the battles, fighting, and worrying, to notice what was happening around us." Kenchi strode to the window and gazed out onto the courtyard below. "As soon as you left I was arrested and thrown in here, no warning, no indication of their deceit." His hands balled into fists on the window ledge. "I tried to reason with Haruto. He called me a wet behind the ears puppy, and I should thank him for taking the responsibility of ruling the domain off my hands."

"He said the same thing to me." Amelia swung to her mother. "No one hurt you, did they, Mother?" she asked. "If anyone did, I'll have their heads on a pole and displayed outside the castle's walls if it's the last thing I do."

Mochitoyao-san gasped at the vehemence in Amelia's voice. "Oh, no," the old woman hurried to assured her daughter. "The men were very polite to me. Asked me to come in here. I did, and then they locked the door." She pointed a gnarled finger to the table. "Brought me a pot of tea."

Amelia walked to the window next to Kenchi and looked out. "No way of escape," she asked without much hope of an affirmative answer. "Can we scale the wall?"

"One hundred *shaku* straight down, no handholds, nothing in here long enough to make a rope. Climbing out was one of the first things I thought of." He chuckled bitterly. "Haruto must have considered the possibility also."

The girl's eyes rose contemplating the situation. Amelia felt the walls of the prison closing in yielding no hope of escape. She asked, "Food, drink?"

"Oh, our captors feed us, no problem there," Kenchi replied. He nodded to the pot of tea. "I was in the process of inventorying the stores when I was arrested. The old warlord's people took almost everything, but what remains, mostly rice, arrives in small quantities. I saw a farmer's wagon approach the castle yesterday, bringing fresh vegetables."

Amelia leaned against the windowsill and looked down, the weight of hopelessness stabbing her chest. In the courtyard, still patiently standing was Lan Ying. *"Lan Ying—Lan Ying. UP HERE."* Amelia frantically waved at the unicorn hoping her friend would hear.

The filly's ears perked up at the sound of her name. *"Are you coming down? You never told me when you would return."*

"I can't," Amelia shouted back. "I'm being held prisoner." A wild idea of the unicorn fighting her way up the stairs speeded though Amelia's mind. She dismissed the thought. Even though Lan Ying was a tough fighter, the guards would kill her before the filly struggled halfway to the top of the keep. Instead, Amelia yelled, "Can you bring help?" She tried to project an image of guards on the staircases and before the door, so the unicorn would not attempt to storm the castle. Instead, she tried to picture her soldiers returning with Lan Ying in the lead.

Lan Ying paused, studied the fortress and tower intensely, saying nothing; instead, the unicorn trotted in a tight circle, debating in her mind what to do. As if arriving at a decision, the filly bobbed her horn, wheeled about, and galloped toward Mount Fuji.

"Did Lan Ying say anything?" Kenchi asked eagerly. "Is she going to bring our army back?"

"I don't know," Amelia replied, puzzled. "I didn't ask her to bring the army, they're scattered all over the dominion, and Lan Ying doesn't talk to men, anyway. I did think about our soldiers marching here but she didn't answer, either. I really don't know what she can do, but it's a chance. A slim one. All we can do is hope."

Amelia, her mother, and Kenchi waited. The young samurai paced nervously back and forth across the small chamber. Amelia's mother said nothing, her attention switching from her daughter to Kenchi as if hoping one or the other would devise a solution to their captivity. Amelia sat at the table opposite her mother, thinking up escape plans and dismissing them as quickly as they came. A knock rapped on the door and two soldiers brought in bowls of pottage along with a pot of steaming green tea. Amelia debated jumping the servers and attempting to escape, but when she peeked out the door, ten armed guards stood expecting just a sort of move. After the guards left, Amelia kept jumping up; staring out the window in the direction Lan Ying ran, hoping to see the unicorn returning.

"It is no use," Kenchi said, after Amelia peered out the window for the tenth time. "The day grows dark, and if the unicorn located a part of our army, the number would not be sufficient to take this castle."

Amelia refused to believe rescue was not on the way, and continued to gaze across the landscape. As the light faded, sentries from the castle silently closed the massive gates of the fortress against intruders during the night.

"Kenchi is right," Mochitoyao-san said, placing her arm around Amelia's shoulder. "You wear yourself out by worrying about things you have no control over. Your unicorn will return in her own time, whether with friends or not." She led Amelia to one of the beds. "Sleep; in the morning maybe your unicorn will release us." As Amelia lay down her mother added half-jokingly, "Who knows? There are even bugs that eat knotweed."

Amelia smiled in return at the old Japanese saying. "I hope so, but unicorns do not eat knotweed."

Amelia woke at daybreak before the others. The first thing she did was rush to the window and peered out. A red sun was cresting the trees, leaving crimson streamers on the clouds overhead. Amelia scanned the open vista as far as the dark forest hoping to see signs of a rescue.

Lan Ying, where are you? You haven't deserted me, have you?

As if to answer Amelia's unspoken plea, a point of light appeared in the darkness, and to her amazement, another next to the first. Two unicorns emerged from the trees, Lan Ying, and a pure white stallion.

"Kenchi—Mother. Look."

"Huh?" Kenchi stumbled upright from his bed and ran to the window, Mochitoyao-san a step behind, rubbing her eyes. "What is the matter?"

Amelia pointed a shaking finger out the window. "Lan Ying has returned, and she's brought a male, a big one."

"The stallion is the same one who reared to us at the battle," Kenchi exclaimed, squinting at the two as the unicorns drew near. "I am positive."

Amelia looked closer. "You're right. I wonder what he's doing here?" She scanned the forest. "I don't see the rest of the herd."

Mochitoyao-san glanced at Amelia. "What are they going to do?"

"I don't know, Mother. We'll have to see."

The three didn't have long to wonder. The unicorns trampled over the drawbridge, and approached the main gate of the castle. The stallion sniffed the closed portal cautiously, swung about, and hurling a terrific kick of his hind-legs, smashed the wooden doors to splinters, knocking the gates off the hinges. The barrier crashed inward, landing on the stone pavement. With a snort of satisfaction, he and Lan Ying gingerly stepped over the remains and entered the courtyard.

Startled soldiers ran from the castle to investigate the noise. Bugling a ringing challenge, the stallion charged the warriors, head lowered, scattering the confused men in panic. Lan Ying trailed closely, protecting the stallion's rear with her sharp horn and back hooves.

"The unicorns are attempting to free us," Kenchi said, awed.

"Oh, I hope they don't get hurt," Amelia replied. "I would never forgive myself if anything happened to either one."

The two unicorns dropped from view clattering up the castle steps. From outside the door of their room, the trumpeting of the stallion and the stomping of hooves echoed up the staircase, growing louder. Mingled among the confusion of noise, shouts rang out from soldiers, combined with screams of pain as the hoof beats drew steadily nearer.

Amelia pressed her ear to the door listening intently, her face stitched in worry. A noise like thunder shook the tower and she leaped backward, snatching her mother and flattening against the wall. "Watch out. They're right on the other side!" Amelia shouted at Kenchi. The warrior sprang sideways and the next moment the door shattered at a kick, revealing the hind-legs, rump, and bobbing tail of the stallion.

Lan Ying poked her head in next and sent one rapid thought to Amelia. *"Hurry."*

"Mother, you stay in the middle," Amelia ordered as she took the lead. "Kenchi, guard our rear." She searched around for a weapon, spotted a shattered board splintered into a sharp point at one end, and snatched the makeshift spear up, racing behind the unicorns who already clambered down the staircase in a rush.

Red smeared the walls of the steps. Amelia spied a sword dropped by one of the guards, bent and grabbed the hilt while still running. Ten steps lower she spotted another and shouted, *"Kenchi—Sword!"* and hoped he'd heard and seized the weapon.

Breathing in sharp gasps of wind racing through the main hall, Amelia skidded to a sudden halt. Hung on the wall like some battle trophy was her father's katana. Without hesitation, she dropped the sword she carried and sprinted to the partition, dragging the blade off the hooks and slamming the weapon into her empty scabbard.

Only once did they face opposition. Two warriors carrying *naginatas* stood at the exit to the main hall. The stallion bellowed a scream of defiance, rearing on back legs and waving front hooves like a boxer. The soldiers blanched, arms trembling, and stepped backward in terror. The male unicorn slammed his front hooves down on the floor. An explosion of noise erupted like the detonation of a barrel of gunpowder. The wooden planks buckled upward, tossing the two soldiers into the air. As the guards landed in a heap, the stallion charged, horn down, trampling the warriors into bloody rags. The five sped through the courtyard and bolted out the broken gate, Kenchi half-supporting Mochitoyao-san as the old woman stumbled and slowed, gasping for breath as she struggled, approaching the drawbridge.

Past the moat, Amelia and Kenchi raced across the open expanse surrounding the castle, casting worried glances over their shoulders expecting pursuit. When none was forthcoming, they slowed to a fast walk. "Why aren't the guards chasing us?" Amelia panted as she took her mother's other arm.

"The soldiers are afraid of the stallion and Lan Ying. Look." Kenchi waved to the battlements. The warriors lined the walkways, bows in hand, nervously staring in all directions. "Haruto and Sota remember the charge of the unicorns at the last battle against the warlord and fear the same will happen again. They worry if they send troops from the fortress the herd will descend and crush the whole troop."

The unicorn stallion slowed, stopped. He rose on his hind legs flashing his front hooves, facing the castle, and trumpeted a reverberating challenge. He then swung to Lan Ying, thrusting his head back, and tossed his long mane while blowing a loud neigh. The filly nickered back and nibbled him on the neck. Calling a parting bugle of victory, the stallion whirled and trotted into the forest with tail held high.

Amelia threw her arms around Lan Ying's neck in a bear hug. "You did it. You rescued us. I didn't think you would make it! How?" She waved vaguely toward the trees where the unicorn stallion dropped out of view.

"Oh, coaxing the male into helping was easy, really," Lan Ying replied, half in amusement, half in contempt. *"If you are a filly you can make a stallion do anything as long as you bat your eyes, tell the male how brave and muscular he is, and swish your tail."* The unicorn chuckled. *"After, I asked 'Please.' I told you, please always works."*

Chapter Sixteen

"Now what?" Kenchi swung his attention from the girl and unicorn back to the castle and the soldiers on the stone throwing shelf. Haruto and Sota stalked along the top of the wall, directing the soldiers, angrily waving hands to prepare for an onslaught of unicorns. "We cannot remain here. Soon those two will realize no one joins us, and then send out pursuit. Should we try and gather our troops and return?"

"Yes, Daughter, let us flee before we are captured again." Mochitoyao-san cast frightened eyes at the warriors on the battlements who watched the four closely.

"It will take us weeks to gather enough troops to assault the castle," Amelia fretted. "I wish we had some other choice. Who knows what will happen between now and then?"

"Too bad we do not have the troops now. The vegetables in our potage were the same the farmer brought yesterday. When I inventoried the provisions there was only enough to last a week providing deliveries arrive. We could lay siege to the fortress and starve Haruto and Sota out." Kenchi traced Mochitoyao-san's gaze. "It doesn't matter anymore. We must leave before troops are sent out for us."

Amelia swung her attention to the unicorn. "Lan Ying, can you do anything? Maybe ask the stallion to return and guard the castle so no food enters?" She doubted a lone unicorn, even the stallion, could watch the whole perimeter of the fortress by himself, but asking was worth a try.

"He would not return. By now he is in a cool green pasture, grazing and boasting to his friends. Stallions enjoy

showing off, but he is arrogant, also lazy, just like all males. He will consider guard duty below his dignity, and the other males would laugh at him." The filly issued a deep sigh and shook her head. *"I have friends, however, who may be willing to help. Shall I ask?"*

Amelia exhaled heavily with relief. She checked over her shoulder. The soldiers had withdrawn from the battlements. Their absence could only mean one thing—they were preparing to exit the fortress and attack. "Yes, of course, and quickly, too. We don't have much time." Her heart raced. To have won so far and have all the gains stripped away was more than she could bear.

"Humph. Of course, unicorns never dawdle. We are creatures of nature and very prompt." Lan Ying raised her muzzle into the air, released a loud whinny rising up the scale of hearing and melting away into the air.

An inquiring nicker answered her, vibrating in the atmosphere surrounding Amelia and Lan Ying.

"Now we wait," Lan Ying commented. *"It will take a few minutes for the herd to arrive."*

"What is she doing?" Kenchi asked nervously. "We must leave now."

"Hush. Lan Ying is calling her friends. This may be exactly what we need."

The unicorn cocked her head, listening. *"My friends approach."*

The ground rumbled; excited trumpets flew through the air. A score of unicorns appeared, all galloping toward Lan Ying. She pranced out to meet the small herd, calling over her shoulder, *"These are my age mates, all born in the spring as I was—my fillies."*

The girl unicorns crowded around Lan Ying, jostling each other and uttering happy nickers. She replied in kind and then told Amelia, *"They wish to meet you."*

Amelia started forward, Kenchi following. The unicorns lifted their heads, sounds of distress flying back and forth. *"The man may not approach,"* Lan Ying snorted. *"My fillies do not like or trust men. Your mother may draw near, but not too close."*

"Kenchi, you must stay back," Amelia warned. She threw her hand up, palm out to stop him from walking any farther toward the fillies. "You're making the unicorns nervous. Mother, Lan Ying says you can come, but not too near."

Kenchi halted in his tracks, a surprised look on his face. Mochitoyao-san took a hesitant step forward and stopped next to Kenchi. "I will watch from here, Daughter. You go ahead. I do not wish to bother the unicorns."

Amelia strolled into the middle of the herd. Immediately the unicorns greeted her with delighted neighs. Wet noses nuzzled her and she broke out into a fit of giggling when a soft muzzle sniffed under her arm, almost jostling Amelia off her feet. "Oh, stop, please. You're tickling." She eased the curious nose away with a scratch behind the ears and a pet on the head. Still laughing, Amelia said to Lan Ying, "Your herd is friendly enough, but will they help us? I need your age mates to encircle the fortress so men and supplies can't enter."

"My friends already agreed to," Lan Ying announced proudly. *"Fillies, take your posts."*

As if the unicorns practiced this maneuver a hundred times, they peeled off in two lines and galloped in the direction of the castle, splitting half to the right and the rest to the left. Within a matter of minutes, the unicorns enclosed the fortress, pacing around the perimeter in a continuous watch, issuing snorts and pawing of the earth.

"Is it safe for me to walk over there now?" Kenchi called to Amelia.

She looked at Lan Ying who bobbed her horn in the affirmative. "Yes."

Kenchi and Mochitoyao-san hurried to Amelia. "Thank you, Lan Ying," the young warrior said to the unicorn, bowing low. "You have solved our problems." He said to Amelia, "How long do you think gathering our army will take?"

Amelia pursed her lips. "Two, maybe three weeks. As fast as Lan Ying runs, I might be able to locate enough soldiers in ten days."

After Kenchi's compliment, Lan Ying stood with head raised and tail swishing. When Amelia stated the time to gather the troops, the unicorn shook her horn sharply. *"My fillies cannot stay here more than five days. They will be missed from the herd and yelled at by the lead mare."*

The elation Amelia felt died. "Five days? It will take more than five days for the closes troops to march here, and even so will not be enough to storm the castle."

Banging from the direction of the fortress interrupted their discussion. Soldiers busily hammered away, repairing the broken main gate and hoisting the barrier back into place straining at pulleys and ropes. In the courtyard, Amelia made out the figure of Sota directing the construction before the doors rose and he dropped from view.

"You must hurry then, my daughter," Amelia's mother said. "A handful of rice is better than an empty belly."

"I cannot leave either," Lan Ying told Amelia. *"My friends would think I desert the herd, and depart."*

"Oh, dear." Amelia looked from the unicorn, to the castle, and then at Kenchi. "Lan Ying can't go. That leaves us five days for the three of us to figure out how to assault the fortress, or force Haruto and Sota to surrender."

"Well, I know one thing for sure," Kenchi said. He watched the soldiers completing repairs on the gate and swinging the doors shut. "We cannot remain here for five days without food and shelter." He jingled a string of coins. "My money was never taken away. I have coppers and silver aplenty here. There are farmhouses not far from the castle. Let me see what I can buy if we are to stay."

"Do you want me to go with you?" Amelia asked anxiously.

"No. You remain here and protect your mother," Kenchi said. "Lan Ying might need you too. I can carry whatever I find." He studied the sun estimating the time. "If I have luck I will return before dark."

"Okay, be careful. Mother? Let's explore the forest and gather wood so we can have a fire tonight when Kenchi returns."

As the sun brushed the tops of the trees shooting pinks and oranges into the sky, Kenchi trudged up the road, sweating profusely and pulling an old rickshaw behind him. "I was in luck," he shouted, waving and beaming at Amelia. "The first house I went to was empty. The people must have been part of those who evacuated the area when we marched our army in." He stopped next to the small fire Amelia started and dropped the handles of the rickshaw, wiping his forehead. "Look what I found." From the top of the floorboards, he dragged out a bundle of torn blankets and cloth. "The farmer was in a hurry, or his wife decided these were too worn to bring and left the rags as garbage."

Mochitoyao-san picked up the largest piece of cloth and shook the fabric out. "We can make a small tent out of this," she exclaimed. The old woman wagged her head. "There is luck even in the leftovers."

Amelia rose on her toes and peered into the rickshaw. "Did you find any food, though? That's what you went searching for. I'm hungry."

"Plenty," The warrior replied. He held up a bunch of onions by their stalks and waved the clump toward the battlements of the castle where the soldiers stood watching. He rubbed his stomach and laughed when onlookers made angry gestures back at him. "The next house I stopped at, the farmer was eager to sell me as much as I wanted,"

Kenchi said turning back to Amelia. "He wanted to load up his cart and make a delivery to the castle. I told him to wait a week. The fortress was not buying any more supplies at this time. He appeared dubious, but I explained this was the new daimyo's orders. " His lips bent down and he groaned in exasperation. "Have you thought out a plan yet? I can think of nothing."

"No." Amelia began examining the foodstuff while she and her mother unloaded the rickshaw. "Perhaps the thought of hunger will drive the men out before the food actually ends." Amelia tried lifting a sack of rice, grunting. Kenchi jumped to take the bag from her. "We will see."

The next morning while Amelia and Mochitoyao-san prepared a simple breakfast, a farmer approached, traveling the road to the fortress leading an ox-cart. The castle gates swung open to welcome him.

"What the…?" Kenchi leaped up from the fire and ran at the farmer, the same one he'd talk to the night before. *"Go away,"* he screamed furiously, waving his hands. "You were told, you are not welcome here—GO."

The farmer stopped in confusion, gaping at Kenchi and then at the open gate. "But…."

The young warrior drew his sword. At the same time, Lan Ying sprang between the gate and the cart, her age mates raced to her issuing neighs of fury. The farmer stood frozen to the spot he stood on, too terrified to do more than clutch at the halter of his oxen, trembling, his mouth open. Amelia ran up and shook him by the arm. "Go. If you do not, your life is forfeited."

Confronted by steel and spiral horns the farmer hastily tugged on the halter of the oxen and swung his cart around, to the groans of the soldiers standing at the gate. The men eyed the cart, debating if they should dash for the supplies, and then glared at the unicorns. With disgruntled curses, the warriors reentered the castle and the doors slammed shut.

As the farmer ambled down the road, Kenchi said to Amelia, "I should have imprisoned the man. We are in trouble now."

Amelia divided her attention between the road and fortress, assuring herself soldiers did not attempt a sortie from over the wall, or the farmer double back to the rear of the castle. "Why? He cannot do anything. You don't think he'll try and sneak into the castle at night to bring the traitors vegetables, do you?"

Kenchi blinked at Amelia and his mouth tightened. "He will do worse. He will tell his neighbors what he saw here today. They will gossip to their acquaintances and friends. Within a week, every daimyo in every han surrounding this domain will know of the feud dividing us and descend on our land like flies devouring a rotting carcass, attempting to take advantage of our plight."

"Oh, you're right. I never thought of that." Amelia's shoulders slumped. She exhaled deeply.

More fighting. More killing. When will the battles end? Please Buddha tell me—when will the slaughter all stop?

Her weary soul could stand no more. Breathing a mute sob, Amelia gazed at her feet, rubbing her forehead as tears leaked from her eyes. "The brutality never halts, does it—the constant warfare and violence?"

A red blaze of anger darkened Kenchi's face. His body stiffened, filling with resolve. "Yes, the slaughter halts now. For better or worse the fighting and bloodshed ceases right this minute." Before Amelia could hold him back, Kenchi strode away toward the gate of the castle. When he was within earshot of the soldiers on the battlement he called out, "Haruto, I know you can hear me. I challenge you to a duel. If you are a coward you will hide behind these walls. If you a man you will accept my offer and fight me like a warrior and samurai." He squatted on the ground and folded his legs under him, waiting for a reply. His eyes firmly locked on the gate, face impassive as a stone image.

"Kenchi—NO!" Amelia rushed to him, trying to draw him up by his arm. "You cannot stand against him. Haruto will kill you."

Amelia's mother pulled her away. "There is nothing you can do now. He has issued a challenge. Kenchi will lose face if he does not fight."

Amelia scratched at her face, staring at the fortress, dreading what was about to occur. "He will be dead if he does," she wailed.

The gates of the castle opened and Haruto stepped out wearing his sword, Sota walked behind.

The unicorn fillies stopped their patrolling and formed an arch behind the men to watch. Soldiers lined the battlements to view the fight, not wishing to miss a single detail of the battle to tell their children and friends.

Kenchi stood and bowed, keeping his eyes on the man.

Haruto kept walking until he was within arm's length of the young warrior, and then returned the bow, smirking. "So the puppy wants to be a dog, huh?" he barked sarcastically, his lips curling up in a sneer.

Kenchi said nothing, but the sides of his mouth flickered upward at the corners.

With the suddenness of a striking dragon, Haruto drew his sword, flashing the tip at Kenchi's belly; but the young man was prepared. He leaped backwards, drawing his own blade as the point whipped past his kimono. The two men circled warily, each hoping for an opening.

Amelia held her breath, hands balling into fists at her side. *Be prepared for anything. The man is a master. Remember every trick my father taught you.*

The older warrior leaped back in, raining a steel curtain of death around Kenchi. The younger man parried each thrust, backing up as he sought to preserve his life from the flashing sword.

Haruto's furious assault could not last long. He paused and took a deep breath. "Are you going to fight, or run? I see I must chase you down like a chicken for the pot."

Kenchi said nothing, but his smile broadened and eyes narrowed into mere slits. Before Haruto could say anything else, the young warrior swung his blade. Haruto countered and the two stood toe-to-toe, exchanging sword strokes.

Haruto stepped close, drawing his leg up to kick Kenchi in the ribs with a knee. Kenchi brought the hilt of his sword down, smashing the warrior's kneecap. Haruto release a yelp of pain, limping backward while rubbing his leg. "So the puppy has learned to bite I see, huh?"

For the first time Kenchi spoke. "You taught me that one yourself. How is your sword arm? The blade growing heavy?"

Haruto's lips turned upward. "Heavy, yes, but not heavy enough so I cannot finish a pup." He swung his blade horizontally and the tip ripped through Kenchi's kimono, leaving a bloody slice on his thigh. "How does my snap feel, pup? A good enough nibble for an old dog, huh?"

Kenchi clenched his teeth, wincing at the pain. He took a step back and gave a short bow. "An old dog still has one nip left in him and sharp teeth."

Kenchi drove on the offensive, slashing overhead blows and thrusting at Haruto's stomach. Even though Kenchi was the one wounded, each time, the older warrior's parries were slower, barely catching Kenchi's blade. The sun hung high in the sky, each man covered in a thin layer of perspiration, Kenchi's kimono soaked in scarlet. Through the ringing of steel on steel, the gasping of the older man breath bellowed as he breathed heavily through his mouth, sucking in air and swiping at his face to brush the sweat out from his eyes.

Kenchi jabbed at Haruto's leg. The warrior lowered his sword and caught the thrust on the blade. He whipped his hand up to strike a blow and his katana slipped out of his damp fingers, clattering into the dirt.

"Pick up your weapon and let us finish this." Kenchi took a step backward to allow Haruto time to retrieve his sword.

The old warrior staggered as he bent over, almost collapsing to the earth before he straightened himself, and squinted at Kenchi through sweat-filled eyes. He said quietly, "Yes, let us finish this." He fell to his knees and pulled his *tanto*. Before anyone could stop him, he thrust the knife into his belly and with a quick motion cut left and right.

Mochitoyao-san released a shriek. Amelia gasped in shock. Kenchi's face hardened. He raised his sword high, chopping into the warrior's neck.

Kenchi broke the stillness. "He fought like a man and died like a samurai." The young warrior switched his attention to Sota. "Now your turn." He limped toward the other man, bearing his weight on his good leg.

"He's mine," Amelia said holding back Kenchi. She grasped her father's sword and half drew the blade from the scabbard. "You are tired and wounded. The battle would not be a fair fight."

The unicorns gathered closer.

Sota stared from Kenchi to Amelia and dropped to his knees. In one swift motion, he snatched the *tanto* from Haruto's dead fingers and held the tip against his stomach. "I thought we did right," he murmured, and plunged the blade into his belly. Amelia's jaw muscles tightened. She stepped forward and delivered grace.

"Are we all done with this nonsense now," Lan Ying asked, sniffing at the dead bodies. *"I really do not*

know what all the fuss was about. They are, after all, only men." The unicorn swung her sight to the battlement of the fortress. *"See? The rest line the wall, staring, mouths wide open."*

"Yes, for now we are all done," Amelia muttered, releasing a deep breath she didn't realized she held. She closed her eyes, opened them and inhaled deep, turning her gaze on Kenchi. "I hope." He looked back, the intensity of his stare sending shivers through her body.

"For now, anyway," Kenchi replied, his voice hardly above a whisper.

The clattering of steel against stone rang from the direction of the castle, the noise of the soldiers lining the walls dropping their swords and bows in surrender. Amelia said to Lan Ying, "The battle is finished. Thank your friends for their help. We couldn't have won without the support they gave us."

"Of course not. This is why age mates stay together." Lan Ying trumpeted. The unicorns' heads snapped up in response blowing inquiring snorts. She issued a whinny and the fillies nickered back, rising on their hind legs, clashing front hooves together in celebration. As one, the herd bowed to Amelia who bowed back. With a thundering of hoofbeats and wild neighs, they galloped off.

Amelia watched the small herd swallowed up in a cloud of dust, stricken into silence by the beauty of the animals, their shining coats, flowing manes and tails. Long after the unicorns disappeared, Amelia stood, wishing she were on Lan Ying's back, racing on the filly over the earth as she'd done in the past.

Kenchi touched Amelia's shoulder and gently spun her around. "Now will you marry me?"

"Huh?" The sight of the unicorns still preoccupied Amelia. When she realized what Kenchi asked, she froze in silence.

Of course, I want to marry you. I love you. I love Lan Ying and the unicorns, too. Why do I have to make this choice?

Amelia stared at the young man before her, and then the two dead bodies on the ground. She looked at Lan Ying. "I'm sorry. I love you. I will always love you."

"Of course, you love me, and I love you. What is there to be sorry about? We will always belong to each other."

***

The wedding ceremony was short. The celebration, however, was long and noisy, with hundreds attending, lasting well into the night. Eventually the guests departed or were settle into rooms in the castle for the evening. Lan Ying stood patiently in the courtyard for Amelia to come and tell her about the party inside the fortress.

The servants straightened up the main hall, swept, put away food, and went to sleep. The cooks cleaned the kitchen, banked the fires in the stoves, and wandered off to slumber. The stronghold returned to normal. Sentries kept watch on the battlements and patrolled the corridors. One by one, the lanterns in the lower rooms of the fortress winked out until only the lights in the highest part of the bedroom keep remained. Then they too faded.

Lan Ying turned and silently trotted into the dark forest.

Epilogue

Amelia and Kenchi ruled their small domain for many years. The Onin War raged on, until both sides stopped their fighting in exhaustion, the imperial capital in ruins and thousands killed. With a weak shogun and emperor unable to stop the carnage, small warlords carved out territories in the land and sought to conquer as much as they could hold by force of arms. Amelia and Kenchi protected their people throughout the war, invasions, and raids by rival daimyos. The couple brought peace, security, and harmony to the population. Their small portion of Japan prospered and grew wealthy.

Amelia and Kenchi had a baby daughter and named her Yasmin. A beautiful and precocious child forever getting into mischief, she had long black hair and a quick smile like her mother. The girl was the bane of the cooks, especially when making *uiro,* or steam cakes; strawberry as her favorite. They knew to make extra, for Yasmin always volunteered to help, eating twice as many as she made, but so beloved was the child, the kitchen staff hid their faces and laughed whenever Yasmin's cheeks bulged.

On Yasmin's fifteenth birthday, the girl raced into the castle library where Amelia sat reading a book of poetry and trying to compose her own. "Mother—Look." She seized Amelia's hand, hopping from one foot to the other in excitement. "Quick, outside the castle walls, standing there in plain sight—Unicorns, two of 'em!" She tugged Amelia to the window, squealing in delight and pointed a finger. "See?"

"Unicorns?" *Lan Ying?*

Outside the walls, two unicorns stood, a large one, a mare, and a smaller version of the first, a filly by her side, as pure white as her dame was.

"Oh, Mother, they're so beautiful," Yasmin exclaimed, unable to contain herself. "Can we go and see them, pleassse?"

"Of course, honey." Amelia took Yasmin's hand and the two raced down the steps and outside the gate. Yasmin ran a few paces past her mother and fell to her knees, arms outstretched to the small unicorn.

"You are both so beautiful," the young girl cried. She waved her fingers. "Come here, baby girl, and let me pet you."

Lan Ying nudged the filly beside her with a prod of her horn. The young unicorn advanced slowly on skittish legs, and many backward glances at her dame, until she stood before Yasmin. The filly sniffed the girl's outstretched fingers cautiously and dropped to her knees, resting her head on Yasmin's shoulder uttering a contented sigh.

"Mother, she likes me," the girl exclaimed in awe, voice shining. "She even told me her name. Is she my birthday present? Can I keep her forever? Can I *ride* her?"

Amelia barely heard her daughter speaking, her eyes locked with Lan Ying's in yearning of a time long past. An invisible hand clutched at her throat making it hard to breathe. Amelia whispered back, "Of course you can, Yasmin." *But only for a time.* Wetness dripped down Amelia's cheeks she didn't wipe away. *For don't you know? Only a virgin may ride a unicorn.*

The End

About Arthur Butt

Army Veteran, graduate of Florida State University, former police officer and plant manager. Native Long Islander now living in Florida was wife, two puppies and SnoopyCat. (And yes, a coffee drinker!)

Social Media

Twitter: https://twitter.com/artyny59 @artyny59

Facebook / Author Page:
https://www.facebook.com/pages/Arthur-Butt-The-Fantasy-SyFi-Author/1528729850734703

Amazon link:
http://www.amazon.com/s/ref=nb_sb_noss?url=search-alias%3Ddigital-text&field-keywords=Books+by+arthur+butt

Goodreads link:
https://www.goodreads.com/search?utf8=%E2%9C%93&query=Arthur+Butt

Instagram Link:
https://www.instagram.com/artyny59/

Acknowledgments

Yasmin B. for the inspiration, Editor in Chief K.C. Sprayberry, and all the people at Solstice Publishing, and as always, to my wife Susie.

If you enjoyed this story, check out these other Solstice Publishing books by Arthur Butt:

Dragonkiller

Hope is a monster killer, First Family of her town, and condemned to death if people knew she is the mother of a half-human, half-dragon child. When summoned to another dimension, she discovers love, and a man who accepts her son. In order to stay, however, she must vanquish a demon army that threatens to destroy this new land, and the old world she is leaving behind.

http://bookgoodies.com/a/B00USNA7TI

The Girl Who Rode Dragons

All Jackie wanted was equal treatment and to ride a dragon. When her cruel brother-in-law takes over as head of household, and makes her quit school, she is forced to do all the chores, and collect wood in the forest. Jackie finds a dragon's egg, and although law forbids girls to ride dragons, she secretly hatches the egg, and dons boy's clothes. After she brings the gift of fire to the dragonriders, she becomes an accepted member of their band.

Civil wars breaks out, dragonrider against dragonrider. Jackie leads the loyalist faction against the rebels. The stakes—the fate of the kingdom and the life of her and the man she has grown to love.

http://bookgoodies.com/a/B0117QI24Q

Gail is Gaea

To the people who enslaved her she is a priestess trained in the art of prophecy. To the new land she escapes to, she is an outlaw. To the natives she leads in revolt, she is a goddess.

http://bookgoodies.com/a/B0193QH2SE

Caitlyn

A father and husband commits suicide for a murder he never did. A wife devastated by the death of her husband and sister. Two families left wondering why.

http://bookgoodies.com/a/B01N0KCSO5

A Kingdom by the Sea

Kenya wants to be a singer. When she is cast into another world, she learns magic is in the power of her songs.

https://bookgoodies.com/a/B074JF6WN6